Mys Booth, Claire.
FIC
Boo The Branson beauty

BID $26
DUE DATE 7/16 25.99

DB

THE
BRANSON BEAUTY

THE
BRANSON BEAUTY

CLAIRE BOOTH

Minotaur Books
New York

This is a work of fiction. All of the characters, organizations, and events portrayed in this novel are either products of the author's imagination or are used fictitiously.

www.minotaurbooks.com

Designed by Omar Chapa

Library of Congress Cataloging-in-Publication Data

Names: Booth, Claire, author.
Title: The Branson beauty / Claire Booth.
Description: First edition. | New York: Minotaur Books, 2016. |
    Series: Sheriff Hank Worth mysteries; 1
Identifiers: LCCN 2016001429| ISBN 9781250084385 (hardback) |
    ISBN 9781250084392 (e-book)
Subjects: LCSH: Rescue work—Fiction. | Murder—Investigation—
    Fiction. | Branson (Mo.)—Fiction. | Mystery fiction. | BISAC:
    FICTION / Mystery & Detective / Traditional British. | FICTION /
    Mystery & Detective / Police Procedural.
Classification: LCC PS3602.O663 B73 2016 | DDC 813/.6—dc23
LC record available at http://lccn.loc.gov/2016001429

Our books may be purchased in bulk for promotional, educational, or business use. Please contact your local bookseller or the Macmillan Corporate and Premium Sales Department at 1-800-221-7945, extension 5442, or by e-mail at MacmillanSpecialMarkets@macmillan.com.

First Edition: July 2016

10 9 8 7 6 5 4 3 2 1

For Joe

ACKNOWLEDGMENTS

This is a work of fiction, but it would not have been possible without the very real help and support of many people. First, a huge thank-you to my wonderful readers, whose constructively critical eyes helped make this book ten times better than it was before they got ahold of it—Kristi Belcamino, Paige Kneeland, Bridget Gray, and Claudia and Michael Brown; and to my technical consultants, Zachary Heyde and Mandi Fanchar, who generously (and patiently) shared their different areas of expertise with me.

I also want to thank Jim McCarthy, my fantastic agent, who wholeheartedly encouraged my switch from nonfiction to novels; my wonderful editor at Minotaur, Elizabeth Lacks, whose support and enthusiasm I deeply appreciate; and David Rotstein, who created the gorgeous cover art.

I've been a writer in many different ways for a long time, and I'm very lucky to have always had the unconditional support of my family, including my parents and grandparents.

Thank you. I also owe a debt of gratitude to my in-laws. Without them, I never would have discovered Branson in the first place, and without them, I wouldn't have the most important person in my life. Thank you for my husband.

To my husband and my children—you made this possible. I couldn't have done it without you. You are my everything.

THE
BRANSON BEAUTY

CHAPTER

1

His feet crunched on the snow as he stumbled behind the Company Man. The guy had loafers on and still managed to keep his footing as they scrambled down the incline toward the lake. Hank's heavy-duty snow boots, on the other hand, were not living up to their billing, he thought, as his feet went in opposite directions on a patch of ice.

Finally, he skidded to a stop at the edge of the water. The lake wasn't a terribly wide one, but it was pretty. It lay like a shard of glass in the middle of the granite Ozark Mountains, its surface that glassy sheen only possible when it's a degree or two from freezing solid.

It was, he thought, nature at its finest. Except for the boat. That was nature at its worst. Or human stupidity at its worst. His guess was the latter.

"It seems to have run aground," the Company Man said. He had the grace to sheepishly clear his throat.

Hank fished his binoculars from inside his parka. He

raised them toward the huge, immobile paddlewheel, which he judged was about five hundred yards from where they stood on the shore.

"Yep. Seems that way," Hank said, still looking through the binoculars. He could see some movement through the windows, but no one was out on the deck. At least the passengers seemed to have some sense.

"How often does the boat go out?" Hank asked.

The Company Man cleared his throat again.

"Every day except Thursdays," he said.

"New captain?"

"Uh, no. It's Albert Eberhardt. He's the same one's been doing it for almost twenty years."

"New route?"

The Company Man sighed. "No. Same route as always. It was windy earlier, though, so we think maybe the boat got blown this way and stuck on the rocks."

"You take it out when it's windy?"

"Um, well. It is up to the captain's discretion."

"And he decided to? He's the only one who makes that decision?"

The Company Man frowned.

"Not anymore, he's not."

Hank snorted. He aimed the binoculars to the left. The nearest shore to the boat appeared to be only about one hundred yards to the east. That wouldn't be fun, though. They'd have to carve a road through the woods to reach that spot. Then they would need something that could coast right up onto the shore. Maybe rubber dinghies? All those little old ladies out for their luncheon cruises bobbing instead on the near-frozen water like so many corks in a barrel. He tried not to grin and hid behind the binoculars.

"Um, Sheriff? We, uh, we were hoping to keep this quiet." The Company Man smiled eagerly.

Hank lowered the binoculars.

"Quiet? There're a hundred and twenty tourists on that boat. My guess is they're not satisfied customers at this point."

"Yes, but they're out of cell range right now," the Company Man replied. "It took a radio transmission for the boat to notify us about this at the home office. No one else knows about it."

Now Hank was starting to get irritated. He hoped the guy's feet were cold.

"Unless you think that the two of us alone are somehow going to either unstick that boat or swim all those people to shore, I don't think this is going to stay quiet."

The Company Man sighed again. Hank started hoping for frostbite.

"We would just rather this not turn into a public relations disaster. You know, something that would reflect badly on the company."

Hank decided it would not be wise to smack the guy with the binoculars. Instead, he reached for his own radio.

"Unless you want to get those shoes wet, I'm calling in the cavalry."

Hank's radio call notified not only every one of his deputies, but the highway patrol, the state water patrol, the mayor, the Coast Guard, the television stations that bothered to listen to police scanners, and Lovinia Smithson, the widow who lived just west of Branson and had bought her own scanner a few years back.

She got there first.

"Hey, Lovinia," Hank said.

She grinned at him. Even her little puffs of breath seemed excited.

"Beautiful day, isn't it, Sheriff?"

Yeah, it was beautiful like the North Pole was beautiful—something best viewed in a picture, not in person. He was pretty sure his nostril hairs were frozen.

"Just stay out of the way, okay, Lovinia?" he asked. "I've got to go meet the EM guys at the road."

She nodded and plopped down on a boulder that would afford her a good view of the whole operation. How she'd avoid having her pants freeze directly to the rock, he had no idea.

He climbed back up the incline to the road, which was the nearest access point. So they'd have to start hacking through the woods toward the boat from here. His boots hit the mercifully plowed surface, and he paused to take a deep breath. He spotted the Company Man standing dejectedly at the road's curve as a big blue sedan slowly pulled up.

As the back door swung open, the Company Man squared his shoulders and stepped forward. Hank couldn't help but cringe for him. It looked like the boss had arrived.

Henry Gallagher unfolded himself from the car and stood in the middle of the road. He listened to the Company Man for a few seconds, then held up his hand and turned toward Hank.

"Worth," he called.

Here we go, Hank thought, and walked toward Gallagher.

"Hello, Mr. Gallagher. I assume he . . ." Hank realized he hadn't paid attention to the Company Man's actual name. He pointed instead. "I assume he's explained the situation?"

"Yes." Gallagher's voice was about as cold as the surrounding air. He visibly got a grip on himself and softened his tone. "Of course, the company will assist in every way possible to get these poor people off my boat. I have a passenger manifest with me."

Good. It would be quite helpful to know exactly how many people he was going to have to shuttle to shore. Maybe this would be easier than he thought. Gallagher handed him a crisply folded sheaf of papers.

"The asterisks denote those in wheelchairs," he said.

Maybe not.

As they talked, the emergency vehicles started pulling up. The county emergency district chief leaned out the window of his rig.

"Hey, Hank." He could barely talk as he tried to choke back laughter. "Did I get your broadcast right? The *Branson Beauty* ran aground? On the lake it's been sailing for more than thirty years?"

Gallagher scowled. The Company Man swooned a little and stifled a groan. Hank grinned.

"Yep, Larry, that's what happened." He tried to focus the conversation on the task at hand. "How many guys you got who can help?"

"Oh, I've called everybody in. And Thompson over in the next county said he'd loan us anybody extra he's got."

"Good," Hank said. He jerked his thumb toward the woods. "Why don't you go park and start talking with the road department guys about cutting through those trees."

"Sure thing," Larry said merrily. "I'm glad I decided not to take vacation this week. This is gonna be a fun one."

As the rig pulled away, Hank was sure he heard Larry whistling the *Gilligan's Island* theme. From the pinched look on Gallagher's face, he'd heard it, too. Hank pasted on his best try at a diplomatic smile.

"Sir, if I could get you to stand off to the side here," he said. "Oh, and perhaps you should start talking with this gentleman."

Hank pointed toward a man who had just climbed out of a Ford F-150 truck with a Bass Pro fish logo magnet on the side. Gallagher raised an eyebrow.

"You don't have the resources to rescue these people by yourselves?" he asked.

Hank stared at him for a long second. What world had he been living in lately? We barely have the resources to pay for the gas to get out here, he thought. He took a deep breath through his frozen nose.

"No, sir, we do not have thirty or forty boats sitting in a warehouse just waiting for the opportunity to rescue your stranded tourists. However, this nice gentleman does."

He pointed at the Bass Pro man, who was giddily pulling a store catalog out of his coat pocket.

"I'll send a water patrol officer over to help you pick the appropriate watercraft for our needs," Hank said evenly. "Then I'm sure Bass Pro will be happy to take a check."

He turned on his heel and walked away. He fought the urge to swear. Then he fought the urge to whistle. *A three-hour tour . . .*

He stepped away from the water patrol officers. It seemed they needed to get out to the boat a bit more quickly than they had thought. They'd been informed through the company's radio communications that situations were developing aboard the *Beauty*. Several passengers were complaining of heart palpitations. A diabetic's insulin supply was running low. And they were almost out of coffee.

He crunched through the snow over to Larry.

"I need at least two of your paramedics. That's all we'll have room for in the boat we're taking out there," he said. "Stock them with everything they could possibly need. I think I'll have to leave them on the *Beauty* until everybody's off. There will only be more medical issues as this thing drags on."

"Yeah," Larry said. "I saw the asterisks."

One of the water patrol guys gave a shout. A tiny motorboat was gliding into the nearest dock, which thankfully wasn't too far from the original spot Hank and the Company Man had hiked to earlier. Two paramedics jogged up, juggling what had to be hundreds of pounds of gear. They wrestled the huge bags on board, then hopped on. The boat already held the water patrol officer most familiar with the lake and a ramrod-straight Coast Guard commander. There was room for one more. Hank sighed and swung his leg over the side.

They pulled away from shore and headed toward the *Branson Beauty*. With its two tiers of white gingerbread railings crowned with an ornate wheelhouse and giant red paddlewheel wedged on a rock, it looked for all the world like a beached whale in a prom dress.

Hank shaded his eyes. He'd forgotten his sunglasses, and the glare off the water was brutal. It was like there was no atmosphere when it was this cold. The sun shone through as if you were standing five feet away from it. Except for the warmth, of course. There was none of that. His breath rose in clouds.

He turned and scanned the shore. He spotted Lovinia, still sitting on her rock. He wondered if her clothing had frozen to it yet. She gave him an energetic wave. He turned back around as the water patrol's Bill Freedman cut the engine and their boat glided up next to the *Beauty*. He hit his mark exactly, coming to a stop directly in front of the gate in the gingerbread railing where a slight young man in a *Beauty* uniform waited. The kid swung open the gate, caught sight of Commander Ramrod's officious-looking blue Coast Guard uniform, and gulped. His hand went to his forehead in a hesitant salute. Bill, in his much more modest water patrol jacket, smirked at Hank.

"Son," Bill drawled, "permission to come aboard?"

"Sir! Yes, sir!" Another salute.

The three men climbed through the gate. They turned back to hoist the gear the paramedics handed up. Man, that stuff was heavy. Bill lashed his little boat to the *Beauty*, and the group set off toward the front of the boat. The kid led them to large double doors that opened into the main salon. Dozens of round tables sat between them and the huge stage at the other end of the room. About half the tables had people at them. Some were playing cards, some talking. There were a few older women in a prayer circle off to the side. One man was stretched out on the floor asleep, using what appeared to be a wadded tablecloth as a pillow.

A young teenager saw them first. He shouted and pointed, and the room burst into applause.

"We're rescued!" the teen shouted. Bill looked at Hank.

"I'm just here for the boat, man," he muttered. "You're here for the people."

"Yep," Hank said. He arranged his face into what he hoped was a reassuring smile and stepped forward.

"Ladies and gentlemen," he said. "My name is Hank Worth, and I am the Branson County Sheriff. We are here to help, but—"

He was interrupted by more applause. Maybe he should take the stage at the other end of the room. He smiled some more.

"But . . ." he continued, "we need to do this in order of priority." The longer he could go without mentioning that no one was getting off the boat anytime soon, the better.

"First, is there anyone who needs medical attention? We have two paramedics here who will be able to help anyone in need."

He felt a tap on his shoulder. He turned around and looked at the kid who'd brought them on board. Then he noticed one of the paramedics was missing.

"Sir," the kid said, then coughed nervously. "I already sent one of your medics to the second deck. That's where the diabetic is resting, and a lady who's been having breathing problems. I hope that's okay."

Huh. He'd underestimated the boy.

"What's your name?"

"Tony, sir. Tony Sampson. I'm, uh, the first mate."

"Okay, Tony. How many more people are on the boat other than the ones in this room?"

Tony's mouth twisted in thought as he did a few mental calculations.

"There are about a hundred here. And maybe twenty up with the other medic. Then there are the cast members and the serving staff and the kitchen folks. So all together probably a hundred and sixty, a hundred and seventy people."

Shoot. The staff had not been on the manifest. Hank had not factored them into his rubber dinghy rescue plan. Well, that meant an even happier Bass Pro man, at least. It always surprised him how many people it took to run a tourist attraction. So many waiters, cooks, maids. And then on something like the *Beauty*, there was the show—a big, skirt-twirling, fiddle-playing, tap-dancing extravaganza that took at least another couple dozen people to put on. He should have thought of that. He and Maggie had taken a dinner cruise last year for their anniversary. She had loved it. He had thought the salmon was rubbery.

He shook his head and refocused on the one hundred people in front of him. Several were beginning to gravitate toward Commander Ramrod, asking breathless questions about rescue. He didn't think so. The Guard, like Bill, was here to examine the technicalities of the boat's problem. Just because the guy could keep his uniform spotless didn't mean he was in charge of the people aspect of the deal. Hank cleared his throat loudly and held up his hand.

"Ladies and gentlemen," he repeated, "I need to ask for your patience. We do not yet know the best way to get you off this boat and safely to shore. That's why the Missouri Water Patrol"—he purposefully pointed to Bill first—"and the Coast Guard are here. They are going to assess the situation. In the meantime, I need you to do exactly what you have been doing. Remain calm, relax, and know that we are doing everything we can."

There was no applause this time. A few women stifled sobs, several others went back to praying, and the dude on the floor rolled over and started snoring.

Tony unlocked a door and led Hank upstairs to the second deck, where Medic One was busy treating the people clustered together in the observation lounge. Several lay on the long bench seats. One older woman was getting oxygen through a non-rebreather mask as her weary-looking companion patted her hand. A petite middle-aged brunette paced along the back wall of windows. A well-dressed man about the same age stood in the corner jabbing viciously at his cell phone. And there were a few teenagers sprawled out on the floor, looking bored. None of them appeared to be attacking their phones, though.

The youth contingent would not counteract the senior citizens when it came to rescue, Hank thought. Not only were there a lot of folks in wheelchairs here and downstairs, but several others looked like they needed them. He began to think that his rubber dinghy plan was not going to float.

"I don't think ferrying these people to shore is going to work," said a voice behind him. Hank turned and saw that the commander had followed them upstairs. "Now, I don't know the currents on this lake like the water patrol does," he said, "but I do have a tugboat."

"Can it get in this far?" Hank asked. "Could it dislodge this thing?"

"That's what we need to figure out," the commander said. "I've ordered it out here just in case. I'll go find Freedman and see if we can take a look at that paddlewheel."

He spun on his heel and marched out of the room. Several

little old ladies sighed after him. Tony looked at Hank and grinned.

"Uniforms sure do the trick, don't they, sir?"

Hank looked at Tony's navy blue shirt with the absurd gold piping and smiled.

"How long you been doing this, kid?"

"This is my second season, sir."

"And pardon me for asking, but are you really the first mate? Or are you, uh, the 'first mate' cast member?"

Tony grinned again. "Good question, sir. I'm not technically a cast member—not part of the entertainment at all. I'm the assistant to the captain."

That was good. Seemed like the kid's abilities would have been wasted if he . . . wait a minute. The captain. Where was Albert the Moron? He needed to get on that pronto.

"Where is your captain?" he asked quickly.

Tony gave a start. Then he looked down at his feet. "Um. Yeah. Well, he was up in the pilothouse. I don't know how he's doing . . ."

Hank raised an eyebrow."You mean now that he's run the boat aground?"

Tony continued to stare at his feet. "Yeah. He's pretty bad . . . I dunno."

"Take me to the wheelhouse," Hank said.

Tony, still looking at his feet, cleared his throat and mumbled, "Pilothouse, sir," as he left the lounge and headed down a plush corridor. Hank's feet sank into blue carpet held down with brass fittings. The lake and the snow-covered shoreline glittered through windows on the left. They passed a couple of doors and windows with the shades pulled on the right, and then Tony swung one open at the end of the hall.

A narrow set of stairs led straight up. Tony lightly trotted ahead. Hank grabbed the cold metal rail and followed. They came up at the back of the wheel-, er, pilothouse. Tony pushed open another door and there they were, with a panoramic view of Table Rock Lake. And the back of a man's head.

Tony nervously cleared his throat. The man did not move. Hank stepped around the first mate and pivoted in the small space to stand directly in front of him. Albert looked like something out of a '70s biker movie. Beat-up leather bomber jacket with the collar turned up, faded jeans, sailor cap pulled low over his face. Aviator sunglasses hid the rest. He hadn't so much as twitched.

Hank leaned down until he was pretty sure he filled Albert's entire field of vision.

"Sir?" Hank drew out the word into one long, exasperated growl. Albert remained a statue. He was breathing, at least. Hank resisted the urge to poke him in the chest.

"Are you all right?" Hank growled.

The boat creaked against the rocks. Tony's shallow panting grew more rapid. There was no other sound. Then Albert peeled his sweaty palm off his leather armrest. The ripping noise made Tony jump back into the doorway. Hank just scowled. Albert slowly raised his hand and took off his sunglasses. His eyes were huge. Bloodshot, watery messes. He blinked once. Then he carefully replaced the sunglasses and did not move again.

Hank did not take his eyes from Albert's face. He pointed in Tony's direction. "Go get a medic. Tell him I'm going to need a blood draw."

CHAPTER

2

Hank stood wedged in a corner of the tiny pilothouse as Medic One took Albert's vital signs. He was not letting this guy out of his sight until they figured out what the hell was wrong with him. Albert still had not moved of his own accord; the medic was manhandling him into the blood-pressure cuff. It did not appear that he would be able—or willing—to consent to having his blood taken for a drug and alcohol screen.

Hank sighed. He'd have to get a warrant. And the longer that took, the less there would be in that idiot's blood to test. He reached for his radio. He considered stepping outside, but at this point, he didn't care if the guy heard him or not. Plus, it was cold out there.

"Sheila, come in, please. This is Hank. Over." The radio crackled loudly in the small space.

"Yeah, I read you. How's it going out there?"

He filled Sheila in.

"Glad to have something to do," she said, "seeing as I'm the only one stuck here in the damn boring office."

"Hey, somebody's got to mind the store."

She laughed. "Oh, sugar, there's nobody here to care. Everybody's figured out where the action is—seems like the whole town is down on the docks watching this thing."

Great.

He signed off, dug his binoculars out of his coat, and started to scan the shore. There was Lovinia. And the dock he and Bill had set sail from, now bustling with rescue personnel. Well, they hadn't set sail; it was a motorboat. Whatever. He turned slightly and saw them. A few other private piers, and then the big park shoreline. All of them were packed with people. Several satellite truck poles sprouted behind them. How on earth had those things made it out here in the snow?

He shoved the binoculars back in his coat and turned around. Medic One looked up at him.

"This dude is something else. His heart rate is high, but otherwise, he seems to be fine. He's just not movin'."

"Any idea how we can get him out of here?" Hank asked.

"Well, I'd suggest a round of talk therapy, but I don't think that fits your style," he said.

Hank grinned. "I am not in the touchy-feely business," he agreed. He thought for a moment. The challenges of moving Albert would be different depending on which rescue scenario the water boys chose. Despite his vow not to leave the moron, he knew he'd have to go see what they'd decided.

"You," he said, jabbing his finger at Medic One, "are not to take your eyes off this guy. Nobody comes in here, and he sure as heck doesn't leave. Got it?"

"No problem," said Medic One.

Hank headed down the stairs, avoiding the cold handrail this time. He strode back past the observation lounge. Everyone looked calm now. Medic Two was busy flirting with a blond teenager, so there couldn't be anyone in too much medical distress anymore. Good.

He took the next set of stairs two at a time. When he hit the bottom level, he pushed the separating door open wide and headed toward the stern and the paddlewheel, where he could see Commander Ramrod's immaculate uniform. The sounds of yelling and crying hit him as he passed the doors to the main showroom. He did not stop.

". . if you're sure your boat can do it," Freedman was saying.

The commander got even starchier. "I've been saying repeatedly that my boat can do it. We can even push this sorry hulk all the way to shore if it's too damaged to make it on its own. I—"

Hank interrupted. "When might that happen? I don't think we have much longer before things start to get really ugly in there. These old folks expected to be gone for two, two-and-a-half hours, tops. It's been almost six. They're running out of food and water. And medicine. And probably toilet paper."

All three men shuddered at that.

"The tug will be here within two hours," the commander said.

Hank sighed with relief and started to turn away.

"Not so fast," Bill said. "It's not going to be that simple."

Hank stopped.

"The tug will push the boat out, but it won't be able to lift this paddlewheel off those rocks."

He pointed, and all three leaned over the back rail. The huge red wheel was locked in between boulders as big as cars. It wasn't going anywhere, regardless of the Coast Guard's tugboat.

"We figure we can detach it, but if we do that in the next two hours, it's going to be pretty ugly. Basically just hacking the supports off, slicing through the hydraulics, that kind of thing," Bill continued.

"Gallagher's not going to like that any," Hank said.

Bill and the commander looked at each other. The commander jerked his head toward Hank as if to say, you tell him.

Bill cleared his throat. "Yeah, well. That's why we figured you would be the best one to have that talk with him. Him being your constituent and all."

They had to be kidding. He didn't know anything about boats. Or water. Or hydraulics. But unfortunately, he did know a few things about Henry Gallagher. The guy hadn't built one of the most successful businesses in southern Missouri by being a pushover. He'd come into town a few years before and bought the *Beauty* and several other entertainment enterprises that had all been owned by local families. Add up all of his new holdings, and he employed more people than anyone else in town. He softened the hard-charging business image with some pretty good philanthropy—sponsoring several charities and single-handedly paying to save the county animal shelter from closure last year. But that didn't mean he would readily sacrifice his assets. Especially a five-ton behemoth painted such a pretty shade of red.

The two men staring at him mistook his silence.

"You're the highest county official we've got," Bill said.

"And we've heard such good things about your, um, tact and diplomacy," the commander said.

Thanks, Ramrod.

"Uh-huh. But you're right. Bill, you take your boat back to the dock to pick up some guys who can hack this thing off. I'll have to come with you. I don't think I can get a secure communication off this boat, and I don't want the world to hear the conversation I'm going to have to have with Gallagher."

He turned. "Commander, as long as you're putting this one on me, you get to make the rounds inside. Reassure everybody that their rescue is coming. Hold some old ladies' hands. Oh, and stop in up at the pilothouse. I don't want anybody moving or talking to that captain until I get back."

The commander nodded and headed for the *Beauty*'s bow. He and Bill made their way to the gate in the railing. There was no Tony this time. The two made it into the boat—Bill jumping lightly in, Hank landing with a thud as his heavy snow boots skidded.

They made the long trip back to the dock in silence. Hank hunched down into his coat, trying to avoid the wind created by the speeding boat. They pulled up alongside the dock. Convinced he was twice as frozen as before he'd left land, Hank eyed the four-foot vault off the boat.

"Chief! Chief! Here, sir!"

Well, thank goodness. For once, he was grateful for the Pup's inexhaustible exuberance. He took the offered hand and hoisted himself onto dry land.

"Good to see you, Chief," said the Pup.

"Thanks, Sam. How long have you been here?"

"Got here right as you were pulling away to go out to the *Beauty*," he said. "I've been coordinating with Larry and the fire guys. Got five other deputies up at the park doing crowd control. The roads guys haven't been very cooperative, though. They're threatening to take their bulldozers and go home."

Nice.

"And the press is screaming for somebody to make a statement," Sam the Pup continued. "They cornered Gallagher a little bit ago, but I got them pushed back to the top of the road. They're not allowed down here at the dock anymore."

Even better. After that, Gallagher would probably be in a fine mood for their little chat.

"Where is Gallagher now?" he asked.

Sam pointed over toward a stand of trees just off the dock. Hank saw the Company Man crouching as he tried to balance a laptop on a rock. Gallagher stood silently over him.

"Thanks, Sam. Now I need you to get me whoever is in charge of the road guys. We don't need the bulldozers, but we do need saws and drills and maybe some sledgehammers. Get the supervisor down here so I can talk to him."

Sam gave a quick head bob, then turned and bolted up the hill. Hank watched him go. After almost six months of working with the kid, Hank still had no idea how he managed not to trip over those enormous feet.

He took a deep breath, which thankfully did not lead to a bout of choking on the frigid air, and strode toward Gallagher.

"Mr. Gallagher. Could I have a word?"

"Of course." They moved off to the side. Hank explained the tugboat and the boulders and the food shortage.

"Why can't you ferry them all to shore in motorboats?" Gallagher asked.

"Several reasons. The wind keeps increasing, and the water is too choppy for all but the healthiest people to handle. And this dock requires a four-foot jump to get up on it from the boat. We need a landing location that can handle a gangplank, and this is not it."

Hank took a breath and continued.

"If we remove the paddlewheel, we can get the boat to a suitable docking location within two or three hours. But we think that's going to mean basically hacking the thing off. If we take the time to do it right, those passengers will still be out there come morning."

Gallagher looked out through the gathering darkness at his boat. The pinched look on his thin face got even worse. Hank stuffed his hands in his pockets and waited. After a very long minute, Gallagher let out a long breath. Hank didn't realize he'd been holding it.

"All right, Sheriff. It is . . ."—he paused—". . . the only good option for my passengers. But I would like to get my maintenance men down here to help with the work. They might know how to salvage at least some of it."

"Of course," Hank said. "We now have two boats capable of taking people out to the *Beauty*. I need to get back out there myself."

"I'll have my men here in fifteen minutes. With equipment." Gallagher spun around and marched toward the Company Man, who had given up on his laptop-balancing act. A few swift sentences, and the Company Man was running up the hill to the road, where he could get a cell signal and call in the death warrant for his boss's boat.

•   •   •

Half an hour later, Hank clambered back onto the *Beauty*. He'd
been forced to hike to the road and give the hovering TV
cameras a statement before coming back. He hoped he hadn't
had frost on his eyebrows. If it was cold before, now it was
almost unbearable. The temperature had to be near zero. And
now the clouds were starting to roll in. There would be a
storm before the night was over. He prayed they'd have the
boat to shore by then.

Tony must have seen them coming. He met them at the
gate. Hank smiled at him and introduced the Pup.

"This is Deputy Samuel Karnes. He's here to help out.
You have a status report for me?"

"Yes, sir. Three more people in the main salon have had to
go on oxygen. We're almost completely out of food, but your
guys did bring out a load of bottled water, which has helped.
The, uh, facilities, um, are starting to back up. Not good, that.
And we had an emergency in the showroom when a lady's
rosary broke, but we managed to string it back together with
dental floss somebody had in her purse."

Well, thank God for that.

"And your captain?"

"Yeah." Tony stared at his feet again. "He's about the same,
sir, from what I hear. I haven't actually gone back up there."

Hank didn't blame the kid. It had been a pretty freaky
sight.

"Well, Tony, we should be off this boat within two or
three hours. I need you to stay here and meet the folks who'll
be coming shortly. They're Gallagher's maintenance men, and
they'll be removing the paddlewheel."

Tony's eyes got wide. "How are they going to do that?"

"That's a very good question. I have no idea. You and Sam make sure they have what they need, though, okay?"

Tony straightened. "You bet, sir."

Hank set off for the showroom, where he found a decidedly more cranky group than he'd seen earlier. Still, they weren't doing too badly, considering. Several card games were going at different tables. The guy on the floor had awakened and was doing a series of yoga poses in a corner of the room. Hank gave the crowd the new timetable, which was met with scattered grumbles. He gave them his best smile and was turning to leave when an image of his wife's yoga workout videos popped into his head. She was always happier after she did one of them. He walked over and spoke quietly to Sleepy Guy, then headed upstairs.

The folks in the lounge were in better moods, but worse health. One of the teenagers was crying.

"I'm glad you're back."

Hank turned to see the commander walk in. "The medic is in the staff break room downstairs," Ramrod said. "One of the waitresses collapsed."

Hank grunted. "Three hours, max, until we're out of here."

"Thank God," the commander said. "I'll go find Freedman and see what we can do down at the paddlewheel. Oh, and you, ah, might want to check in on your guy upstairs."

Hank nodded. That was definitely his next stop. He stepped into the pilothouse and was met with the sound of sobbing. Medic One, looking quite harassed, pointed at Albert.

"He started this about a half hour ago. Won't stop. It's driving me crazy."

Albert still had the sunglasses on, but he had hunched

forward and was rocking back and forth. Hank pulled a piece of paper out of his inside coat pocket. Sheila the miracle worker had somehow gotten it down to the lake and into Sam's hands before they'd come back out to the *Beauty*.

"Sir. I have here a court order that allows us to draw blood from your person. I need to ask for your cooperation now."

Medic One eagerly reached for a needle. Hank shot him a warning look, and he slowed down before maneuvering it into the captain's arm. Albert stopped rocking, but the sobbing continued. Hank sighed and looked out the window. Someone had turned the big boat's floodlights on, pushing back the darkness. He saw another small boat coast up to the *Beauty*. It was packed with men and some big sawlike equipment. And Henry Gallagher. He stood stickstraight in the bow, with his perfectly tailored overcoat fluttering in the now-gusting wind.

"Okay," the medic said behind him. "Here you go."

He started to hand Hank a vial of blood, but Hank shook his head and pulled a set of stickers out of his pocket. "You have to seal it, sign across the sticker, and then initial here," he said. "Chain of custody." He glanced at the still-rocking Albert. "Something tells me you'll have to testify to this at some point."

The medic chuckled. "Yeah, when all these people sue this joker. You don't ruin a bunch of old people's lunch cruise without there being serious consequences, man."

Hank grinned in agreement. Tailored coat or not, he would not want to be Henry Gallagher right now. He wondered what the big boss was doing.

"I've got to go check on the paddlewheel removal," he said. "I'm going to have to ask you to stay with him."

Medic One frowned, but Hank was already out the door. By the time he'd made his way down to the paddlewheel, he could hear the whine of saws. The men wielding them looked to be having a great time attacking the huge wooden beams. Bill and Commander Ramrod stood off to the side.

"Where's Gallagher?" Hank asked.

"I think he went upstairs," Bill said. "Something about checking on his guests."

Sam appeared at Hank's elbow. The little group watched with a certain wicked enjoyment as the paddlewheel was severed from the boat. As the workers got to the last connecting piece, a horn blast cut through the frigid air.

"That would be my tug," the commander said with a smile.

It nosed in slowly and bumped against the *Beauty*. The commander nodded, and the two men holding the saw gave one last slice. The *Beauty* swung free.

The snow fell in devilish swirls around the passengers as they slowly filed down the walkways to a long gangplank that led them—finally—to solid ground. All of Larry's guys and every available gurney in the county had come aboard first; no matter how crotchety and independent, no old folks had any desire to roll their wheelchairs through the icy gusts and onto shore. They submitted to the firefighters' transport with a minimum of grumbling. Small favors, Hank thought. He found Tony putting masking-tape name tags on the many chairs left behind.

"Come on," he said. "I need you to take me through the whole boat. We have to make sure everyone's off."

Tony hesitated and looked down at the roll of tape in his

hands. "Yes, sir," he said. He stuffed the tape roll in his pocket and led the way.

The main showroom was empty. Abandoned water bottles and coffee cups littered the tables. Many of the chairs and tables had been pushed back against the walls. "It was pretty cool, sir," Tony said. "They were all doing yoga. That one skinny guy with the ponytail had the idea. He got up on the stage and had them doing all kinds of stuff. It really calmed everybody down. Do you know there's something called a downward dog?"

Hank just smiled. "What's behind the stage?" he asked. Tony led him through the maze of kitchens and dressing rooms. There was no one left. They headed upstairs. There were only three passengers and two medics left in the observation lounge. A very old lady was sitting regally on a gurney.

". . . and there is no way, young man, that I have any intention of lying down and being carted off this snake-bit ship like an invalid. If you want me on this thing, I'm going like this." She folded her hands in her lap with a definitiveness that signaled that the conversation was over.

Hank had no desire to start it up again. He yanked Tony's sleeve and the two backed out of the door. They turned in the corridor to see someone who was obviously not in any condition to argue about his transport off the boat. Albert the Moron was completely prone and meticulously strapped to the gurney that Medic One and a colleague were about to take down the last flight of stairs. He was still moaning—loudly.

"The elevator's not working," growled Medic One. He glared at Hank. "You are going to owe me one heck of a drink after today."

"Yep," Hank said over Albert's moans. "Probably two.

Get him to the hospital. Make sure that one of my deputies goes with you and stays with him."

"What else is on this deck?" he asked Tony.

"Just the captain's dining room and the private kitchen," Tony said, pointing at the closed white door with a gold anchor painted on it. Hank tried the knob. It was locked. He turned to Tony, who was standing just behind him.

"Huh," Tony said. "That's weird." He dug in his pocket and pulled out a jumble of keys. It took him several minutes of searching to find the right one. Hank occupied himself by looking out the wall of windows at the activity down below. Somehow the television camera crews had managed to sneak back down to the shoreline. Their bright lights illuminated every bedraggled passenger staggering off in the whipping snow. They started to bob like summertime fireflies as they caught Albert in their beams. Hank wasn't sure if he felt sorry for him or not.

"There!" Tony finally got the door unlocked. He pushed it open, and Hank stepped inside, flipping on the light switch. One long rectangular banquet table covered by an embroidered white cloth stretched the length of the room. Aside from a few crystal water glasses and crumpled cloth napkins, it was bare. Deep blue carpet anchored with brass fittings covered the floor, and a huge wooden ship's wheel hung on the back wall. Every window had the shade drawn.

And then he saw the hand. Long, elegant, and white, it peeked out from an edge of the tablecloth. Hank stepped forward and around the end of the table. A woman lay behind it. Her brown hair spread around her on the blue carpet as if she were underwater. Her green dress billowed around her knees, and her red, hemorrhaged eyes stared at the gold-detailed ceiling. A ring of bruises circled her neck. Rigor was setting in.

Hank stood over her and stared. This . . . well, this was unexpected. Behind him, Tony let out a little shriek. Hank did not take his eyes from the body. He slowly raised his arm and pointed toward the door.

"Get out of here. Go get Deputy Karnes, and don't let anyone else up on this deck at all." Tony did not move. "Go!"

Tony moved backward toward the door, just as Sam's cheery face poked around the doorjamb.

"Hey, Chief!" he said. "Everyone is off and safe and on their way home."

Perfect.

CHAPTER

3

The room was very cold. Hank squatted down next to her and felt for a pulse, although it was quite obvious he would not find one. The big boat creaked in the wind, and the snow pelted the windows. He stood. Sam was standing stock still on the opposite side of the banquet table from the body.

"Let's step outside," Hank said.

Sam backed out through the door, then visibly got a grip on himself.

"I should call for the coroner," he said, reaching for his radio. Hank stopped him. Better not to broadcast this over the scanner settings while the media was twenty feet away.

"Just walk down and tell Larry personally to come up here. We'll have him call it, then we'll get the coroner down here. And the crime-scene techs."

They also needed to ID her. There had been no purse, no wallet in the room. Hank walked up and down the hallway before he found Tony sitting in the lounge, his arms wrapped around his middle.

"Hey," Hank said. "Do you know who that is? Do you recognize her?"

Tony looked at him as though he were an idiot. "You mean you don't?"

Hank raised an eyebrow. "You mean I should?"

"It's Mandy Bryson. She was almost homecoming queen last year. She's friends with my little sister. She spoke at graduation. Everybody knows her. She's, you know, she's the one. She's . . ." He trailed off.

"When did you last see her?" Hank asked.

Tony stared at him. Hank repeated the question. Tony shook his head. "I didn't even know she was on the boat."

Did anybody? Hank frowned.

"Hey." Hank turned as Larry appeared beside him. "Sammy said you needed me up here 'right frickin' now,' but he wouldn't say why."

Hank rose and walked back into the dining room. Larry followed, muttering. They walked around the table and the muttering stopped.

"Oh, shit," said Larry.

"I didn't want this out over the scanner until the TV cameras left and we could close all access to the dock without a huge fuss," Hank said.

"Good call," Larry said. "I got this. You go get your CSI guys." Larry had also worked up north, and thankfully had seen enough homicides to know exactly what he was doing.

By the time Hank made it down to the dock, the TV cameras were gone. So was the Pup. Then he heard something crashing down the hill from the road.

"Chief!" Sam panted up to him. "I went up and got enough of a signal to call Sheila on my cell. She's getting Kurt and Alice and heading out here."

Hank nodded. He figured the media were far enough away that it was safe to use the scanner frequency, as long as he didn't get too specific. He radioed that he wanted every deputy in the area on the dock immediately. He'd have Sam lead another search of the boat.

"I want every closet and cupboard searched. You look under every table, in every drawer, you got it?"

The Pup gave a floppy nod and ran off.

"Why," said a pinched voice, "is that necessary?"

Gallagher. Hank had noticed the showboat's owner appear on the dock seconds earlier. The Company Man was not with him.

"I'd like to have my men do a damage assessment here," the *Beauty*'s owner said. "We don't need your deputies getting in the way of that. I'd like a look at my poor boat."

Hank blew on his hands. The wind gusted in whistling bursts down the hill, and he decided maybe he should raise his voice.

"Sir. As of right now, this is my boat. The entire thing is now a crime scene, and no one—no one—goes aboard without my permission."

Gallagher started to protest. Hank continued.

"There is a dead girl in your dining room. It appears she was murdered."

Gallagher's jaw dropped so far that his chin hit the upturned wool collar of his coat. He did not close it as Hank rattled off a list of all the information he was going to need from his company. It was still open—but blessedly silent—as

Hank finished, drew his frozen body up to its full height, and turned back to the boat. He had work to do.

The crime scene, now roped off with tape and crowded with techs, was apparently the captain's dining room. It could be reserved for small private parties that wished to enjoy Table Rock Lake without being subjected to skirt-twirling, fiddle-playing, tap-dancing extravaganzas. Or the hoi polloi who enjoyed such things.

It had been booked today for Frances Honneffer's eighti-eth birthday. Twenty-two people had attended. And according to Tony, all of them had ended up in the observation lounge next door after the boat ran aground. Except Miss Mandy Bryson. Who had clearly been strangled. And probably hit on the head, as well.

Mandy's identity had been confirmed by Kurt, the crime-scene tech, who had a kid in last year's graduating class at the high school. He and his fingerprint powder were now focused on a well-camouflaged box on the wall in the back corner. His partner Alice was busy photographing the area around the body. Larry walked around her and over to Hank.

"It's going to be hard to establish a time of death. Some-body turned the heat off. It's a de facto refrigerator in here. Kurt finally found the thermostat."

Hank nodded.

"I'm pretty sure she was killed here, though. There's a little bit of blood on this chair," he said, pointing to the cor-ner of an overturned banquet chair near her head. "We took a sample to confirm it's hers, but I'm sure it will be. She's got to have a cut somewhere. We haven't turned her over yet, though."

Hank nodded again. "Could have bumped the chair as she was getting forced down to the ground."

Larry agreed. "And did you see her right hand? It's still grabbing the edge of the tablecloth."

Both men jerked up as the door to the dining room popped open. Sheila sailed through. She was wearing an enormous white parka with some odd kind of fake fur around the hood. It went down almost to her knees and made her look like the unfortunate offspring of a hairy penguin and a marshmallow. Hank was envious.

The hood was cinched tight around her mahogany-colored face. She yanked it back and shoved a travel mug at him. An adamant finger followed. "This is the only time—ever—that I will get you coffee. Ever. Got it?" The finger jabbed his chest.

She could smack him upside the head for all he cared. The warmth of the mug began to penetrate his icy hands. He took a long, grateful swallow.

"And I'm going to want my mug back."

"Uh-huh," Hank said between slurps.

She started to walk away, but he stopped her.

"Put on your best momma bear face and go take a full statement from Tony Sampson. He's the kid sitting in the lounge at the front of the boat. He's had a rough day. Be nice."

Sheila rolled her eyes. "I'm always nice."

Hank was about to reply when a thud caused both of them to look toward the corridor. A gurney had hit the doorjamb; two of Larry's guys repositioned it and made it through.

"We're ready to move her," Larry said.

"Wait just a sec," said Hank. The coffee was thawing his brain and making it capable of higher thought again. "Let me take one more look around." He handed the coffee mug to Sheila and stood quietly in the doorway for a minute. He walked forward, imagining the path Mandy Bryson had taken into the room. He moved to the end of the table. Then he took a step back and into the killer's shoes. From the direction of the bruises on her neck, it appeared that Mandy had been facing the person. The killer must have stepped forward, shoving her into the corner of the table, then down to the floor. That was when she grabbed the tablecloth. Right before the end.

He knelt down beside her and gently lifted her shoulder, rolling her onto her side. He moved aside the spot of blood-crusted hair on the back of her skull and found a vertical cut, rough but not deep. He rolled her back and raised up on his knees until he was eye-level with the top of the dining table. There was nothing on it that could have caused that kind of injury. It hadn't been the chair. That was for sure.

Hank rose and slowly walked around the table, then in a wider circle around the edge of the room. He stared thoughtfully at the thermostat box for a moment—who would have the presence of mind to turn the temperature down? Everyone in the room stood still, watching. He walked the perimeter again, examining the ceiling, the floor, the walls, the blinds over the windows. Every killer left something behind. Even if it was just an emotion. He looked again at the beautiful girl dead on the floor. There was a lot of emotion there in the bruises around her neck, but which one? Hate? Fear? Panic? Love?

His circuit ended back by the doorway. He retrieved the coffee from Sheila and nodded. The medics wheeled the gurney forward. They carefully lifted the body and laid it down as Alice made the sign of the cross. Larry gently zipped the plastic bag closed, and they slowly rolled Mandy Bryson out of the room and down into the storm.

Sam's team had not turned up anything during its search of the boat. Hank left Sheila and the Pup in charge of the scene and, armed with a list of Tony's best recollection of who had been at the birthday luncheon in the captain's dining room, went to find Gallagher.

He found the *Beauty*'s owner sitting in the backseat of his big blue car up on the road. He knocked on the window. Gallagher opened the door and slid over. Hank climbed in. It was blissfully warm. Gallagher cleared his throat. His driver sighed and got out to stand in the middle of the deserted road.

"I saw the ambulance leave," Gallagher said. He was staring straight ahead. "Who was it?"

"Her name was Mandy Bryson. She was a local teenager."

That was all Gallagher needed to know at this point. Hank listed everything he wanted to know about the boat staff and their access to different parts of the boat. And then he remembered something. "I need to ask you where exactly you were during the time you were on the boat today. You were not supervising the paddlewheel removal. Where did you go?"

The only sound in the car was the hum of the engine and the whir of the heater. But that was not as hot as the hostility now radiating from the man next to him, Hank thought. He sniffed—his nostril hairs were finally defrosting, and now his nose was starting to run. He waited for Gallagher to answer, fighting a surge of annoyance. Gallagher would have been a key source of information about the workings of the *Beauty*. Now everything he said was suspect.

"I was checking in on my guests, and my employees," he said haughtily.

"Where'd you go?"

Gallagher paused. "The showroom, the main kitchen, the staff break room, the dressing rooms backstage, the observation lounge on the upper deck. I was not allowed into the pilothouse."

"Did you go into the captain's dining room?"

"No."

"Why not?"

"It was locked. I did not have a key. Plus, everyone was accounted for—they were all in the lounge. Oh, and the cook, the waiter, and the show captain were in the private kitchen."

"Did anyone accompany you to all of these places?"

Gallagher's nostrils flared. "It's my boat. I don't need an escort."

No, he certainly did not. But it sure would have been better if he'd had one. Even if his story was true, there was still part of his time that could not be accounted for.

"When can you get me that list of staff crew members?" Hank said calmly.

"By morning," he said. "I'll have it emailed to your office. Am I otherwise free to leave?"

Hank briefly thought about trying for his best thanks-for-your-help smile, but decided it wouldn't fool anybody. He opened the car door and stepped out. Gallagher reached forward to close the door and gave him a hard stare.

"You're no Darrell Gibbons," he said evenly.

"No. I'm not."

The door slammed shut. Gallagher's driver—who had been jogging in place to stay warm—jumped in the front seat, and the car glided away through the snow. Hank headed for his own car, which was still where he had parked it on the shoulder more than ten hours ago. He used his arm to swipe most of the snow off the windshield before he climbed inside and cranked up the heat. Not all of his suspects had vanished into the night. One of them should be in a hospital bed by now. It was time for a chat with Albert.

CHAPTER

4

The elevator doors slid open and Hank walked onto the floor, illuminated by the pulsing fluorescent glow that only happens in hospitals in the dead of night. Hank started down the hallway. As he neared the corner, he heard one of his deputies. Duane's voice was shaking, and getting gradually louder. "I can't, sir. As I said, no one is allowed in this room. I have orders. I can't let you in, even though you're . . ."

He trailed off as someone else started talking. The voice was much quieter, but had the kind of ingrained authority that eluded poor Duane.

It was the same tone he'd used with Hank only an hour before.

"Young man, you know exactly who I am. And you will let me in there to talk to my employee, or I will have you writing parking tickets for the rest of your career."

That did it. He didn't have the howling wind as an

excuse for raising his voice with Gallagher this time, but he was past caring.

"Mr. Gallagher," he intoned loudly as he stepped into the doorway. "I believe I made it quite clear that my investigatory needs take full precedence. You are not to speak with anyone—not your employees and not your guests—at all. For any reason. Until I tell you otherwise. Got it?"

Duane sagged against the wall with relief. Gallagher got that pinched look that was becoming all too familiar to Hank. He looked Hank right in the eyes. "I will not let this harm my company," he said.

Hank leaned forward. "Then perhaps you should consider the consequences of your company's president getting thrown in jail for hindering an investigation and evidence tampering."

"You wouldn't dare," Gallagher spat.

"Oh, yeah?" Hank drawled as he leaned against the doorjamb.

"If you want to keep this new job of yours, you'd be wise not to threaten your constituents."

"Oh, no," Hank said, as he straightened and stepped forward until he was inches away from Gallagher. "That wasn't a threat. It was a . . . a diplomatically delivered advisement. A . . . preliminary notification. Or maybe just some friendly advice for one of the *many* constituents I serve." He stepped to the side and swept his arm toward the doorway. "Good night."

Gallagher opened his mouth, then quickly snapped it closed. He slowly walked out and around the corner toward the elevators.

"Wow," Duane exhaled.

"You did fine." Hank slapped him on the shoulder. "I know that wasn't easy."

Duane swallowed visibly. "My mom works for him. Out at the resort. God."

Hank hadn't known that. He made a mental note to transfer Duane off his regular parking patrol duties by next week. Give the kid more to do. He'd earned it. He pulled Duane out of the room.

"Yes, sir. I'll wait out here, sir."

"No. I want you to come in. Sit in the corner and don't say anything. Just pay attention."

Duane beamed. "Yes, sir."

They walked in and Hank pulled a chair up close to the head of Albert's bed. He looked frail and old now that he didn't have his bomber jacket and his big captain's chair. He had several IVs snaking out of him, and the hospital gown was bunched up where he'd been clutching it across his chest. His eyes, though, looked the same as they had on the boat.

"Mr. Eberhardt, sir. I need to ask you some questions. And I need you to listen carefully and answer me. Do you understand?"

Albert blinked at him. Not promising. Hank was dying to know what those tox screen results were going to be.

"How did your boat run aground?"

Albert looked down at his hands. When he finally spoke, his voice sounded like ice cracking under a great weight.

"Don't know what happened. Little windy. Then we were on the rocks. My *Beauty*." He looked like he wanted to start rocking back and forth again but didn't have the strength.

"What is so upsetting to you?" Hank asked very slowly. "Why did today have this effect on you?"

Albert turned and looked him full in the face. "What I did. What I did. I'm so ashamed." He choked on the last word. Then his hand fell from the twisted gown on his chest, and his head slumped to the side.

"Jesus," Hank said. He looked up; Duane seemed as startled as he was. "Push the button for the nurse." The two men looked around frantically until they found the call button up to the right of Albert's unmoving head. Duane held it until they heard footsteps pounding down the hall.

"Good heavens," the nurse panted.

They both gestured futilely at Albert. She glowered at them. "He's not dead. The doctor sedated him. It's finally kicking in. The patient was almost hysterical. Other than that, there isn't a darn thing physically wrong with him. Doctor wants to keep him here overnight for observation, though," she sniffed. She clearly thought that was unnecessary. "Seems to me he just needs a good talking-to," she muttered under her breath. "And you two"—she glowered some more—"do not push that button again unless something catches fire. I got computers down at my station. I see everything about this fool. I don't need you panicking at every twitch."

She gave them one last glare and stomped off down the hall. Hank and Duane looked at each other. Hank started laughing and couldn't stop. His sides began to hurt. Duane wasn't any help—he was wiping away tears as he tried to keep quiet. Hank swung the door closed until they both regained their composure. When they finally pulled themselves together, Hank felt better than he had all day. Sometimes a break in the cold came when you least expected it.

"I've got to go track down a lot more people," he told

Duane. "I need you to stay here. And don't piss that woman off again. I don't need another homicide today."

He left to the sound of Duane laughing again. He knew the back stairs were in the opposite direction from the nurse's station. He headed for them.

What I did. It was either a confession, or a captain mourning the loss of his command—and his career. Hank seriously doubted he was lucky enough to have it be the former. Once the sedation wore off, Albert the Moron could easily say that it was drug-induced rambling, or that he was referring to the paddlewheel. Hank drummed his fingers on the steering wheel. His squad car was now nice and toasty. He just needed to decide where to drive it next.

His phone buzzed, and he dug it out of his pocket to find a voice mail from home. He knew it wasn't Maggie—she was on duty. That left only one cantankerous possibility. He hit play, and his father-in-law did not disappoint.

"You still down at that boat thing? The kids saw you on the news. Now they won't shut up about it. Wanted to talk to you before they went to bed. All riled up now, they are, so thanks for that. They— wait, Benny, will you stop yelling? Your daddy's not on the phone. I'm leaving a message. Stop that—"

A call beeped in and Hank gratefully cut off the voice mail. It was Sam, who had tracked down last year's Branson Valley High School yearbook and confirmed Tony Sampson and CSI Kurt's ID—it was Mandy Bryson in the morgue. There was no reason to put off notifying her family any longer. He had Sam read him the address; her parents didn't live far from the hospital. By the time he got there, his gut was churning and he was glad he hadn't eaten anything since lunch.

He pulled into the long driveway of a house huddled against a stand of trees. It was on a quiet, unlit street where the lots were a couple of acres, but only because the people who'd built there had done so long before Branson became "Branson." When the country music stars began building theaters and drawing tourists from all over the place in the mid '80s, the town boomed, and the price of land skyrocketed.

The walkway had been shoveled already—the snow was less than an inch, compared with the six or seven already on the lawn. The porch light was off for the night. They weren't expecting anyone. Hank tried to swallow and rang the bell. It took three rings before he heard scraping footsteps coming toward the door. An inside light flipped on, and he could see the person block it as he peered through the peephole. He made sure his badge was visible. The door swung open.

A disheveled man in his sixties stood there. The two stared at each other through the glass storm door for what seemed like an eternity to Hank but couldn't have been more than two or three seconds. The temporary lines of puzzlement and worry on the man's face grew deeper. Hank knew that as soon as he started talking, they would become permanent.

"Sir, my name is Hank Worth, and I am the Branson County Sheriff. Are you Mr. William Bryson?"

The lines burrowed deeper into the man's forehead.

"Oh, God. Has she been in an accident?"

"Sir—are you William Bryson?"

"Yes, yes. Is it Mandy? Where's Mandy?"

"What about Mandy?" a sharp female voice asked from the entryway behind William Bryson. "What's wrong? Bill?"

Gina Bryson's face appeared over her husband's shoulder. Hank still couldn't swallow.

"Mr. and Mrs. Bryson, I need to speak with you. May I come inside?"

Bill Bryson moved back with a start. "Of course, of course. I'm sorry—please, this way."

No one said anything else until they were all sitting on stiff formal sofas in the living room. Hank leaned forward and rested his elbows on his knees; in his experience, it was the best posture for delivering bad news. Authoritative, but not intimidating.

"Sir, ma'am. I have some bad news."

"It was a car crash, wasn't it?" said Mrs. Bryson. "She was in a car crash. Is she hurt? Is she . . ."

Mr. Bryson quietly took her hand, and she stopped talking. His eyes had not left Hank's face. "If she were just hurt, the university would have called us," he said in a cracked voice. "She's dead, isn't she?"

Hank nodded. He'd given up trying to swallow.

"Yes, sir, she is. I'm very sorry to have to tell you this. And also, I need to tell you that it was not an accident. We are investigating, but it appears that Mandy was the victim of foul play."

The Brysons stared at him. They didn't move, they didn't blink, they didn't breathe. They just sat on the couch they saved for company and stared, holding hands.

"She was found on the *Branson Beauty* during the rescue operation today," Hank continued. That jolted Mr. Bryson out of his silence.

"She wasn't at school? She was here? Why was she here? She should have been at school." His voice stayed the same volume but rose in pitch. "Why?" he squeaked.

"I was hoping you could tell me that, sir. I don't know why she was here. She went to the University of Oklahoma, didn't she?"

"Yes, yes. She's a freshman. She just started her second semester. She . . . she has two tests next week . . ."

"Can you think of any reason she would have come up to Branson this weekend?"

Mr. Bryson shook his head.

"Yes."

Both men looked at Mrs. Bryson. Her sharp edges had dissolved and everything seemed watery and smudged. Even her grip on her husband's hand had melted away. "Yes, I can," she whispered. "Was Ryan there?"

There had been several Ryans on the passenger manifest, but Hank was pretty sure he knew which one she meant.

"Ryan who, ma'am?"

"Ryan Nelson. They're dating. They have been since the summer before their senior year."

"But she just saw him. Over Christmas. Why would she come back so soon?" said Mr. Bryson. His voice had returned to normal. Mrs. Bryson's had not. Hers gasped and faded as if she were trying to swim through a very deep sea.

"Because she was in love, Bill." She turned to Hank. "Was Ryan in town, too?"

"I believe so, ma'am. I have not talked with him, yet. Is there anything you think I should know before I do?"

Mrs. Bryson thought for a minute. As she started to speak, her husband seemed to finally connect everything Hank had said so far.

"What do you mean, 'anything you think I should know'?

Is he a suspect? Do you have suspects? Do you know who did it? Who did this? Who would . . ."

Hank put his hands up in front of him to stop the torrent of questions. He decided the generic answer was the best he could do at the moment.

"Right now, we do not know who killed her, and we do not have any suspects. Anything you can tell me would be helpful."

The Brysons looked at each other. Mrs. Bryson took several short, quick breaths before she seemed to acquire enough oxygen to speak. She gave Hank the names of Mandy's friends who were still in town, and tried to sketch out her daughter's new college life as best she could. She was only the mom, she didn't know everything, and she knew it. Her pain seemed an almost physical presence in the room. Hank carefully wrote it all down. He did not want to have to ask her again.

Mr. Bryson left his wife drowning on the couch and walked Hank to the door. Once they were in the entryway and out of her sight, he grabbed Hank's arm. His hand was shaking. "How, Sheriff . . . how did it happen?" The last word was a whisper.

Hank spent a long time exhaling through his stuffy nose. Sometimes he hated this job. He made himself look Bill Bryson straight in the eye. "It appears that she was strangled."

Bill slumped against the wall. "Was she . . . was she . . ."

Hank saved them both from hearing the words.

"No, sir, there's no indication of that," he said. Just in case . . . "But we won't know for sure until the doctor does an autopsy."

Mr. Bryson nodded. "You'll keep us . . . keep us updated? If you find anything out?"

Hank nodded. He gently removed Mr. Bryson's hand from his arm and shook it. He walked out onto the porch and left him silhouetted in the doorway, nothing now but a shadow with all the light behind him.

CHAPTER

5

Hank pulled up to the house of Ryan the Boyfriend. The lots in this newer neighborhood were small and overwhelmed by the houses, hulking collections of brick and windows that all looked the same. He double-checked the house number. The driveway had a few tire tracks but was otherwise unplowed, so he chose a street spot around the corner that was mostly clear of snow. He waded through the growing drifts on the front walk. It was very late by now, but this time, he did not feel the least bit sorry about disturbing the occupants. Ryan the Boyfriend had some explaining to do.

He banged on the door and waited. Two more poundings finally brought an answer. It was a middle-aged blond woman he recognized from the observation lounge. She had obviously been asleep. Hank introduced himself. He needed to talk to both her and her son.

"He's asleep," she snapped. "Why on earth do you need to talk to him at this hour? We've had a very trying day. As you well know, Sheriff. Surely anything you need to know about our ordeal on that boat can wait until tomorrow."

Hank's eyes narrowed. "I am not here about your ordeal, ma'am. I am here about Mandy Bryson."

"Mandy? What has she got to do with anything? She was dating my son, but . . ." Ryan's mother trailed off, her eyes still bleary with sleep. She waved her hand in the air vaguely as if to dismiss the subject. Her use of the past tense had not gone unnoticed.

"May I come in, ma'am." It was not a question.

Ryan's mother scowled at him. "I don't see why that's necessary at this hour."

If she wasn't going to be nice, then neither was he. He drew himself out of the hunch he'd folded himself into underneath his parka and raised up to his full height.

"Mandy Bryson was found dead on the *Branson Beauty* this evening. In the private dining room reserved by your family. This is a homicide investigation, and I'm going to ask you once again—may I come in?"

Michelle Nelson stared at him, her mouth wide open. The look did not change as she slowly moved aside so he could enter the echoing foyer. They stood there staring at each other until she gave a start and turned toward the nearest doorway. It led to a formal dining room with ceiling-to-floor windows and a long table that reminded Hank of the one on the boat. She didn't bother to turn on a light, just sank into a chair and stared up at him. He helped himself to a seat away from the wall of windows, which let in slanted beams from the outside streetlamps, and sat down.

"Why were you and your family on the boat today, ma'am?" he asked.

"It was my mother's birthday luncheon. She turned seventy-five a few days ago. We rented the private dining room."

"And who was in attendance?"

"Mother. Me. Several of her friends. Bridge club, the church prayer group—I don't know. My brother, Jeffrey, and his wife, Patricia. Ashley—their daughter. Ryan. He's home from St. Louis. With Kelly."

She ended her list and just sat there, staring limply at him.

"And who is Kelly?" he prompted.

"Oh. Yes, ah. She's the girl he's seeing. They came down from school together for the holiday weekend."

"He wasn't seeing Mandy anymore?"

"Well, no." She cleared her throat. "That's what makes this a bit awkward. They had broken up, you see. I can't imagine what she was doing on the boat."

"Did you know she was on the boat today?"

"Heavens, no. I never saw her. I had no idea."

Hank sat back and gazed out the windows at the falling snow.

"When did you find out that this Kelly was coming down with your son?"

Michelle Nelson thought for a moment. "It must have been when he called last week to confirm that he could make it to Mother's party. He said he was bringing her. Yes, that was when."

"And had he mentioned Kelly before that?"

Michelle pursed her lips. "No, actually. I don't think so. He said he was bringing her, and that he and Mandy had broken up."

"And how did you feel about that?"

"How did I—? I don't understand."

This woman was starting to make his head hurt.

"How did you feel about your son breaking up with his girlfriend?" Hank said slowly.

"Well, it really wasn't any of my business, was it? He's a big boy. He does what he thinks is best."

Let's try this from a different direction, he thought.

"Did you like Mandy?"

"Yes." That was it. She stared at him some more. He needed an aspirin.

"How long had you known her?"

"Forever, I suppose. They'd always gone to school together."

"When did they start dating?"

"Hmmm. I think at the beginning of senior year. I know they were going together by homecoming. She was up for homecoming queen. I remember that. She didn't get it. Ryan was very disappointed."

Hank suppressed a sigh.

"Did they see each other over Christmas break?"

Michelle pursed her lips again. It was not that long ago. How hard could it be to remember?

"Yes. I think he had dinner over at her parents' house. He went somewhere all dressed up, too. Maybe that was New Year's. Yes, yes, they did go out on New Year's Eve."

"Do you know where?"

She shrugged. "No. I don't remember."

Maybe her short-term memory was better.

"Today, ma'am, on the boat. Did your luncheon start off in the dining room?"

"Oh." She blinked several times at the switch in topics.

"Ah, yes. We were in the dining room until the ship ran aground. We had just finished the food."

"Then what happened?"

"We all went out into the corridor to try to see better what was going on. What kind of idiot steers a ship into the rocks?"

Hank had to give her that one. He leaned forward and rested his elbows on the shiny table.

"What did you do then?"

"They were clearing the dining room, so we went into the observation lounge. We just stayed there. There was no point going anywhere else."

"Did everyone stay in the lounge the whole time?"

"Well, yes, I just said that."

Hank took a deep breath. "Did anyone leave the room at any point, ma'am? To go back to the dining room, perhaps? Or take a walk?"

"Oh. I see. I don't know. People did leave, to use the rest-room, I suppose."

"Did you?"

She glared at him. "We were on that boat for more than eight hours. Yes, I used the restroom. No, I did not keep track of whether other people did. I am not a hall monitor."

That was quite obvious.

"Was the restroom the only place you went?" Hank asked. "Did you go back into the dining room? Or to another deck?"

"No, I didn't go back to the dining room. It looked like they shut it down. All the shades were drawn. And why would I want to go downstairs? The main room was packed with people." She gave a little shudder. "At least the lounge was comfortable and only had us in it."

"And did you at any point see Mandy?"

"No. I told you that."

"Did you hear anyone talk about her?"

"No. Her name did not come up."

Hank sighed. A conversation about Mandy could have oc-curred two feet away from this lady and she would not have noticed. He was forming his next question when he saw a car slowly grind through the snow on the street outside. The headlight beams sliced through the windows as it turned and pulled into the driveway, barely making it over the drifts before it came to a stop. Both he and Mrs. Nelson stared as a jacketed figure got out and plowed to the door.

"What the hell is he doing?" she said as she got to her feet. She strode to the front door and jerked it open. Fum-bling for his keys on the other side stood Ryan the Boyfriend.

He jumped back and almost toppled into a snow-covered shrub.

"Mom! Jesus! What are you doing? Why are you up?"

"Why are you out there?" she snapped back. "I thought you were in bed."

"I went for a drive," Ryan said. "I couldn't sleep."

He stepped into the foyer and flung the door shut behind him. Then he saw Hank. His keys slipped from his hand and clattered across the tile floor. Hank didn't say a word, just stood there in the shadows of the massive foyer with his arms folded across his chest.

Ryan swallowed. "New boyfriend, Mom?" he said with a weak grin.

"This is the sheriff, you idiot," she said. Apparently, her brain only fully turned on when she was pissed. "He's here because Mandy's dead. And he wants to talk to you."

Ryan froze in the act of bending toward his keys.

"Mandy? What? Mandy? Dead? Mandy's dead?"

Hank watched very closely. He didn't feel it necessary to jump into the conversation quite yet.

"Did you know she was on the boat? DID YOU?" Michelle Nelson's demand rang through the foyer. Hank thought he heard the chandelier rattle. He didn't look up, however, instead keeping his eyes on young Ryan's face. The shock on it—just for an instant—changed to hostility as he stared at his mother. Then it was gone and the nice, Polo-shirted, hair-gelled college boy was back. He patted an errant strand back into place, picked up his keys, and straightened. It was just enough time to gather his thoughts.

"She . . . she was on the boat? Today? Was that where she was . . ." He trailed off.

"Did. You. Know." Mrs. Nelson spat the words at him. The animosity flickered across his face again.

"No. No! Happy?" he shouted. "I didn't know. Why the hell should I?"

"Because she was your girlfriend, for Chrissakes," she shouted back.

The two glared at each other as the echoes subsided. Perhaps Mrs. Nelson was more fond of Mandy than she admitted earlier, Hank thought. The foyer fell into silence. He waited. Certainly, the young lady at the top of the stairs would have something to say about all this.

"Your *girlfriend* was on the boat?" she hissed.

Ryan and his mother jerked around, their heads swiveling up toward the second floor, where one of the pretty blond teenagers from the observation lounge was standing. She was wearing nothing but a St. Louis University T-shirt and a look of very angry surprise. Hank considered pulling a chair out of the dining room and making himself comfortable. That might disrupt the flow of things, though. He did not want to interrupt.

"You have a girlfriend?" she said from above.

Ryan spread his arms wide. "Baby, no. Of course not. We broke up. It was over. It—" He stopped himself and had the decency to wince at that. She seized on the silence.

"What's she doing here? Are you going to see her? What does she mean to you?"

All very good questions, Hank thought. He was going to make sure Ryan answered them one way or another. But the blond replacement had obviously not emerged from her room in time to hear that Mandy was dead. He glanced at Mrs. Nelson. Her jaw clenched.

"Ryan's *ex*-girlfriend is dead. She was murdered on the boat. Today," Mrs. Nelson said as she craned her neck to look up at the blonde. The anger drained out of her face, leaving only surprise.

"My God. That's . . . that's horrible." She stepped back from the railing and started to turn back into the upstairs hallway. "Now I'm really sorry I came," she muttered.

Hank had no intention of letting her go back to her room and her cell phone so she could start texting everyone she knew to complain about her terrible weekend. He cleared his throat. All three froze. Then they turned as one to stare at him, still standing in the shadows.

"Kelly?" he said. "Miss, if you would stay right where you are. I'm going to need to ask you some questions. You, too, Ryan."

They all continued to stare at him. He stifled a sigh of exasperation and gestured up toward the blonde.

"Miss, if you would be so good as to get dressed. But first, I'm going to need for you to bring me your purse and your cell phone."

Kelly snapped out of her stupor. "What? Why? Are you going to search me?"

Now Hank stifled a chuckle. No way would he be that stupid. "No, I'm not," he said. "I also am not going to search your purse. But I am going to ask you to let me hold your cell phone. I need to ask you a few questions before you use it to call anyone and tell them about what has happened. You, too, Ryan."

He held out his hand toward Ryan, who had not moved from the spot where he'd dropped his keys. This time, there was no attempt to disguise the hostility. He glared as he dug into the pocket of his khakis. He slapped the phone into Hank's hand and moved back toward his mother. Hank turned to look up the stairs. Kelly was just starting to stomp down them, which was impressive considering that she now wore big fuzzy slippers that should have muffled her footsteps. She walked forward and dropped her purse on the table in the middle of the foyer. She set her phone next to it.

"We can just go back in there," Mrs. Nelson said, pointing toward the dining room. Hank shook his head and turned to Kelly. "If you would be so good as to get dressed—and bring your coat," he said. She stomped back up the stairs.

"Where are you taking her?" Ryan asked.

"She—and you—need to come down to the station with me," Hank said. The farther this kid was away from his mother, the better his interview would be. And he certainly didn't need Mrs. Nelson having a heart-to-heart with the replacement girlfriend while they were gone, so Kelly needed to come, too.

"The station," Mrs. Nelson squawked. "Is he a suspect? What the hell? You can't talk to him without me. I'm his mother. I have parental rights."

"How old are you?" Hank said to Ryan.

"Nineteen."

"Then, no, ma'am, you do not have the right to be present. You may certainly drive yourself and wait at the station for our talk to be over with, but that's it."

She started toward him with her fists clenched at her sides, before taking a breath and pulling herself back. "Then I want a lawyer. You can't talk to him without a lawyer."

"Why?" Hank hoped his face registered a look of innocent surprise. "I just need to find out as much about Mandy as I can." Pause. "We just need to have a chat. Don't we, son?"

Ryan glanced from Hank to his mother and then longingly out toward the car he'd just parked in the driveway. He looked back.

"Just a chat." Hank smiled.

Ryan swallowed. "Okay," he said. "I'll go."

"Ryan!"

He turned toward his mother and whispered furiously, "If I don't go, he's going to think I have something to hide."

Oh, how Hank loved that line of reasoning. Now he had to hustle the kid out of here before Mrs. Nelson talked sense into him. More stomping from the direction of the stairs signaled that Replacement Kelly was ready.

"Everyone bundled up?" he said and swung the door

open. Mrs. Nelson, a shaking pillar of fury in a bathrobe, lost no time slamming it shut behind them. The motion triggered the front walkway's sensor light and flooded the entire yard with searing fluorescence that bounced off the swirling snowflakes, blinding him. Momentarily, he hoped.

CHAPTER
6

He and Ryan sat staring at each other. Hank had left Kelly with Sheila once they arrived at the substation on Shepherd of the Hills Expressway. It was a little outpost of a building that had a shoebox-sized lobby, two offices, and a holding cell. It came in handy when it wasn't practical to make the long, twisty drive to the main office in Forsyth. Like tonight.

"Where were you this evening?" Hank asked. Ryan started; he obviously had not expected that to be the first question.

"Uh . . . uh. I went for a drive," he stammered.

"In a snowstorm?"

"Yeah, well. Um. I went up to the high school and just, you know, sat and thought for a while."

"Thought about what?"

Ryan shrugged. "Stuff."

He was as forthcoming as his mother had been. Great.

"How long where you up there?"

"Hmm. An hour or two."

"Your mom didn't know you went out?"

Ryan looked at him like he was stupid. Good.

"Obviously not. You were there, right?"

Hank nodded. And waited. Ryan eventually filled the silence.

"I left after she and Kelly went to bed. Mom's pretty old-fashioned, so we were in separate bedrooms. Kelly didn't know I'd left, either."

Maybe Mrs. Nelson is a better mother than I gave her credit for, Hank thought.

"What stuff?"

"Huh?"

"What stuff where you thinking about . . . up at the high school?"

"Oh, right. I don't know. School. Kelly. It's all pretty stressful. A lot more stressful than I thought it'd be."

"How so?"

He shrugged again. "It's so much work. And Mom's calling all the time. Always telling me I'd better be getting her money's worth up there. Having all kinds of experiences and taking all kinds of classes. But then she wants me to come home all the time, too. She can . . . well, she can be a pain."

Hank could only imagine.

"When was the last time you were home—before this weekend?" Hank asked.

"Christmas break," he said. "I knew I'd be coming back this weekend for Gran's birthday. That's not something you miss."

"And this is your second semester at St. Louis University?"

"Yeah."

"And is that where you met Kelly?"

"Yeah. We had our University 101 orientation together. She's in a sorority." He grinned.

"How long have you been seeing her?"

"Oh, about a month or two. Since right after—" He stopped. He'd figured out they were circling around to Mandy.

"Right after what?"

"Right after Christmas break," he said slowly.

"And when, exactly, did you and Mandy break up?"

Ryan fidgeted in his seat. Hank waited.

"Right around then . . ." he said eventually.

Hank's eyebrow went up. "Right around when, exactly?"

Ryan yanked at the lock of hair that kept falling into his eyes. He looked out the window. He chewed his lip. Then he pushed at the hair again.

"She . . . we . . . it's complicated."

Hank almost snorted. If this kid thought life with two living girlfriends was complicated, wait until he had to deal with the reality of one who had been murdered and one who knew she'd been two-timed. Add to that the fact that he was currently Hank's top suspect, and Ryan the Boyfriend's life was not looking simple.

Ryan got a grip on himself. He straightened in his chair and cleared his throat. "We broke up two weeks ago. It was a mutual decision."

"Then can you explain to me why she was five hours away from her university, without her parents knowing, and in the same place where your family was having a large celebration?"

"No," Ryan said flatly. "I can't."

Hank leaned forward and put his arms on the desk in front of him.

"Did you know she was on the boat?"

"No."

"Did you know she was in Branson at all?"

"No."

"When was the last time you saw her?"

"Christmas break."

"When was the last time you talked to her?"

"Two weeks ago."

"Was that when you broke up?"

"Yes."

"Who broke up with whom?"

"*Whom*? Really?" He paused and gritted his teeth. "I said it was mutual."

"But you didn't tell your mother."

"Yes, I did."

"Not when it happened."

"Well, I guess not. I was . . . I was getting over it."

"With Kelly?"

Ryan shoved his hair out of his face again.

"Why didn't you tell your mother?"

"I didn't want to, okay? You've met her. I didn't want a lecture."

"And she would have lectured you?"

"No. But she would have told Gran. And Gran would have lectured me."

"But your gran was okay with you bringing someone else to her party?"

The shrug again. "I didn't ask. I just figured if I showed

up with Kelly, there was nothing anyone could do, and they'd all just have to be cool about it."

"Is that why you brought her? To give you cover from your gran?"

"Pretty much, yeah."

Hank did not see much of a future for the two of them after Kelly found all this out. And she was the lucky one. He suddenly felt very tired.

"I'm going to ask you this one more time, Ryan. Did you know that Mandy Bryson came up from the University of Oklahoma this weekend?"

"No."

"Did you know she was on the *Branson Beauty* today?"

"No."

"Did you see her on the *Branson Beauty* today?"

"No."

"Did you kill her?"

"No."

Hank leaned back, away from the desk. The kid had looked him right in the eye during every one of those answers. Except the last one. Just hiding the tears suddenly in his eyes, or hiding the lie? That was the question, wasn't it?

A door slammed, and they heard Sheila talking to someone. Then Mrs. Nelson's voice cut through everything. Ryan sagged in his chair and actually looked relieved. Hank was surprised it had taken her this long. He'd had more time with her son than he had expected he would. Maybe he should have been grateful for the snow after all.

The door to the office popped open, and Hank turned to smile at Mrs. Nelson. She was still furious, but that had not prevented her from taking the time to put on a nicely pressed pantsuit and a full face of makeup. Behind her hovered a man who had to be the defense lawyer.

"Ryan, there you are. Sheriff, this interview is over."

How very TV-sounding. Hank's smile got bigger.

"Of course, Mrs. Nelson. Your son and I were just finishing up. Thank you for coming to get him. That was very kind of you."

The fuel yanked from her fire, Mrs. Nelson stopped halfway into the room. The lawyer, whose own outfit looked as if it had been pulled out of the clothes hamper five minutes before, bumped into her, and the two stumbled forward. Now Hank's smile was genuine. Keep everyone off-balance.

Sheila stepped into the doorway. "I've already told them that no one leaves town until we say they can."

Hank nodded. Both he and Sheila knew they couldn't physically keep the family Nelson from leaving Branson, but Ryan and his mother didn't need to know that. With a bustle of coats and indignant mutterings, they left. Hank resisted the urge to lay his head down on the desk and got up to get a cup of coffee instead.

Sheila's talk with Kelly had confirmed that the two had been dating since before Christmas. And she'd had no idea Ryan had another girlfriend. And boy, Sheila had said with a chuckle, was she pissed off about it.

Hank pondered all the information from Sheila as he drove home, tapping the steering wheel as the heat blew on high. Ryan had invited Kelly just on Friday to come down for his grandmother's party on Sunday. She hadn't wanted to—she had a math test on Tuesday—but he had really seemed to want her to come.

Kelly had not seen anyone matching Mandy's description on the boat. She had not heard anyone talking about Mandy, although Ryan's cousin and his old high school friends had acted strangely toward her, which made sense now that she knew the situation into which he'd forced her. His grandmother had been perfectly sweet to her, but when she thought about it, the old lady had not said anything at all to Ryan after he introduced her as his girlfriend.

Well, Hank thought, at least the grandmother appears to be placing blame on the proper person. Now it just remained for Hank to figure out whether Ryan was the proper person for his purposes, too. He knew he wouldn't get another crack at the kid now that Mrs. Nelson had lawyered him up, but he hoped the old lady would be helpful. He'd get to her first thing in the morning. That and have a chat with the coroner, whom he really hoped would be able to tell him a lot more about Mandy Bryson's death than he knew right now.

He slowly pulled up to the house and into the shoveled driveway. Good God, had Duncan been out doing that? The guy was seventy-one years old. That was all he needed—his father-in-law dropping dead of a heart attack just so Hank could park closer to the house. He jabbed at the garage door opener, but the door didn't rise. Must have been frozen shut. He left the car in the driveway and made sure there wasn't a stubborn Scotsman collapsed in a snow drift on his way to the front door. He let himself in quietly, automatically avoiding the squeaky floorboard in the entryway. He stopped and just stood there, inhaling the faint scent of a now-extinguished wood fire and the chicken stew that Dunc must have fixed for dinner. The clock ticked in the hallway. It had to be past four. He sat down on the floor—the bench and the big shoe brush were in the mudroom attached to the garage, where they all usually came in—and wrestled off his snow boots and then his coat. Then he padded into the kitchen to see if there was any stew left.

There was. He stuck some in the microwave and then tip-toed down the hallway to the kids' room. They were both sound asleep, like any sensible human being should be at this hour, he thought. He pulled Benny's covers up over him and then turned to Maribel, who was bathed in the blue and yellow light from that ridiculous smiley moon night-light she loved so much. His throat tightened and he turned quickly away.

He headed back for his stew, ate it quickly, and then crawled into bed. Maggie, as usual, didn't even stir. He lay there, staring at the shadows on the ceiling, until his body finally overruled his racing mind and he slept.

At six thirty he staggered out into the kitchen, where his Cheerios-chomping children greeted him with grins and Maggie shoved a mug of coffee into his hand.

"What time did you end up getting home?" she asked.

Hank shrugged. "I don't know. Four something."

"You want some eggs or something, or do you have to go straight back in?"

"I should go. I ordered a briefing at seven thirty."

"Hank." Maggie put her hands on her hips. "Can't someone else get that boat off the lake? Isn't it Gallagher's problem now? What's so urgent?"

Hank took another swallow of coffee and glanced at the kids.

"Actually, I haven't technically released the boat back to Gallagher."

Maggie had been a cop's wife for long enough to know what that meant.

"It's a crime scene? What happened? Nobody was hurt. We cleared everybody they brought into the hospital." She stared at him, waiting for an explanation. He jerked his head toward the mudroom. Once they were inside, he closed the door.

"There was a murder. A teenage girl, dead in the private dining room. We only found her after the boat docked."

Maggie gasped and then just stared at him. Despite the awfulness of it, Hank grinned. It wasn't often he struck her speechless. He watched her gather herself.

"Well, you're right. No breakfast for you. Get going." She put her hand on the doorknob and then stopped. "Was she . . . did she go to Branson Valley High?"

"Yeah," Hank said. "She graduated last year."

Maggie nodded. "Mom would have known her, then." She flung open the door and strode back into the kitchen. "Okay, who needs more cereal?"

Hank went out the opposite door, into the garage to find an ice scraper for his squad car. He almost tripped over the snowblower.

"Careful there. That thing's almost as old as you are."

Hank turned to see Duncan leaning against the doorjamb in his bathrobe. "You own a snowblower? How did I not know that?"

Duncan shrugged. "There hasn't been a need for it since you moved down here. Pulled it out of the shed early yesterday. Haven't used it since, hmm, must have been that big one four or five years ago. Little dusty, but it still fires up just fine."

The same could be said for you, Hank thought. Probably

just as gassy, too. "Thanks for doing the driveway last night. I might need it again to get back out, though."

Duncan smiled. "Probably. Holler and I'll show you how to start it. The switch has gotten a little balky." He turned to go inside. "Oh, and the ice scraper is up against the back wall."

Once again, Hank was glad he'd ceded the garage to Duncan when they all moved into the house. He kept it as spotless and organized as one of Maggie's operating rooms. He managed to fit two cars in there, along with the kids' bikes and all of their other outside toys. And, apparently, a snow-blower. Hank shook his head, grabbed the ice scraper, and headed back into the house.

Half an hour later he finally extricated his car from the driveway—and he only lost control of the snowblower once, to the delight of Maribel and Benny watching from the window. Those two had a nice, snuggly Presidents' Day holiday ahead of them, playing by the fire and drinking entirely too much of Grandpop's hot cocoa.

He was not so lucky. By the time he got to the substation, he'd already pulled over two different drivers for going too fast on the icy roads. He stomped into the office and found the Pup putting on a pot of coffee.

"Hey, Chief," he said and pointed toward the computer behind the counter. "I was just surfing around. Everybody has stories on the *Beauty*, but no one has anything on the murder. Are we going to be the ones who have to release it?"

Hank thought for a moment. Usually, somebody tipped off reporters on stuff like this, and all he'd ever had to do was confirm it. Or pass them off to the department spokesperson. But as the Branson County Sheriff's Department had no flak, he would have to be the one to do the talking. Ugh. Maybe he could convince Sheila to do it. No, the risk of her poking some reporter in the chest for asking a "fool question" was too high. He sighed, poured himself a cup of coffee, and walked back to his office.

It was cold and dark and bare. He wasn't here all that often, and so he hadn't bothered to bring in anything personal to take the edge off. Metal desk, metal lamp, metal filing cabinet. Metal miniblinds. No point opening those. He sat down and fired up the computer on the desk. Might as well get started on that press release. Sam and Sheila came in.

"Just us," Sheila said. "Everyone else is out digging fool drivers out of snowdrifts. And there's an accident out on Seventy-six." She walked over to the window and yanked up the blinds. Hank sighed.

"Okay," he started. "Mandy's parents did not know she was coming down this weekend. We need to find out if any of her friends at the University of Oklahoma knew. And what they knew about her relationship with Ryan Nelson."

They both nodded at him.

"So, who wants to go to Norman?"

No nods this time.

"Someone needs to go to Norman," he said.

"There's, um, a blizzard going on, Chief," Sam said. This time Sheila did nod. Hank scowled and turned to jab at the computer.

"Ah, yes. But the forecast says it's expected to blow out of here by noon. And the next couple of days are supposed to be clear."

"Clear all the way to Norman?" Sheila asked. Hank nodded. She primly adjusted the glasses on the end of her nose.

"It's five hours just to get down there," she said. "Then all the interviews. I'd have to stay over. Pack a suitcase."

Hank nodded again. Sam watched her out of the corner of his eye and held his breath. She took her glasses off, looked at them carefully, and then placed them back exactly where they had been on her nose. The two men waited. She sniffed.

"Tyrone will not be expecting this," she said.

Hank nodded with what he hoped looked like solemn agreement, even though he knew Sheila's husband was perfectly capable of handling an unexpected absence.

"He's going to have to take care of the dogs all on his own," she said, talking more to herself now than to the men in the office with her. "He'll have to remember to put out the recycling, and . . ." She trailed off, although she was obviously still making a mental list of everything poor Tyrone would be responsible for if she left.

"He'll be fine, Sheila," Sam said in an attempt to be helpful and reassuring at the same time. "He was fine when you went to Comic-Con two years ago, remember?"

Hank sat bolt upright in his chair.

"*You* went to Comic-Con?"

Sheila gave Sam a look that should have turned him to stone right then and there. "How. Did. You. Know. That's. Where. I. Went?"

"Ah . . . um. Yeah. Well." He wouldn't look directly at her. "You wouldn't tell me, and I was practicing my investigative skills—like you told me I should be doing—so I tracked your itinerary, and . . ." He ended in an unintelligible mumble and stared at his shoes.

Hank was dying to press it. What comic was she such a devotee of that she would travel sixteen hundred miles to go to a fan convention? But the look on her face did not invite questioning. And that was putting it mildly.

"Okay," Hank said. "We were talking about Oklahoma. And the weather clearing up. And the interviews that need to be done."

He smiled brightly at Sheila. She let out a sigh that sounded more like a growl. Sam scooted his chair away from her.

"All right. I'll go. I think I'd be the best one to talk to her friends. Should be a woman doing it. They might open up to me more."

Hank nodded. He thought the same thing. Sheila knew exactly how to approach an interview. She could pull out the maternal caretaker or the girlfriend conspirator, whichever suited the situation.

"I'll call you with more information as I get it, but you'd better get going," he said.

She left the room and only then did Sam exhale. Hank grinned. "Think we'll survive without her?"

"You won't," she yelled from the lobby. The outside door slammed shut.

Hank got the Pup started on setting up appointments for the workers on the boat to come in and be interviewed. "Make them think it's just about running aground—don't tell them about the murder," he said. But there were other interviews that were too important to be scheduled. He needed to get the lay of the land, figure out the dynamics surrounding the luncheon and its guests. And the best place to start was the birthday girl. It was barely seven thirty in the morning, but Hank had a feeling that Frances Honneffer would be up.

CHAPTER

7

Hank sipped his tea and looked across the coffee table at Frances Honneffer. She sat on the edge of a lumpy easy chair, her back perfectly straight and her hands folded in her lap. She had probably had her hair done just before yesterday's party, and the white curls still looked immaculate. She was already dressed—complete with earrings and a flower brooch pinned to her blouse—and had tried to hide the tearstains on her face with makeup. Her daughter had called her at four in the morning with the news. Hank suspected she'd been ready and waiting for him ever since.

"Tell me what I can do to help, Sheriff," she said. "I cannot believe this . . . Mandy . . . Do you have a suspect? Do you know what happened? I cannot believe . . ."

Hank chose not to bring up her grandson quite yet. He set down his teacup.

"Did you know she was on the boat?" he asked.

She stared at him in puzzlement. "Well, of course I did. I invited her."

Hallelujah. Somebody was finally admitting to knowing something. He nodded encouragingly.

"I mailed her an invitation to my party several weeks ago. I got a very nice note back—I don't use the email—saying she would try to be there. She had some obligation at school the night before, so she said she would try to drive in early Sunday morning and come straight to the *Beauty* for the luncheon. I was so pleased she might come."

"Did you tell Ryan that she was coming?"

She thought for a moment. "No, I don't suppose I did, now that I think about it. I guess I just assumed that he knew she would be coming—that she would have told him. I thought they were still a couple." There was no small amount of temper in the last sentence.

"When did you find out they weren't?"

Her voice crackled. "When he brought that blond coed on board. I was astounded. First, he had not asked to bring her. Second, no one knew he was seeing someone else. Mandy certainly didn't know. She was devastated."

"What happened?" Hank was literally on the edge of his seat. Please.

Mrs. Honneffer straightened the crease in her trouser leg.

"Jeffrey and I—that's my son—we got to the *Beauty* dock early, so we could make sure all of the arrangements were in place. We were there when Mandy arrived. She was the first guest. She popped out of her little car and gave me a big hug. Talking a mile a minute. Telling me all about her track training, and her roommate failing a class, and all sorts of things. She said she had just gotten into town. Had left school at something like six in the morning. I told her that made me feel very special, that she would make such an effort to come see me. She teased me—she was always teasing me, but in such a kind way—and said that I wasn't her only stop. She was going to surprise her parents after we were done with the boat cruise.

"We went up onto the boat together and took a look at the dining room. It was beautifully set. Crystal and linens and those wondrous windows looking out onto everything. Mandy—you could tell she was delighted with it, but she put on airs that she wasn't impressed. 'Where are the birthday balloons, then? You call this decorated? Where's the clown?' Oh, she could make me laugh."

Mrs. Honneffer's voice caught on the last word and refused to go any further. Her hands turned white as they gripped each other in her lap. She stared at Hank. He stared back. She managed to swallow and start again.

"We were in there a few minutes, and then Jeffrey poked his head in and said that guests were starting to arrive. We went out into the hallway and looked down at the dock. We saw Ryan walk up with his arm around that blond coed. He was making quite a show of it, stroking her hair, kissing her cheek, that sort of thing.

"Mandy had been holding my arm—I can be a little unsteady on my feet—but she slowly detached herself and placed my hand on the railing instead. She turned so pale, as if she were about to be ill. I . . . I didn't know what to say. It was absolutely horrible, watching someone's heart break right before your eyes.

"She looked around and said she had to get out of there. By then, they had opened that door to the stairway and everyone was either climbing the stairs or heading for the elevator. She couldn't get down without everyone seeing her. And I could tell she was just mortified and still in shock. She couldn't face him then. She backed away from the windows and almost ran into a waiter who was coming out of a door that was right there, next to the one that went into the dining room. She looked at me and whispered 'Happy birthday,' and then she bolted through that door. That . . . that was the last time I saw her."

Hank sipped his tea and waited for Mrs. Honneffer to battle back the tears filling her eyes. He set down his teacup.

"Who attended your luncheon?" he asked. He had the list of descriptions provided by Tony Sampson on the boat, but he needed names—and personalities—to go with it.

"Well," she said with renewed strength, obviously glad to stop talking about Mandy, "my son, Jeffrey, who arrived with me. His wife, Patricia, and their daughter, Ashley. She's twelve, looks like her mother. They arrived separately, after Jeffrey and I did."

"And they knew Mandy?"

"Oh, yes. The whole family knew Mandy. She was always around, before they both went off to school. Ashley adored her. I think they really related to each other, both being only children and all."

"And Jeffrey and Patricia? They have a good marriage?"

"Oh, why, yes, I suppose. A perfectly ordinary one, at least. They've been married twenty-five years. Waited a bit too long to have Ashley, if you ask me, but they were both very invested in their careers. Jeffrey is a lawyer up in Springfield, and Patricia runs the law office for him."

A lawyer. Great.

"He was terribly agitated when the boat ran aground. He had several clients he appeared to desperately need to contact, but there was no cell phone reception. He was ridiculous—moving all over the lounge, trying to get a signal. I think he even went outside on the deck at one point. At least he kept the damn thing in his pocket during lunch. He is my polite child." She looked pointedly at Hank. He chose not to take the bait.

"Other guests?" he asked.

"My daughter, whom you've met. And honestly, it's her I would have expected to show up with an uninvited date. She's always got some boyfriend or other. That's why I was so happy with Ryan and Mandy. They were going steady. They were stable. I so hoped Ryan wasn't going to turn out like his mother."

"So she's divorced from Ryan's father?" Hank asked.

"Yes. They divorced when Ryan was five. She played around for a while, then she married that idiot Barney Lambert. Oh, I begged her not to. Anybody could see it wouldn't last. And it didn't. Two years. I took my wedding present back."

She paused and took a sip of tea.

"It really hurt Ryan. He had just gotten attached to Barney when Michelle ended the whole thing. The only good thing to come out of it was the money. She took him for half of everything, which was much more than I'd ever thought he was worth. After that, she's been able to afford the lifestyle she always wanted—not working, lots of travel, nice clothes. You saw that monstrous house she lives in, didn't you?"

Hank nodded. Mrs. Honneffer continued. "And the money has certainly helped her relationship with Jeffrey and

Patricia. She was always hinting that they should be more generous with her, help her out financially, since he was the big-
time lawyer. And Jeffrey always believed, as I'm sure he'd tell
you, that she should get a damn job. Since her divorce, though,
that has stopped. She doesn't pester him, and he doesn't
lecture her. That's been nice."

"And how did Michelle feel about Mandy?" Hank steered
the conversation back.

"As far as I know, she liked her fine. I think she genu-
inely couldn't understand why Ryan would want to stay with
one person for so long, especially at his age, but she liked
Mandy anyway."

They both took drinks of tea. Mrs. Honneffer kept her
hands, swollen and bent from arthritis, curled around her cup
as Hank asked who else had attended the party.

"Several of my friends. Doris and Leonard Dovecoat. She
was in fairly dire straits by the time you arrived. She never
could handle stress. Thank God the paramedics had oxygen.
I thought she was going to pass out.

"Eight ladies from church. I can get you their full names.
And Regina Price and Lois Campbell. They're both in
wheelchairs. As is Malcolm Turner, who broke his hip last
month, poor man. Can't even get out of his wheelchair
without a hoist. I don't think he went to the bathroom the
entire time."

"Did you?"

Mrs. Honneffer looked puzzled. "Did I what?"

"Did you use the restroom? Did you leave the lounge
at all?"

"Oh," she said. "Why yes, of course. You know how long
we were stranded out there."

"Did you see others leave the lounge also?"

"Yes. I'd guess everyone did at some point or another. You had to go out into the hallway to get to the restrooms. But no one was gone for very long. I don't think anyone had any desire to go down into the main dining room, or outside onto the deck. We were content—" She smiled weakly. "Relatively speaking, of course—we were content to stay right where we were."

She took another sip of tea and glanced at his cup. "Do you need more, Sheriff?"

"No, thank you, ma'am," he said. The stuff was obviously decaf and not doing him a bit of good. He'd have to stop for coffee somewhere. "Was there anyone else on your guest list?" So far, she hadn't mentioned any of the teenagers he'd seen sulking on the floor.

"Oh, yes. I'm sorry. I got sidetracked. Ryan had friends. Since he was only down for the weekend, he had asked if he could invite a few people he'd been in high school with, friends who have stayed down here instead of going to school. There were two of them. I don't remember their names. One of them was a very pretty blonde who didn't say a word until the paramedic showed up. She must like a man in uniform. I know I did."

He had to go. He had so much work to do. So many people to interview. He picked up his cold cup of decaffeinated tea and settled back in his chair. "Really?"

Mrs. Honneffer smiled, and he saw the wrinkled remnants of what her man in uniform must have known so long ago.

"Frank was so handsome. He'd just gotten back from Korea, where he'd been a lieutenant in the army. We met at a welcome-back-the-troops dance. I was twenty-two. Quite long in the tooth, you know. My mother made me go. She said it was my last shot at a husband. I was so peeved that I vowed I wouldn't talk to any man at all. Then I saw Frank. We were married three months later."

Hank let her go on, about the kids, the lean years, the eventual success with the furniture store, the retirement, the declining health, and then Frank's death at seventy-three from a stroke. Talking about that well-worn sorrow helped her shift her attention away from today's fresh grief. He left her with that.

Back in the car, he read a text from Sam. Albert the Moron was still practically comatose at the hospital. Hank sighed. There was no point in going back there, then. Another message came in as he sat there staring at his phone. A reporter had called, asking about the murder. Fantastic. He called Sam, who was still at the station.

"What's up, Chief?"

"How'd the reporter find out?"

"Nobody here. But the body is up in Springfield for the autopsy. Could've been someone on that end. I didn't tell him anything. I swear."

Hank grunted. He couldn't put off that press release any longer. He'd go back to the office and get that over with before he headed up to Springfield himself. At least going there would put him out of the reach of the media. He wanted to talk to a reporter about as much as he wanted to talk to Michelle Nelson again.

The roads were getting better. He made it back to the station in half the time it had taken him to get out to Mrs. Honneffer's house, and he only had to pull one driver over for using the road like a personal slalom course. Maybe things were looking up. He walked into the office and found Tony Sampson, the boat's first mate, sitting in one of the cheap plastic chairs in the lobby. The kid leapt to his feet.

"Hello, sir. How are you today, sir?"

Hank grinned. "Just fine, Tony. You here to finish giving your statement?"

"Yes, sir. I was told to come in. Will it be that lady I talked to on the boat?"

"No," Hank said. "She's not here right now. You'll be speaking to Deputy Karnes. He should be out in a minute." He glanced up at the clock on the wall. It had stopped. Cheap government junk. Tony noticed and poked at the phone in his hand. It looked bigger than the smartphones Hank was used to seeing. Headphones dangled from it.

"It's eight fifty-five A.M.," Tony said.

"What were you listening to?" Hank asked.

"Oh." Tony paused. "Different stuff." He waved the phone enthusiastically. "This is the brand-new one. It has enough space to hold thousands of songs, or at least a couple of movies. It's awesome."

"Come in handy on the boat?" Hank asked.

"Heck, yeah," Tony replied. "I just download them before work, and I'm all set."

The Pup bounded around the corner.

"I'm ready for you, Mr. Sampson."

"Hold up, Sam. I need to talk to you first." Hank pointed toward the back offices. Tony remained standing, looking from Hank to Sam, unsure of what to do. His eyes finally rested on Hank and he sank slowly into his chair.

"We'll have you out of here soon, Tony," Hank said as he

walked away. Once in his office, he wrote the press release with Sam hanging over his shoulder offering suggestions.

"I knew a girl in college who was in communications, and she always said that you start with the who, what, when, where, and why," Sam said.

"She went to *college* to learn that?" Hank asked.

"Well, more than that, of course," said Sam, ignoring the sarcasm. "But it seemed worth bringing up, cuz right now, you've got three long sentences, and you haven't even said yet who was killed or where."

Hank scowled at the screen. The Pup was right. He deleted his useless sentences and started over.

". . . and then her senior year, she decided to go into PR, and by that time—wait, shouldn't you put that the victim was a student at OU?"

Hank smacked the return key. "No. Let them figure that out on their own. I'm not making their job any easier." He moved out of Sam's way and jabbed his finger at the screen. "Would your PR friend approve of that?"

Sam skimmed it and nodded. "You've got the four we know. In the first two sentences, so that's definitely better." He leaned back from the computer. "I sure wish we had a *why*, though. We'd be a lot closer to solving it."

For a twenty-five-year-old pup who still insists on Froot Loops for breakfast and continues to trip over his own feet, Sam comes up with some surprisingly mature conclusions sometimes, Hank thought as he emailed the press release out to the various local news desks.

Then he ran down the staffing situation, which was as bleak as he'd feared. Everyone he had was out dealing with weather-related ridiculousness, except for him and Sam, road-tripping Sheila, Duane—who was still stuck at the hospital guarding the *Beauty*'s captain—and the deputy they'd stationed out to watch the boat itself at the deserted dock. It was basically just the two of them to interview God knew how many people.

And he needed to go to Springfield. He was tempted to avoid the normally half hour drive up there and just call the doctor for the results, but he'd always gone to these things in person at his old job. He wasn't going to start cutting corners now. Not with his first Branson County case.

Hank walked down the hallway and into the morgue. None of the counties in southwest Missouri created enough business (thank God) to employ their own forensic pathologists. Instead, they all used Dr. Whittaker, who apparently had been doing it forever. Hank had never met him.

"Well, hello there," boomed a deep voice as Hank swung open the door. He blinked at the short, very old, roly-poly man. The overhead lights bounced off a bald head so shiny Hank suspected the good doctor actually polished it. He peeled off an exam glove and stuck out his hand. "You must be the new sheriff in town."

Like Hank hadn't heard that one before. He shook hands and gestured toward the sheet-covered body. "Shall we get started?"

Whittaker went on as if he hadn't heard. Maybe he hadn't. Hank was having trouble pinpointing how old the man was.

"So you're the one the county commissioners thought so highly of. Dazzled them with your big-city experience, did you?"

"I did work for the police department in Kansas City, yes," Hank said.

Whittaker gave him a once-over with blue eyes that were going a little rheumy but still managed to appear sharp. Hank felt as if he were going through the job interview all over again.

"And they figured you'd be a good one to finish out Darrell Gibbons's term, did they?"

"Yes, sir," Hank replied.

"How's he doing up in the legislature, anyway?"

"I wouldn't know," Hank said. "He . . . ah . . . he seems to be busy. We have not had a chance to talk."

Whittaker nodded knowingly. Hank wondered how close he had been to Gibbons. They must have worked together for years.

"Good ol' Darrell. He's very suited for that political life. What about you?" Whittaker asked cheerfully. "You going to run for sheriff next year? Get elected instead of just appointed?"

Hank tried not to frown. "I hadn't really given it much thought," he said. "I've been a little busy." Again, he pointed toward the occupied exam table.

"Oh. Oh, yes. The autopsy. Yes, yes." Whittaker chuckled and bounced across the room. "Let's get started, shall we?"

He pulled back the sheet and started pointing.

"I'll do the whole thing, of course, but it's pretty obvious she was strangled." He moved her hair out of the way. "Bruising on the throat, petechial hemorrhages in the eyes."

Hank stood with his hands in his pockets as Whittaker moved around the head of the table, gesturing dramatically with his hands.

"Cut on the back of the skull. Prior to death. Heavy object, not particularly sharp. The start of some bruising, but not much, so she was killed pretty quickly after."

"So she was hit from behind. What about when she was strangled? Was the killer facing her?"

Whittaker lifted up her head to take a look at the bruising on the back of her neck, then laid her back down with a *clunk* that made Hank wince.

"I'd say so. Whoever did this had to have been looking straight at her."

CHAPTER

8

After finishing with the good doctor, Hank stopped by the law office of Honneffer & Boskins, which was not closed for the holiday, or the weather. At least they had the heat going and served some pretty good coffee.

Jeffrey gave substantially the same version of events as his mother had earlier. But he had not seen Mandy flee into one of the other rooms because he had gone ahead of her and Mrs. Honneffer to welcome the arriving guests downstairs. After seeing his nephew hanging all over the blonde, he assumed Mandy had left the boat altogether after witnessing the same thing. He'd had no idea she was still aboard until his sister called at four in the morning to yell news of the murder at him and demand he come down and represent Ryan.

"I declined," Jeffrey said in a clipped tone. "I am not a criminal defense lawyer. And I was not going to drive back down to Branson in a blinding snowstorm just to spend two seconds telling some two-bit local cop to stop questioning him."

Hank smiled winningly.

"Oh," Jeffrey said. "That was probably you, wasn't it?"

Hank nodded.

"Sorry."

"Do you think he did it?" Hank asked.

"Ryan? No," Jeffrey said immediately, then paused. "No," he repeated slowly. He thought for a moment. "I think he was too entranced with that new girl. And I don't know that he even knew Mandy was on the boat."

"Did he leave the dining room, or the lounge, at all?" Hank said.

"The dining room—no. I don't recall anyone leaving the dining room during lunch. And it was very soon after that when we ran aground. That captain fellow came in and had us all move to the lounge at that point. No one knew what was going on. There was a huge sound of cracking wood from the back, and we just jolted to a stop. Everyone was stunned."

"What captain fellow?" Hank asked. He resisted the urge to lean forward.

Jeffrey chuckled. "Oh, that ridiculous actor. He plays 'the captain.'" He made quote marks in the air. "He was included in the luncheon package. Apparently he usually dines with the guests and narrates the trip around the lake. I told him when we came aboard, however, that his services would not be needed. I wanted a nice environment for Mother's party, not a cheesy sideshow."

An actor. Not Albert the Moron. Hank mentally slumped

back in his chair. It would have been nice to know Eberhardt's condition when the boat crashed.

"Once we were in the lounge," Jeffrey continued, "people did leave to go down the hallway to the restrooms. We were there for several hours before you even came aboard."

"Did you go?"

"Well, of course," he said. "I'd just had lunch, after all."

"Did you leave the lounge at any other point?" Hank asked.

"I don't think so—wait. I did go outside on the deck to try to get cell reception. That was about two hours into it. I needed to make some business calls and send a few emails. I had not expected to be on the boat all day."

"Were you able to make the calls?" Hank asked.

Jeffrey frowned. "No. Not a one. I couldn't get any kind of signal, no matter where I stood. It was like the whole boat was just a black hole."

Hank went back to one of Jeffrey's earlier statements. "How do you know people just went down the hallway to the bathrooms? Couldn't they have gone somewhere else?"

Jeffrey snorted with laughter. "Half of them—no way. The elevator went out when we hit those rocks. None of the old folks could get off our level after that. On the way to the lounge after the crash, Leonard Dovecoat and I checked. The cables or rails or whatever were messed up. The doors weren't working, so we pulled them open a little bit—who knew if we were going to have to flee a sinking ship, right?—and we saw it stuck a couple of feet down. It wasn't going anywhere."

"What about the stairway?"

"I guess someone could have gone down that. No one could have come up it, though. It had one of those fire doors.

I had to prop it open when all of our guests were boarding. Otherwise it locks from that side—to keep us safe from the riffraff down below, I suppose."

Normally it would have been a mostly harmless toss-off attempt at humor. Instead, as soon as he uttered it, Jeffrey Honneffer cringed. The two men stared at each other as an expensive clock in the corner ticked away the silence.

"Actually, then," Hank said quietly, "it appears the riff-raff was among you."

Jeffrey swallowed and his mouth tightened. "Look, I'm sorry. I don't mean to make light of any of this. Mandy was a beautiful girl. This is . . . this is just horrible. I cannot imagine who would do this. . . ."

He trailed off. Hank leaned forward.

"Did *you?*"

Jeffrey's jaw started to drop, but he stopped it and slapped on his best lawyer face. "My God, sir. Of course not," he said. He tried to continue, but Hank was rising to his feet. An indignant speech would not be informative. And he didn't have time. His phone was vibrating with text alerts. Since Patricia Honneffer managed her husband's law firm, he asked Jeffrey where her office was and dug his phone out of his jeans pocket as he headed down the hall.

Victim still alive right b4 crash. Hanging out in kitchen.

Hank's face split in a genuine smile. Now that was something. That pinpointed things better than the old doc had, that's for sure. Sam must be interviewing the waitstaff. He stopped in the middle of the hallway and texted back.

Who says?

Waiter. Cook up next. Will let u know whats up.

A very feminine cough had him jerking his head up from

his phone. The petite brunette from the lounge stood in front of him. She had been crying. The makeup around her eyes was smudged, and the corner of a tissue poked out from the pocket of her dress slacks.

She led him into her office, which was as luxuriously appointed as her husband's, only slightly smaller and with more filing cabinets. She sat behind her desk and waved a hand at the chair on the other side. Hank lowered himself into it, and it was as stiff and uncomfortable as it looked. He was fairly certain he was sitting where her employees did when they were about to be reprimanded or fired.

She folded her hands in front of her and waited. She still had not said a word. Hank figured she was the type of person who did not like having her time wasted. He dived in.

"Do you know who killed Mandy?"

She shook her head.

"Did you know she was on the boat?"

Another silent shake.

"How long had you known her?" he asked.

She started to speak but choked on the tears she had apparently been trying to suppress. She tried again.

"Since she started dating Ryan. So I guess about a year and a half. They started dating the summer before their senior year, I think. She was . . . she was absolutely wonderful. Charming and funny and so kind. She really took to Ashley— that's my daughter. Mandy would always make time for her, treat her as an equal. Ashley just adored her."

Hank's chest tightened. "How is Ashley doing?"

That did it. Patricia started to sob. She fumbled for the tissue in her pocket, but it did little good once she found it.

Hank waited. Finally, she regained enough control to speak again.

"My little girl." Patricia tried to mop up the makeup dissolving under her eyes. "My little girl. She's devastated. We told her this morning after we confirmed it with Frances. How do you tell a child that happened? How do you explain that a person could be so evil? That a person would want to do that to someone you love? I don't know how we did it. I don't even remember the words. Just the look on her face . . . I remember that."

Hank waited a minute and tried to swallow.

"Ma'am, I'm going to need to talk to Ashley. About yesterday." Patricia stared at him. Her eyes narrowed, and her hands, which before had been merely clutching the tissue, now balled into fists. There was no clock in this office to break the silence.

"You have got to be kidding," she finally said.

"I wish I didn't have to," Hank said. That was certainly an understatement. "She might have seen or heard something important. I know how horrible this is, but, Mrs. Honneffer, I have to. Is she here at the office with you?"

Patricia continued to glare at him. She shoved her chair back and stood.

"Since it is a school holiday, yes, she is here with us." She paused before walking out the office door. "You will be gentle. And I will be here the whole time." Neither was a question. Hank nodded and she stalked out of the room. Ten minutes later she returned, holding the hand of a crying twelve-year-old with the same petite frame and brown hair as her mother. Patricia led the child around the desk and sat her in the chair she had just vacated. Ashley was wearing a Sooner Track sweatshirt.

Hank introduced himself and explained why he was there. She looked at him with huge fawnlike eyes, and Hank felt like shit.

"I need to ask you about the lunch, Ashley. Okay? Can you tell me about it?"

"It was Gran's birthday party. There weren't any other kids. Just adults. And stupid Ryan and his friends. They didn't pay any attention to me. Ryan only does when he's by himself. I kept wishing that Mandy had come. She would have talked to me . . ."

"Did you know she was on the boat?"

Ashley shook her head. Her eyes never left Hank's face. He took her through the lunch and the crash. Nothing she said added to what he'd already heard. Then he asked about the lounge.

"All the teenagers sat in the middle of the room. They were laughing and talking the whole time. I think they were glad that they were gonna have a cool story about a boat crash that they could tell when they went back to school."

"They were like that the whole time?" Hank said.

"Yeah—wait. No," she said. "Ryan was way upset when he came back from the bathroom. He pouted over by the windows for a while. I guess Gran musta yelled at him."

"Why do you say that?"

"Because she came back into the lounge right after he did. She wasn't gone as long as he was, though. I hope she yelled at him. I think something was up with that blond chick. Why did he bring her? Why didn't he bring Mandy? Was he cheating on her? Do you know?"

"I'm trying to figure all that out," Hank said. "Did you ask him about it?"

"Yeah. I tried to. He blew me off. Said it wasn't any of my business. That what's-her-face was his friend and I should stop bothering him. Jerk."

Hank hid a smile. "Did you notice anyone else who was upset, or gone for a really long time?"

She cracked a split-second smile. "My dad. He was so ticked when he couldn't make those calls he needed to. He even went outside to try, which was stupid, because it was really, really cold.

"And Gran's friend Doris. She and her husband—I don't know his name, but he's funny, I like him—they were gone to the bathroom for a long time, too. But they're old." She shrugged. "Probably takes them a long time to, you know . . ."

Hank did smile at that one.

"And there was Ryan's friend. The tall one. He left for a while. Kinda the same time as Doris did. I remember, cuz when he came back he asked if there was any coffee left. There wasn't, and he got all huffy, said he needed some bad. Like he was a grown-up." She rolled her eyes. "Whatever."

The door behind Hank opened, and Jeffrey came in. Ashley looked at her father and started crying again. Hank knew he'd been lucky to get what he had before she broke down. He leaned forward.

"Ashley, honey? Thank you for talking with me. If you remember anything else later that you think is important, I need you to call me, okay?" He slid one of his business cards across the desk. Through the sheen of tears, her eyes lit up. The kid just wanted to be treated with some respect. Like Mandy had evidently done.

She left the room with Jeffrey, and it was once again just
Hank and Patricia. He asked his questions as quickly as he
could. Nothing she said differed from what her husband and
daughter had told him, although she did rat out Jeffrey. He
apparently had tried to send a few emails during the lunch
itself, while his mother wasn't looking. Two had gotten
through right after they'd said grace at the beginning of the
meal, she said, but the rest had failed.

Hank gave her another of his business cards, thanked her
for her time, and fought the urge to ask for a cup of coffee to
go. She walked him to the door.

"You will catch this person, won't you, Sheriff?" she
asked.

He paused with his hand on the shiny brass knob.
"Ma'am, I will do everything I can," he said. "And that's
a lot."

She stared up at him and nodded. He stepped outside,
yanked his wool hat down over his ears, and strode through
the falling snow to his car.

A cup of gas station coffee steamed in the squad car's cup
holder. It tasted particularly bad right after the wonderful
stuff Hank had had at the law office. But he didn't have time
to be choosy. He had to get back to Branson. He'd gotten permission from Mandy's parents to search her car, which was
still parked in the lot at the landing where people had boarded
the *Branson Beauty*. The boat, however, remained at the rather
rickety down-shore dock it had been tugged to last night. He
would need to head there, too.

If he didn't have time for decent coffee, there was no way
he could justify stopping at the Russell Stover outlet in Ozark.

He loved pulling in there with the kids on their trips back from Springfield. It was about halfway home, the perfect place to stop for a bathroom break and some Pecan Delights. He'd have to make due with the crappy coffee and the bag of stale chips he'd found under the front seat.

He tossed the chip bag onto the seat next to him and looked out the window. As he drove south, the relatively flat and open land around Springfield started to fold up into real mountains. Highway 65 rolled up and down, over and over, as the trees filled in the valleys and clung to the jutting limestone cliffs.

He usually did this drive as quickly as possible, on his way to or from somewhere. Today he was forced to creep along on the barely plowed roadway. The view coasted sedately by, making him feel guilty he'd forgotten it was there.

He remembered the first time he'd driven to Branson, with Maggie, to meet her folks. It had been a two-lane road then. You had to go slowly, or risk your neck trying to pass someone in all those hills. They'd risked their necks a lot as they sped south that day, laughing and talking as she regaled him with stories of growing up in the Ozarks.

She'd spent her summers swimming in the lakes and playing in the woods with a pack of neighbor kids. She was always the first to try something—climbing a particularly tall tree or leaping over a wide creek no one else wanted to cross. Which meant she was also always the first to end up in the emergency room, where she became known as a regular. Hank had wished for a second that he'd known her then—his playmates didn't sound half as fun—but then again, no. If they had grown up together, they'd be good friends. And as he rode with her down Highway 65, her long, sun-streaked hair

blown by wind from the open window and her smile crin-
kling the flawless skin around her bright brown eyes, he did
not want to be her friend. He wanted to take her face in his
hands and kiss her until . . .

He'd spent the rest of that drive trying to redirect his
thoughts by staring at the scenery. And it had worked, at least
a little bit. He'd been astonished that within a ten-mile stretch,
you could go from standard rolling Missouri farmland to
these craggy, ancient rock formations splitting the earth like
some geologist's dream, and forests that seemed determined
to one day overgrow them.

They had only been living in Branson for six months, he
chided himself, and he'd already let his senses numb to the
breathtaking landscape. And then, a twenty-foot-high hillbilly
burst out of the snow at him. That, he thought with a sigh, is
why the natural beauty has faded to the background. The huge
billboard had survived the snowstorm and continued to ad-
vertise ONE OF THE STRIP'S ORIGINAL SHOWS! It was followed
by dozens of others, on both sides of the highway, that trum-
peted country singers, celebrity impersonators, magic shows,
Chinese acrobats, and some museum that had memorabilia
from the Titanic, which made absolutely no sense in land-
locked Missouri, as far as Hank was concerned.

No wonder he didn't pause to admire the mountains and
valleys anymore. The commercialization was easy to blame,
so he'd stick with that for now. He needed to start thinking
about the case again. He limited his attention to the road in
front of him and carefully made the turns toward the boat
landing, where Mandy's car would hopefully tell him something about why its owner had been strangled to death just
short of her nineteenth birthday.

There were a fair number of cars still in the parking lot as he pulled in, and it had been plowed enough so that the cars might be able to get out. He guessed they all belonged to customers on yesterday's ill-fated voyage who had not yet bothered to come down and get them after they were picked up at the emergency docking point last night. Mandy's little Ford sat close to the boarding ramp. Made sense—she had been one of the first to get there. Bright crime-scene ribbon was draped all over it, and evidence tape covered every door handle. Thank God Sheila thought to stop here before she went back to the office last night, he thought, as he got out his pocketknife.

Ideally, he'd have the car towed to a nice warm garage somewhere and have it gone over for fingerprints and forensic evidence at the same time. But there were no tow trucks available, and he needed to at least assess what was inside right now. Potential clues could not wait however many hours it would take to get the car somewhere.

A loud crunch of ice had Hank turning from the car to the parking entrance, where he saw a car even smaller than Mandy's trying to get over the bump of snow into the lot. The tires spun uselessly as the car came to rest half in a drift. The driver hit the gas, which only rocked it further into immobility. The engine whine finally stopped, and Kurt managed to get his bulk out of the car and over the drift. He had his camera with him, at least.

"Whew," the crime-scene tech panted as he staggered up to Hank. "I thought I'd never make it."

Hank had thought the same thing. He made a mental note to lay off the Pecan Delights.

"I expected you to be here already," he said.

Kurt nodded and spoke more quickly as he got his breath back. "Me, too. Took forever to dig my car out. Whew. And then getting out here. Good golly. I've never had to drive through that much ice."

Obviously. Hank turned back toward the Ford, which looked kind of festive, if you didn't read what was on the ribbons fluttering in the wind. He moved toward it, pulling on latex gloves as—

"Um, sir? Sirs?" The voice cracked and rose sharply, which made sense as Hank turned to see a boy who couldn't have been more than sixteen standing behind them. Even the thick parka couldn't disguise the gawky limbs that were shaking as the kid stood there, clearly petrified to be confronting two strange men, one of them holding an open pocketknife.

"I . . . I need to ask you . . . ask you not to do that. Sir. Sirs. The police . . . they came and put all that stuff on it." He raised a shaking hand toward the Ford. "You can't . . . can't . . ." He trailed off, and his hand fell to his side.

Hank looked at the Gallagher Enterprises name tag pinned to the parka.

"Ezra? Ezra. Hi. My name is Hank Worth, and I'm the sheriff." He slowly raised his hands. The one with the knife stayed up, and the empty one reached into his pocket for his badge. When he saw the badge, Ezra heaved a sigh so big that his breath formed its own little cloud and floated away.

"Thank the Lord," he said. "I didn't . . . I didn't know what I was going to do."

Hank didn't know what Ezra would have done, either. They were the only people for miles around, and he was fairly certain the kid didn't have any self-defense tricks up his parka sleeve.

"You're the parking lot attendant?"

"Yes, sir."

"I'm going to need to talk to you as soon as we're done here with the car, okay?"

Ezra nodded and didn't move.

"I'll come get you when we're ready," Hank said, probably too gruffly. Ezra flushed red and slunk off toward the hut at the other end of the lot.

Hank sliced through the tape on the driver's side door handle and pulled it open. Here we go, he thought.

A crumpled receipt in the center console—$23.76 for gas and coffee at a Conoco in Norman early Sunday morning. A half-full cup of coffee—frozen solid—in the cup holder. A hairbrush and a couple of CDs on the passenger seat. A *Beginning Psychology* book on the passenger-side floorboard. A necklace or some kind of chain hanging from the rearview mirror. In the glove box, her registration and insurance—both in her parents' names—and an emergency flare, tire pressure gauge, and one of those special hammer things to break a car window if you were trapped. Her father had equipped her well.

The driver's seat was too close to the steering wheel for Hank to fit. Instead, he kneeled in the snow outside the door and stuck his hand under the seat. A lot of crumbs, two gum wrappers, and an unsealed envelope. Hank lifted the flap and stared at a stack of twenties. Two hundred dollars. In an envelope carefully hidden under the seat. What the hell? He carefully tagged it and moved around to the passenger side as Kurt took photos of everything. Once Kurt was done, Hank lowered himself into the seat, carefully lifting the psychology textbook off the floor. Was that what she had planned to major in? Was that one of her tests next week? He fanned through the pages until his gloved thumb caught on a piece of loose-leaf paper. He slowly pulled it out and unfolded it.

Dearest Mandy,
I have been waiting for so long. I know that you need me. I know that you want me. I have waited for you and you have not answered me. You are mine. Not his. Not ever his. No matter how far away you go, you will always be mine. You will come back to me. It is almost time. You are mine only. You need to start acting like it. I am getting tired of the waiting. It is almost time.

—A (SQUIGGLE)

CHAPTER
9

It was a single sheet of paper, and it felt like it weighed a thousand pounds as Hank sat there with it in his hands. He read it again. Typewritten. No spelling mistakes, but no big words, either. He flipped it over. Nothing on the back. It was folded in thirds. There were none of the little headers at the top like you get when you print out an email. It must have been mailed. The creases were still crisp. She hadn't unfolded it much. Why? This wasn't a toss-off letter. This was something that should have been noteworthy. More than a bookmark. This should have scared her.

Unless she was used to them.

Hank yanked his phone out of his pocket.

"Sheila. Are you there yet?"

"What? No. It's a long drive, remember? And there's snow. Where you been?"

"Look, get there as fast as you can," Hank said. "And go through her dorm room. You need to be looking for letters.

Hopefully emails, too. Ask her friends if she was worried. Scared."

There was silence. "Why?" Sheila said slowly. "What'd you find?"

"She had a stalker. I found a letter in her car. It can't be the first one. There have to be more." He prayed that Mandy had kept them. "Call me as soon as you get there."

He cut off the call before Sheila could say anything else and stared at the letter again. He wasn't sure how long he'd been looking at it when he heard Kurt cautiously clear his throat. He looked up.

"You don't look so good, Hank," Kurt said.

"Don't feel so good, either." He unfolded himself from the passenger seat and got out of the car. "You finished with the trunk?"

Kurt hefted his camera and nodded. Hank walked to the back and poked his head inside. He waved his hand out toward Kurt. "Gimme your flashlight."

The little twin bed creaked as Hank sat down on it, trying not to muss the frilly purple bedspread. White iron bed posts matched the curlicue curtain rods. A poster of some country singer, impossibly handsome in his cowboy hat, was taped to the lavender wall over the five-drawer dresser. Another, of Jackie Joyner-Kersee running down a track in her prime, hung over the dainty white desk.

They had to be fairly recent additions. The furniture, though, felt as though it had been picked out by a thirteen-year-old reveling in the newly granted freedom to choose for herself. There wasn't much clutter. A few trophies and some yearbooks on the bookshelf, a basket of old hair ribbons on the desk. He supposed she'd taken everything else to school.

His gaze settled again on the desk. He rose and pulled out the little wicker chair. He didn't quite trust it to hold him, so he moved it aside and knelt in front of the drawers. There had been no other notes in the car. He doubted he'd get lucky enough to find any here.

The top drawer was a jumble of office supplies. The next was packed with what looked like graded high school homework. He paged through all of it. Aside from figuring out that she wasn't very into writing English essays, he learned nothing. The bottom drawer was stuck. He wiggled it back and forth until the obstruction gave way. It was a brochure, now bent from his tugging. He smoothed it out on the desktop.

Calfort's Firing Range and Gun Shop
"Straight Shooters Since 1972."
Well.

He opened it. It listed the shooting range hours of operation and a sampling of the guns for sale. *.380 semiautomatics for concealed carry* was circled in blue pen. He looked at the address and phone number. It was pretty far out of town. He knew there were closer places. Why was she interested in this one? Maybe . . . He whirled toward the bookcase and yanked the most recent yearbook off the shelf. Calfort . . . Calfort. Yep. Callie Calfort. Three pictures down from Mandy.

He snapped the book shut, put the brochure in an evidence sleeve, and laid them both on the purple bedspread. He went through the rest of the room as quickly as possible, but found nothing else. He grabbed the stuff off the bed and headed downstairs.

"Mr. Bryson, may I borrow Mandy's yearbook?" He didn't mention the brochure.

Bill and Gina Bryson were sitting on the same couch as the night before. Hank doubted they'd even gone to bed.

"Yes, of course," he said hoarsely. "Take anything you need. Did you find anything?"

"I don't know yet," Hank fudged. "But I do need to ask you—did Mandy have any hobbies, any other interests?"

They both shook their heads.

"No," Mrs. Bryson said. "Just school and track. She enjoyed going up to the mall in Springfield with her friends, that sort of thing, but otherwise, she didn't have time for other kinds of activities."

"Did she ever have any interest in shooting? Going to the firing range?"

They both stared at him in puzzlement.

"Good heavens, no. What on earth makes you say that?" Mr. Bryson asked.

"Were any of her friends into that kind of thing?"

Mrs. Bryson's soggy face firmed up for a moment. "No. Not at all. Her friends were in-town kids. Kids she knew from sports, or from church."

"Okay," Hank said soothingly. Time to change the subject. "Did Mandy seem worried about anything when she came home at Christmas? Or after that, when you spoke with her at school?"

The Brysons looked at each other.

"She seemed stressed, but not about Ryan. She thought that was going great. It was about her schoolwork," Mrs. Bryson said. "When I asked, she kept saying that she didn't know how people did it, all the schoolwork and competing in a sport at the same time."

"Did she still enjoy track?"

"Oh, yes. Good gracious, yes," Mr. Bryson said. "It was her main outlet. I think she'd die if she couldn't run . . ."

Mrs. Bryson's agonized intake of breath seemed to suck all the air from the room. Mr. Bryson buried his head in his hands. "I'm sorry . . . I'm sorry," he mumbled from behind them as his shoulders started to shake.

"I'll let myself out," Hank said quietly.

He inched his car down the deserted road, carefully keeping it in the only set of tire tracks to have already passed through the unplowed snow. He barely saw the small sign through the trees on the right. Thankfully, it was bright orange. CALFORT'S, with an arrow pointing down a drive that was blocked by a closed gate and a lot of snow. Fantastic.

He stopped the car and looked at the gate. He had tried calling the number on the brochure, but there was no answer. It was the only phone listing for the house, and the Pup had come up empty when he searched for cell phones under the name Calfort. So Hank would be unannounced. This far out of town, that was not a good idea. People did not take kindly to strangers traipsing around their property. Especially cops. He didn't know much about the Ozarks yet, but he sure knew that.

He tapped the steering wheel. He knew he should have a deputy with him for backup. But that would mean waiting at least an hour for someone to break free from the storm response and get out here. And he wanted to talk to Callie Calfort now.

He made sure his badge was visible on his coat, although

he wasn't sure if displaying it would protect him or just make him a more enticing target. His gun, normally a weight he didn't even feel, became an acute and reassuring pressure against his side.

He got out of the car and walked up to the gate, which was not locked. Small favor, that. He got it open enough to squeeze through. The snow was at least a foot deep. He started wading through it. The satellite photos on the internet had been taken during the summer and showed nothing but a canopy of trees, so he had no idea how far in the house was—or the gun shop. He just hoped he wouldn't accidentally walk through the firing range on the way.

The pine trees were tall and thin and bending under the weight of the snow. It was hard to see through them to the gray sky above. He trudged on, pausing when he passed the rusted husk of a VW bus sitting about ten yards off the drive. Snow covered the roof, but it hadn't stuck to the doors, and he could see the scatter of bullet holes. Target practice. That's probably what they did to hippies around here.

He nonchalantly took off his bulky snow gloves and put them in his pockets. Better a cold hand that could fire a gun than a warm hand that couldn't.

He had plowed another fifty feet in when he caught a blur out of the edge of his eye. He didn't even think—just drew his gun as he dropped to one knee and spun to his right. He found himself staring at the muzzle of a rifle and a camouflaged form half-hidden by a shortleaf pine tree. Neither of them moved.

Great.

He hadn't meant to do that—it had happened before his brain even registered what was going on. And he couldn't very well undo it now. If he lowered his gun, he doubted Camo over there was going to do the same and offer to shake hands.

He tried to make out more of the figure behind the tree. A big camouflage parka with a hood, and very steady hands. That rifle hadn't moved an inch from where it was trained on his chest.

"Where is she?"

The voice was feminine. Hank's eyes widened. Okay.

"Where is who?" he asked slowly.

He could almost hear her finger tightening on the trigger.

"I will drop your carcass right here," she said.

Hank didn't doubt it.

"Look, I'm the sheriff. My name's Hank Worth. I'm looking for Callie Calfort. I just need to talk to her. That's all. I'm not here for anything else." He cautiously took his left hand off his gun and held it out to his side. The movement made the badge on his coat visible. He kept the Glock leveled at Camo.

"That a badge?" The rifle moved slightly. Hank was pretty sure it was now trained on his heart.

"Yeah." He paused. "How about we both put our guns down?"

A dismissive snort. "Not until you tell me why you're here. Why do you need Callie?"

"She . . . she might know something about a friend . . . a classmate . . . who needed her help."

"Callie doesn't have classmates anymore. She graduated."

"I know, but there's someone she went to school with last year that I need to talk to her about." He avoided saying Mandy's name. He didn't know who this person was, and he didn't want to possibly get Callie in trouble. He wasn't sure how kindly her people would look upon her socializing with an almost-homecoming queen from in town.

"Why do you care about this person? Is she in trouble? Is she hurt?" This time, the voice quavered just slightly.

All right. All in.

"She's dead."

She gasped. Her rifle slumped toward the ground and she staggered out from behind the pine tree.

"Callie?" Hank asked.

She wobbled toward him, her rifle butt dragging in the snow beside her.

"Mandy's dead?"

Hank slowly lowered his gun and lurched to his feet. She was close enough now for him to see the tears in her eyes. That was all he could see, though. The camo hood and the scarf wrapped around her face covered everything else.

"You are Callie?" he asked. "Would you mind taking off your hood?"

She yanked it back, and he could see it was the same girl—thin face, light brown hair, angry gray eyes—as the one in the yearbook photo.

"What're you doing out here, Callie?"

She sniffed.

"I was supposed to meet Mandy. She's late. I was getting so worried. Oh, God. He got her."

Hank leaned closer.

"Who? Who got her? Who, Callie?"

"I don't know," she wailed. "The pervert. That's what she called him. The guy who kept writing her letters."

Hank's heart felt as if it had stopped mid-beat. Please let

her know something. "What did she tell you about the letters? What did she tell you about the guy?"

"She'd got them for months and . . . wait a minute." She
swung the rifle back up and aimed at Hank again, while his
gun remained pointed politely toward the ground. Shit.

"You talk first, cop. What happened to Mandy?"

Hank scowled. He'd certainly been asked for information
before. He'd had people yell at him, swear at him, sweet-talk
him, try to seduce him, shake their fists at him. One lady had
even whacked him with her purse. But no one had ever held
him at gunpoint. He decided this was definitely his least
favorite means of coercion.

"Put that down," he snapped. He had a feeling that direct hostility would work a lot better with this kid than smooth
words. "I'm not telling you anything until you put that damn
gun down."

She glared at him—no more tears in those eyes—and
lowered the rifle slightly. Now it would just blow out his gut
instead of his heart. He raised his eyebrows and folded his arms
across his chest.

"I'm not shooting you. You're not shooting me, either.
Put it down."

She dug in.

"You're on my land."

"Actually, I'm pretty sure it's your daddy's land. And
everything on it's your daddy's, too. Everything." He drew
out the last word. "I'm not here for him. Right now, I don't
care to involve myself in your daddy's business. But that
means you and me got to play ball. Put the gun on the ground,
and I'll answer your questions. Then you answer mine.
Agreed?"

Camo Callie tilted her head up so she was looking down her nose at him. He didn't move, just stood there waiting—and hoping she wasn't thinking about which ravine on her daddy's property would be the best place to hide a bullet-riddled lawman's body. Their breaths shot streams of white into the air as they stared at each other across ten feet of open snow in between the trees. He had to breathe through his mouth because his nose had frozen again, the snot hardening into what felt like sharp ice crystals digging into his sinuses. His wheezing seemed to echo around them—it was not helping his attempts to appear calm and cool. Camo was the one who looked comfortable, standing in the woods she'd probably played in since she could walk, holding a gun she had probably learned to shoot not long after that. He wished she would hurry up and decide. Lower the gun, or put him out of his misery. At this point, he wasn't sure which one he wanted.

Finally, she swung the rifle up and over her shoulder. "Start talkin'," she said, her head still tilted back.

Hank's breath came a little easier as he explained the *Beauty*'s running aground—which she had not heard about—and then finding Mandy dead in the private dining room.

"She was there for a birthday party. But that wasn't the only reason she came to town this weekend, was it, Callie?"

"No."

Hank waited, but she said nothing else.

"Were you going to give her a gun?" he asked.

More silence. She seemed to be sizing him up—deciding whether she should admit to it. She wouldn't be violating the law—she could sell to a person older than eighteen in a private transaction. But that was if the gun itself was obtained legally. And he would bet it was not.

Camo Callie's silence held. He decided to come at it from another direction. "Can you tell me about the pervert? What did Mandy tell you?"

Her stance softened.

"She started getting the letters real soon after she went down there to school. They came to her dorm room, so he knew where she lived. She said they were just stupid in the beginning—she didn't even save the first one. But then they started getting scary. He was writing stuff that was totally disturbing. And demanding that she do stuff . . . like wear her hair a special way, or put something in her window so he could see that she wanted him. That was when she figured he was watching her, not just sending her the letters.

"At first, she thought he was somebody down at OU. But then the letters started coming with Branson postmarks. Or Springfield. I think one was from Forsyth. She was really freaked-out by the time she came home for Christmas. She didn't know what would happen."

Camo stopped, fighting back tears. "She didn't know what would happen," she repeated in a whisper, then cleared her throat and continued. "That's when she called me." She chuckled sadly. "I think she kept calling the gun shop line and just hung up 'til I finally was the one who answered. She asked me if I could get her a gun.

"We were gonna meet at the Steak 'n Shake in town . . . cuz she knows that's my favorite . . . but she decided at the last minute that it'd be safer if she came out here. Nobody would hear us talking. I met her down by the gate, and she told me what was going on. I . . . uh . . . I suggested a certain . . . um . . ."

She trailed off and looked skeptically at Hank. He smiled.

"I think maybe a .380 . . . for her situation. Don't you?"

"Yeah . . ." she said in a tone that implied that any idiot would know that. "I recommended the Sig P290. She needed a serious piece of self-defense. She could run damn fast, but I don't think she could handle herself in, you know, close quarters, without some help." She stopped and patted her rifle. "That's what happened, isn't it?" She now seemed to be talking more to herself than to Hank. "He got her inside. He probably didn't sneak up on her. He wanted her to see him. See who it was." She leaned toward Hank. "He crashed her into a wall, didn't he? Smacked her head? Or broke her neck?"

Camo Callie had clearly seen a thing or two about what happened when you mixed love and hate.

"Not quite," he said. "He strangled her."

"Bastard."

"Yeah." He paused. "Why didn't you give her the gun at Christmas? Why'd she have to come back?"

Camo scowled. "I didn't have any. I couldn't get it until mid-January. This weekend was the earliest she could get back up here to get it . . . I did get her to take my old Ruger Black-hawk revolver to have until then. She didn't have it with her?"

Hank shook his head. There had been no gun in the car, and certainly no gun on her body. Camo's scowl worsened, which he hadn't thought was possible. "I told her. Never go anywhere without it. Never, ever, ever. Why didn't she have it? Why didn't she use it?"

Hank had no idea. He would certainly be working a very different case if Mandy had been carrying it.

"You gave her a revolver? Nobody uses revolvers any-more."

"*The law* don't use revolvers anymore. They're still

good guns." She was again talking to him as if he were an idiot.

"But had she shot before? That's a serious handgun."

Camo snorted a laugh. "No way. Town girl like her? She had no clue. What's her dad, an accountant or a banker or something? She said she'd never even picked up a gun before. She came out here one day after Christmas and we did some shooting. She wasn't too bad, for a beginner. The Ruger was too much for her, but it was the only one I had that wouldn't be missed right away. I said we'd practice more when she picked up the Sig. That's easier to fire. I was gonna have her try it out on the bus today."

"How much was she going to buy it for?" Hank asked.

"Two hundred. I cut her a deal. I know that's still a lot, but I couldn't explain anything less than that to my dad. It was gonna be tricky enough as it was."

A Sig Sauer P290 for only two hundred bucks. He did not think he wanted to know the provenance of that particular weapon. He was pretty sure they retailed for more than twice that.

"So your dad didn't know about this?"

"I thought you said we weren't gonna talk about my dad." The scowl was back.

"I'm just trying to figure out if anyone else knew Mandy wanted to buy a gun. Or that she had borrowed one from you until she got it." He shot her a half smile. She didn't respond. "Did anyone know that besides you?" he pressed.

"No. Only me. Nobody knew she'd ever been out here. At least not on my end. And Mandy wouldn't talk. She knows . . . she knew," Camo corrected herself, "that would get me in trouble."

So he'd been right about the perils of associating with a popular town girl. He slowly and deliberately holstered his gun and put his hands in his pockets.

"So . . . how long had you two been friends?"

Camo Callie relaxed very slightly—this girl seemed to do everything incrementally, except aim her gun—and smiled just a bit.

"We had English together freshman year."

"Huh," Hank said. "She didn't seem to be that into English."

Camo laughed. "Oh, yeah. Neither was I. So we sat in the back and talked. Mrs. McCleary would get so mad. That was the last year she was teaching before she became the principal. Said we would be the death of her.

"So that's how we knew each other. She never changed, Mandy didn't. Even when she got so good at track, and so pretty that she was up for homecoming queen. She kept, you know, bein' true. She'd always talk to me in the halls, or eat lunch with me if I was by myself. No one else bothered to do that. She was . . . she was . . ."

She couldn't hold the tears back this time. She scrubbed them off her cheeks with the heel of her hand, and looked at Hank.

"You. Will. Catch. This. Person."

He nodded. She pivoted back toward the woods, her rifle still thankfully slung over her shoulder.

"Hey," he said, still standing there with his hands in his pockets. "I will need to talk to you again. How do I reach you . . . without causing you problems?"

She did not turn.

"You don't."

CHAPTER
10

That had gone well—if your definition of "well" was getting summarily dismissed by a semi-educated teenager who could have taken you out with one halfhearted gut shot before you even knew she was there. If your definition of "well" meant arguing with a witness you would never be able to convince to give a formal statement, let alone ever—ever, ever—show up to testify in court. If your definition of "well" included sitting in a freezing car that wouldn't start while wearing jeans soaked from kneeling in the snow like some kind of commando moron. Yeah. It'd gone well.

Hank slowly counted to ten and twisted the key in the ignition again. Nothing. He said a prayer to whoever was the patron saint of automobiles. The car coughed and went silent. He tapped the steering wheel. How about the patron saint of poor, witless policemen? The engine whined loudly for a second and then started chugging normally. Air blasted from the vents, and he breathed deeply. That only made his nose start to run. He was tempted to wipe it on his sleeve like his two-year-old did, but settled for using the empty chip bag in the passenger seat. He was hitting all sorts of new lows today.

His phone vibrated in his pocket. He pulled it out as the car warmed up. From Sam.

Sheila interviewed roommate. Is searching dorm. Will call w/ update @ 6:30.

Good. It was five o'clock now. Hank scrolled down, looking at what he might have missed during his little chat with Camo Callie. A voice mail.

"We're out of marshmallows for the hot cocoa. Pick some up on your way home, will ya?"

Dunc. And another.

"We need some more milk, too. Preferably before dinner."

Hank was starting to think that using his father-in-law instead of sending the kids to day care every day was not such a hot idea. There was also no way in hell he would be home in time for dinner. He thought for a minute, then texted Maggie. She could make the grocery run this time. Even though it was unlikely she'd be home for dinner, either.

Now somewhat certain the car wouldn't die on him, he took it out of park and drove slowly down the snowy road. He swore that the next time he came out here—and he knew there would be a next time, eventually—he would be better prepared.

Hank swung open the door to the office, stomping his snow-covered boots into the already soaked doormat a little harder than was necessary. The Pup bounded out of the hallway clutching a sheaf of papers.

"I got lots of stuff for you, Chief," he said, waving the papers. "Where do you want me to start?"

Hank had no idea. Out of habit, he glanced at the wall clock before remembering that it was broken. He sighed. He might actually have to start wearing a watch. "How long do we have until Sheila calls?"

The Pup looked at his own watch. "About twenty minutes."

At least that left time to make some coffee. Hank turned toward the hallway alcove where they had wedged a rickety end table that held the coffeemaker and a big bowl of sugar. Nobody liked cream, which was a good thing. The office had no refrigerator.

Suddenly, Hank thought of Sheila again and stopped short. Not because she was the one who usually made the coffee—she'd made very clear to him on his first day that just because she was the only woman in the office did not mean she was his secretary and he could darn well make his own darn coffee. No, he stopped because it was Sheila who always figured out the staffing. She knew who was on duty, where they were patrolling, and when they hit overtime. It was the kind of managerial crap that made his head ache, and he had gladly let Sheila take over the whole thing as soon as he'd figured out what a pain it was.

He started the coffee pot and walked into his office to look at the names scrawled on a whiteboard on the wall near his desk.

"This current?" he asked Sam.

"Yeah, I think so."

The guys who'd worked through the night and morning

on the snowstorm were now off. Duane was back on guarding Albert the Moron at the hospital. And Gerald Tucker was
out guarding the *Branson Beauty* at its temporary dock. Hank
frowned. He'd have to do something about that, soon.

He turned to Sam. "What's the most important thing
you've got?"

Sam looked flustered. He had clearly not expected to be
asked to do the prioritizing himself. He bounced on the balls
of his feet for a moment.

"Okay," he said with a rush of breath. Hank envied the
ease with which Sam's sinuses appeared to be working. "I
think this is pretty important—according to all the old folks
I talked to and that Tony guy who works on the boat, the door
up to the second level was some kind of fire door. You could
get out, but it locked from the outside. So if you were outside,
you couldn't get in. All the old folks remember Mrs. Honneffer's son holding the door open for them when they got
there." He looked at the notes still clutched in his hand. "And
Mr. Dovecoat—he's a nice man, very funny—and Mrs. Lois
Campbell, they each told me they saw that at one point,
Mrs. Honneffer's son accidentally let go of the door and
it slammed shut. That's how they know it locked. They
couldn't get in until he opened it again."

Very good, Hank thought. "And why do you think that's
important, Sam?" he asked.

"Well," Sam said slowly, "that means that the second level
was pretty much closed off, right? So the murderer has to be
one of the people already up there, right?"

"Yep," Hank said. "Seems like we can focus on them first
and not have to worry so much about the other hundred
people downstairs, doesn't it?"

The two men grinned at each other. Sam looked down at his notes again.

"I interviewed all the old folks who were at the private party. They all said pretty much the same thing. Nobody acted funny, and they didn't notice anything weird going on. Except for the crash, of course."

Hank thought for a moment. "Did Leonard Dovecoat say anything about the elevator?"

"Oh, yeah. He said it was broken. He and Mrs. Honneffer's son went to look at it after the crash, and it was off its track or something. Wouldn't work. So Mr. Dovecoat said that all the 'old birthday biddies'—I told you he was funny—were stuck up there. Apparently he was the only old person there who could use the stairs. The rest of them had to take the elevator up and then had to be carried down by the paramedics. Makes me glad I'm a cop." He grinned.

"Yeah," Hank said. "But nobody's holding them at gunpoint."

Sam stared at him in puzzlement.

"Never mind," Hank said. He popped out to the coffee machine, poured himself a cup of just-done brew, and came back to the office. "What about the waiter interview?"

Sam shuffled his papers.

"Name is Tim Colard. Should I start at the beginning with him?"

"Yeah," Hank said as he settled in his chair and dug in the desk drawer for the box of tissues Maggie had sent to work with him a few weeks back.

"He arrived at work an hour before the boat was supposed to leave, like he always does. Said because he's got the most seniority, he gets to work the private dining room whenever it's rented out. I guess that's a big deal in waiter-world. Anyway, he was going between the kitchen and the dining room, getting stuff ready, when people started showing up. He was coming out of the kitchen doorway when he bumped into two women in the hallway. One was quite old, and he later figured out that was the birthday guest of honor, Mrs. Honneffer. The other was the victim."

"How does he know it was Mandy?" Hank asked.

"He didn't know her, but when he went back into the kitchen a few minutes later, she was in there. She was sitting at the table crying. Mrs. Pugo—she's the cook—was patting her on the back. Mr. Colard never figured out why she was so upset, but said she stayed in the kitchen with them. Said Mrs. Pugo told him it was one woman protecting another.

"Eventually, the victim calmed down enough to tell Mr. Colard her name. She helped heat up the meal and then played cards with them for a little bit after the boat crashed."

Hank perked up. "Then what?"

Sam started reading directly from his notes. "Ten or fifteen minutes after the crash, the witness—I mean Mr. Colard—and the show captain-slash-actor guy, and Tony Sampson moved all the guests from the dining room to the lounge. They thought a change of scenery would keep them all calm. Also, lunch was over and they didn't have any more food to serve, so they thought it would be best to move them out of the dining room. The witness offered everyone coffee or water, but they were starting to get upset, and he didn't want to deal with that, so he went back into the kitchen. Mrs. Pugo, Mr. Stanton—he's the show captain—and the victim had started playing cards. The witness joined them. After approximately fifteen minutes, the victim started to get fidgety. She said she really needed to get some air. The witness heard Mrs. Pugo tell her to go out the kitchen door and turn right, toward the dining room and away from the lounge, where the guests were located. This seemed quite odd to the reporting witness—I mean Mr. Colard. The victim said thank you and left." Sam looked up. "Mr. Colard did not see the victim again."

Hank leaned back in his chair. "Did you talk to Mrs. Pugo?"

The Pup shook his head and looked slightly apologetic. "She's not answering her phone, and I haven't had a chance to drive over to her house."

"That's fine," Hank said, and meant it. The good Mrs. Pugo was now a much bigger player in this drama, and he wanted to hear her story in person. "I'll be able to do that later. You have her address?"

Sam had just started to dig through his stack when Hank's desk phone rang. They both froze, Sam with a paper in mid-air and Hank with his coffee mug halfway to his mouth. He took a drink before picking up the phone.

"Hey, Sheila."

"Hey. I found them. Well, I found a few of them. The letters. There have to be others, though. Her room was messy. Typical college dorm. She was not the neatest thing, bless her heart. I need to go through it again. I've got three so far."

Hank put her on speakerphone and sent the Pup for a fresh pad of paper to take notes.

"You got them in evidence sleeves?" he asked the phone.

"Of course I do! What am I, a rookie? Geez. You send me down here and then have no faith in me?"

"Okay, okay. Sorry," Hank said as Sam stifled a snicker. "Before you read the notes, I've got a couple of questions for you. Did you find a gun?"

Silence. "What did you say?"

"Did you find a gun in her room?"

"No, I did not. Find a gun. In her room. Would have mentioned that first off, don't you think? I might not have gone through all the stacks of papers yet, but I did search the entire room, and there wasn't any gun," Sheila snapped. "She had one?"

"Yeah," Hank said. "I talked to the girl who loaned it to her. And it wasn't on her body or in her car, and no one found it in the search of the boat."

Everyone silently contemplated that for a moment, until Hank asked about Mandy's roommate.

"Sweet kid. She knew about the stalker. Mandy showed her a letter right before Christmas break. She knew Mandy had gotten more, but said that basically Mandy refused to talk about it, even though it was obviously freaking her out. The two girls who lived next door said the same. She didn't know who it was and seemed to think that if she ignored it, it would all go away.

"The roommate said she seemed much happier when she came back after the break. She talked about Ryan all the time, and about feeling more secure. Hmm. Was that when she got the gun?"

"Yep," Hank said. "What'd she say about coming back to Branson this weekend?"

"She seemed pretty excited. Kept talking about Mrs. Honneffer, and about getting to surprise Ryan. She got up at about five on Sunday morning. She'd had some big track shindig the night before, which was why she didn't go up on Saturday. I'm trying to get ahold of those people now."

Again, silence fell. Hank's chest tightened. He stared at the phone and thought about Bill Bryson's little girl.

"Okay, Sheila. We're ready. Read them."

"I'll read them in order of how they seem to have been sent," Sheila said. "Here goes:

"Dearest Mandy,
I know that my first letter might have come as a surprise to you. This kind of love could surprise anyone. It is that deep and that strong. I watch you walking to class and I ache with longing. I want to touch you. I want to be with you. You are my perfect angel.

Yours forever,"

Sheila stopped. "It's signed with a kind of loopy squiggle. They all are. I can't figure out if it's a symbol or a letter."

"Keep going," Hank said.

"Mandy love,
Why are you not doing what you're supposed to? You walk around in sweats and ponytails. You are not wearing your hair like I asked you to. Your beautiful, wonderful hair that I want to run my fingers through. I am very disappointed that you have not figured everything out yet. The enormous strength of my love should make it obvious to you. You need to show me that you love me, too. Your hair, Mandy love. No more ponytails.

"That's it for that one," Sheila said. "This last one is the one she showed her roommate. Mandy told her she'd gotten a few mailed from different places around Springfield, but this was the first one she'd gotten with a Branson postmark:

"My Mandy,
You may be in college now, but I hope that you are a good enough person to remember where you came from and to know that your true love waits for you. No matter how far away you go, I will always know everything that you do. I always know. You will always be mine. I will have you. It is fate."

No one said anything. Sheila cleared her throat. "Well, that's all I've found so far. I'll go back over her room. There've got to be more."

Hank leaned back in his chair and took a swig of coffee. "Download her hard drive—wait, is it a laptop?"

"Yeah," she said.

"Just bring it back. We've got her parents' permission to take anything we need. We've got to get into her email and her Facebook and whatever else, too. And when you—"

The police radio crackled. Both Hank and the Pup jumped, Hank almost spilling coffee all over his shirt.

"Sir? Sir? Please, sir." Frantic whispering came out of the speaker.

Hank's chair, which had been balanced on its back legs, came down with a loud smack on the hard floor. He leaned forward.

"Duane? What the—"

"He's back, sir. He's back, and he's in the room. I just went

to the bathroom, and I came out and saw him going in, and—"
The whispering stopped.

The Pup stared at the radio in bafflement. "Who's back?"

Hank had already grabbed his coat. He kicked open the office door and spun on his heel toward the lobby.

"Gallagher."

CHAPTER

11

Hank took the stairs two at a time and burst into the quiet hallway, which still smelled like sickness overlaid with a liberal dose of antiseptic. His wet boots squeaked on the green linoleum as he sped toward Albert's room. The arrogant prick was disobeying a direct law enforcement order. *His* direct order. The squeaking grew louder. He got to the closed door and shoved it open. It swung wide and slammed against the wall. Gallagher, who had been leaning over the bed, jumped away and whipped around toward the noise. He saw Hank and froze. The two men stared at each other. Hank moved until Albert's bed was between them.

"Good evening," Hank said very slowly. "I was wondering"—he made a concerted effort to unclench his fists, and his jaw—"what exactly you are doing here, violating my order?"

Gallagher straightened his spine and then took a moment

to smooth the sleeves of his suit jacket. His nice wool over-coat was draped over the room's one chair.

"I had . . . I had just stopped by to check on his health. There was no guard anymore, so I assumed . . . naturally . . . that there would be no problem anymore. I certainly did not intend to stay."

Hank looked pointedly at the coat on the chair and then back at Gallagher, who returned his gaze with a carefully constructed look of mild bemusement. Or maybe it was amusement. Either way, it made Hank even angrier. Which, of course, is exactly what Gallagher wants, Hank thought. He forced a smile.

"I will see you Wednesday at ten A.M. at my substation on the expressway," he said. "We need to go over a few more things about your boat . . . and your business."

Gallagher pasted on his own fake smile. "Of course." He picked up his coat and moved toward the door. He paused and gave one quick—almost involuntary—glance back toward the figure in the bed before disappearing down the hallway.

Hank let out a long, slow breath. Good gravy. It was a miracle he'd kept his temper. He was in the middle of draw-ing in a deep breath when Duane appeared in the doorway. More patience, please.

"What happened, Duane?"

Duane looked like a kid who had just had someone run over his new puppy, or a deputy who had just seen his career similarly flattened.

"I had to pee—er, use the restroom. They'd shut off this one—" He pointed toward the door across the room half hidden by one of those curtains-on-wheels. "Something about plumbing pressure. I don't know. They said I'd have to go down the hall to the main one. I waited as long as I could. Really, I did." The last words came out almost in a wail.

Hank frowned. "How long ago did they tell you about this plumbing problem?"

Duane thought for a minute. "It musta been right after lunch. I remember thinking I should not have just had that big ol' cup of coffee with my sandwich."

Well, Hank could certainly relate to that. He sighed. So Gallagher had either gotten extremely lucky and walked in during the two-minute window when Duane was gone, or he had known the plumbing would be shut off and deliberately waited until nature called Duane away. He had a feeling Gallagher was a man who made his own luck.

He looked at Duane. If he were just the guy's colleague, he'd slap him on the back and crack a joke about bad bladder timing. But he was the boss. This was really the first instance since he'd taken the job when discipline was necessary. The guy had left his post, and hadn't asked the nurse to monitor things while he was gone. Enough said. But . . . he had admitted his mistake and called Hank in as soon as he discovered it. And what kind of matchup was it—a twenty-one-year-old kid on his second day of boring, solitary guard duty against the county's leading businessman and his mom's employer? Hank sighed again. Duane cringed.

"You're the only one I've got right now, Duane," Hank said. "Everyone else is working the storm or investigating the homicide. I need you to step up, okay? Can you do that?"

Duane nodded almost frantically. "Yes, sir."

Hank sighed again and walked over to the bed. Albert the Moron appeared to still be asleep. He was still hooked up to an IV and several monitors. Hank squinted at them, but he only knew enough to tell that, yep, the guy's heart was beating. Helpful. He stared down at the thin figure, perfectly still under the grayish hospital sheet. All sorts of priceless information was lying there, locked up in that sedated brain.

Hank gave himself a shake. He could stand there all day staring at the equivalent of a locked safe, or he could get moving and try to find a key. He turned, gave Duane a rundown of exactly what was expected of him, and left. He turned toward the stairwell but stopped and looked the other way, toward the nurses' station. One nurse sat behind the counter.

As he got closer, he realized it was Nurse Grumpy from the night before. He put on his best church smile.

"Ma'am. Hello there."

She looked up and glowered at him. "Are you planning on making noise again?"

"No, ma'am," he said cheerfully. "I was just wondering . . ." He casually leaned against the counter and put his hand in his jeans pocket, pulling his coat back in the process and revealing his badge. He smiled again. "I was just wondering if you had any problems today. You know, any people bothering you up here that I might be able to help you with."

She raised a very thin eyebrow and pursed her lips. After what seemed like five minutes of studying him, she nodded slightly. He must have passed inspection.

"There was a man lurking around earlier. Refused to tell me what he wanted. I told him he needed to be downstairs if he was waiting for someone. He told me he knew what he needed and I should just go about my duties." The sour look on her face showed exactly what she'd thought of that directive. "Just because you're wearing an expensive suit doesn't mean you're better than anybody else. No, sir. I'm just as good in the eyes of the Lord as he is."

"How long exactly was he up here . . . bothering you?"

"Oh, at least half an hour, if not longer. I went to check on Mrs. Trask in room four—she'd pushed her call button—and when I came back, he was gone." She sniffed. "Good riddance."

Hank wished he could be as easily dismissive of the loiterer, but that would not be a wise idea at this point.

"Ma'am, I can't thank you enough for your time. And if there's ever anything you need help with, you just let me know. My name's Hank."

"Oh." Her eyes widened. "You're the new sheriff, then. Aren't you?"

"Yes, ma'am."

"And your wife, she's Dr. McCleary. Down in the ER?"

Hank nodded.

"Well, good. She's a fine thing, you know. Good doctor. Good to everyone, even the nurses."

"Yes, she is," he agreed and turned toward the elevator. Nurse Not-So-Grumpy stood and stuck out her hand.

"Good to have met you, Mr. McCleary," she said, shaking his hand briskly.

Hank headed for the elevator chuckling. Maybe "Mr. McCleary" would take a detour and stop in downstairs. Say hello to his fine thing.

Hank steered the car toward home, a Country Mart bag with milk and marshmallows on the seat next to him. He had stopped in at the ER to see Maggie. She'd dashed out for the cocoa supplies earlier and planned to take them home in time for dinner, but now had an ice-slipping broken leg to set and a snow-shoveling heart attack on the way in. So he'd gotten nothing but a quick kiss and a bag of groceries shoved at him. That was fine. He couldn't complain—his job was just as bad. Unexpected late nights, missed dinners, preoccupied thoughts. It was just as good, though, too. Adrenaline rushes, new problems to solve every day, challenges that made him feel alive. He pulled into the driveway. At least today he would not have to add another missed dinner to the list.

The kids threw themselves at him before he even had his coat off. They'd had cocoa, watched two whole movies, played Candy Land until Grandpop said no more, eaten grilled cheese for lunch, and gotten to jump on the bed.

"What?" Hank stopped their chattering. "You got to what?"

Dunc came out of the kitchen. "It was either let 'em do that, or throw 'em out in a snowbank. Maggie specifically told me before she left this morning that I couldn't do that, so the bed was the only thing I could think of to burn off some energy."

He grabbed the bag out of Hank's hand and disappeared back into the kitchen. Hank leaned down and whispered to Maribel, "You jumped on Grandpop's bed, right?"

She giggled. "No. Yours and Mommy's. It's way bigger."

Hank scowled, which just sent both kids into fits of laughter. They clung to him as he walked into the kitchen, which smelled of warm bread and some kind of meat.

"I'm trying meatloaf. Marian's recipe. I'm not sure I got it right," Duncan said as he served it up.

Hank took his slice and dug in. Dunc had most definitely not gotten it right. It wasn't inedible, but it was certainly not the meatloaf his mother-in-law used to make. He looked across the table at Dunc, who was taking his own first bite. He made a face and slowly lowered his fork back onto his plate. His eyes filled, and he swallowed hard. Hank looked down quickly and tried to concentrate on his own plate. Both men choked it down in silence until Maribel piped up.

"Benny's playing with his food." She pointed at her brother, who had built an impressive meat mountain studded with green-bean trees. He was so delighted with himself, Hank couldn't get mad.

Duncan guffawed. "That's about what it's good for, kiddo," he said. He turned to Hank. "If I'm going to keep trying to learn to cook, we'd better think about getting a dog. Nobody's going to finish this."

Hank pointed to his almost empty plate. "All I've had today is a bag of stale chips . . . and a couple of marshmallows on the way home. At this point, dinner could be dog food, and I'd still eat it."

Benny chose that moment to flatten his mountain. Green beans went flying, and all four of them burst out laughing.

After Hank had cleaned that up, he wrestled his still-way-too-energetic kids into their pajamas and tucked them into bed. He came out after stories to find Duncan stoking the fire.

"Guess you're heading out again?" he said.

Hank looked longingly at the easy chair by the hearth and the Dick Francis novel on the end table. His father-in-law was settling in for the night.

"Maggie told me you've got a murder. First time that's happened around here in ages. Well, first time where it wasn't some druggie meth heads killing each other outside of town."

Hank wished it was a meth case. Nasty business, but it was always pretty easy to figure out what had gone down. No big-time businessmen, comatose key witnesses, or unidentified stalkers to muddy the waters. He stared at the fire. Dunc settled back in the chair to the left and took a slow sip from his mug. He said nothing, just let Hank stand there and think. Hank turned away. The fire was not helping. Maybe the water would. He gave Dunc a slap on the shoulder as he moved toward the door.

CHAPTER
12

The boat sat motionless in the frigid lake, with nothing more than the long, rickety, temporary gangplank to connect it to the dock like some kind of dubious umbilical cord. There was no creaking of rope or lapping of water. No sound at all. The heavy smell of pine and diesel fuel made the air more stagnant than it should have been, so far out in the pristine Ozarks. And the moonlight—the clouds had finally blown through and the sky was clear—slid along the smooth surface of the lake until it got to the *Beauty*. Then it seemed to not want to go any farther. Only small bits of light penetrated the darkness around the boat, casting haphazard shadows in every direction. The white paint looked dull and gray, and the black smokestacks were almost invisible as they towered over Hank.

A brief spark caught Hank's eye. He turned as a shadow separated itself from the blackness of the forest and moved forward. "You better have a reason to be out here, boy," it said.

Hank turned on his flashlight but kept it pointed at the

ground. The light bounced up and weakly illuminated both their faces.

"Well, do you?" the man asked, a cigarette clamped between his lips. "Got a reason? Who are you?"

Well, now, that was irritating. Granted, he'd only been the sheriff for six months, but he felt that was plenty long enough for his deputies, all of whom he'd met personally—there weren't that many—to recognize him.

"I'm the sheriff," he said. "Thought I'd come have a look at my crime scene."

In the darkness, he could feel more than see the other man stiffen. He resisted the urge to shine the light full in his face. That wouldn't make things any better. Gerald Tucker didn't much care for him, anyway. Hank hadn't liked the vibe off the man—he seemed to have been a favorite of Gibbons, somebody used to getting the best assignments even if he didn't have the right skills. Instead of choosing him as his second-in-command, Hank had gone with Sheila. He had a hunch Tucker had never lost out to a woman before. Especially a black one. Join the twenty-first century, pal. The best qualified wins. And he was pretty sure the best qualified had stuck Good Ol' Boy with night dock duty on purpose. Good for her.

Hank smiled calmly and moved past his deputy toward the boat. He ducked under the crime-scene tape and walked up the gangplank and through the same gate where Tony Sampson had greeted him the first time he'd boarded the *Beauty*. It seemed like that had been years ago, but only thirty-six hours had passed. He pulled on a pair of latex gloves, pointed his flashlight down the wide walkway, and headed toward the big showroom.

There was nothing out of the ordinary there, or in the

backstage area. Costumes were neatly hung, props stacked, and makeup jars lined up neatly under the mirrors. It looked as though the actors had used their run-aground time wisely.

The kitchen had also been tidied, although the appliances— with their sharp corners and black boxy fronts—looked as if they had been there since the boat's original launch in 1983. The only things from this millennium were the newish microwaves along the side wall. He went through everything. Nothing was out of place, and there was no .357 revolver anywhere.

The kitchen exit put Hank out on the walkway on the opposite side of the boat from the dock. In order to get to the stairs leading up to the second deck, he had to go around the stern, which took him past the gaping void where the paddle wheel had been. He leaned over the railing and looked down. His flashlight found holes where beams had been amputated. A mass of cables and wires dangled directly below him. The diesel smell was stronger back here.

He ran his light down and over the water. It refused to penetrate, bounced back and caught him in the eyes. He instinctively squeezed them shut and stepped back, hitting the wall behind him. The impact created a booming thud in the silence. He froze. Great. Now he'd have Tucker up here, demanding to know what was wrong. He waited. Nothing. His eyes adjusted again to the darkness. Still nothing. No Tucker. Hank frowned. He was relieved he didn't have to look like an idiot in front of Good Ol' Boy, yes, but come on. The guy should have at least yelled up to him to see if everything was okay. He was going to be a real pain in the neck.

Hank rounded the corner and stood in front of the door securing the stairway. There was another deck gate back here, where presumably the important passengers could use their own gangplank and avoid mixing with the tourists up front. The door was locked. He dug in his coat pocket and pulled out a key ring. Alice had given it to him after they were done processing the boat yesterday. He wondered which boat staff member she'd taken it from.

The fourth key he tried worked. He pulled open the door. It stayed locked on the outside, but pushed open easily from the inside. He climbed the stairs and stood at the end of the hallway. On the right was the wall of windows looking out over the dock. On the left was the dining room door and its windows, still with the shades tightly drawn. Then the door to the windowless kitchen, the elevator, and up at the front of the boat was the lounge, where the door and windows were all open to the view.

Hank went first to the elevator, which looked exactly as Leonard Dovecoat had described it to Sam. The doors had been pried open about a foot. He pushed them apart a bit more and stuck his head and flashlight in. The elevator was definitely hanging off balance in the shaft and not going anywhere. One more thing Gallagher would have to fix. Hank grinned.

The lounge looked the same as when the boat had been evacuated—somewhat messy with empty water bottles everywhere and chairs shoved in haphazard groups. There was nothing under the furniture, but there were a few loose coins in between the couch cushions. He left them alone and headed for the little kitchen directly off the private dining room.

He stood in the middle of the small room and slowly turned in a circle, realizing he had not actually made it into this room on Sunday night. It had obviously been searched by his deputies—drawers weren't closed all the way and two cupboard doors hung open. He turned again. It wasn't even really a kitchen. It had two microwaves, some kind of weird drawer-type oven, and an ancient-looking refrigerator, but that was not enough to actually cook the full-course meal that VIP guests would expect. The food must have been prepared downstairs and then, what, brought up on the elevator? Hank decided he didn't really care about the food service particulars and shifted his focus. He searched everything again, even looking on the underside of the little table against the wall where Mandy and the cook must have whiled away the time, judging from the playing cards still sitting there. He carefully bagged the deck. It wouldn't hurt to confirm that waiter's statement by making sure Mandy's fingerprints were on the cards.

He ended up back in the middle of the room, no further along than when he'd started. That really is a hideous refrigerator, he thought. It had to be at least twenty-five years old. He pulled it open. It held a few bottles of ketchup and some fancy mustards, but that was it. He shut the door, and his gaze landed on the microwaves. He popped the first one open. Nothing. He hit the button on the second one, and the door swung open. A purse sat there, looking for all the world like it was ready to be cooked.

He whipped his phone out of his pocket and snapped several pictures before he reached in with his still-gloved hand and hooked a finger around the strap. He laid it carefully on the little table and stared at it. It was reasonably good sized and trendy looking, something he guessed a college girl would own. He unzipped it and pulled out the wallet. Yep. Amanda Grace Bryson. Born 2-27-93. 1522 Conifer Street, Branson,

MO. Then her University of Oklahoma ID. A campus dining card and what had to be a key card into her dorm. Six dollars in cash. A bank debit card and only one credit card. A very well-worn Branson library card. He flipped it over. The single word "Mandy" was written on the signature line in trembly block letters. He pictured a little girl excitedly filling it in all those years ago, blinked hard, and put it back in the wallet.

He pulled out her phone and set it aside. They would have to go through that back at the office. Then a handful of hard candy, two sticks of gum, a little mirror. And a gift. He pulled out the small, square package, wrapped in birthday paper. The little folded-over card said, *Happy Birthday to my favorite old bird. Love you always, Mandy.* He took a picture, then carefully unwrapped it. Inside the box was a beautiful brooch, a delicate hummingbird in flight.

He replaced the lid and put the box back in the purse's first compartment. The second was closed with a zipper. He undid it, but he knew what he would see. No gun. The purse didn't weigh enough. Camo Callie's loaner would have fit, perfectly, in that empty divided pocket. He growled in frustration. Where was it?

He sat heavily in one of the kitchen's two chairs and absentmindedly snapped the latex of his gloves as he stared at the purse and its contents. Great discovery, but it didn't help him at all right now. He could hope it was covered with the killer's fingerprints, but the way this case was going, he doubted he'd get that lucky.

He hoisted himself out of the little chair and went to the door that led directly to the dining room. The knob would not move under his hand. He tried to twist it again.

Definitely locked. He quickly walked out the hallway door and down to the dining room entrance. He broke the evidence tape on the door and shoved it open. Ignoring the rest of the room, he went to the kitchen door and knelt in front of it. This side of the knob had a keyhole. He whipped out the key ring and started jamming keys in it. The sixth one worked.

He sat back on his heels and stared at the knob, which was still covered with black fingerprint powder. Alice must have been able to lift some pretty good prints—there were several still clearly visible on the brass finish. Good. Then he turned. The entire room was coated in black powder. Because there were prints everywhere. On the water glasses, the backs of chairs, the walls, the window shades. Everywhere.

He moved around the long table, still on his knees, and stopped where they had found her. He slowly rose and placed his feet where he guessed the killer had stood. One foot forward and one foot back. Better balance that way. He reached his arms out in front of him. The killer had been in front of her. He'd done it face to face. And it had to be a he. The only women on the second deck did not have the strength or mobility to overpower a young person in top physical condition.

He curled his fingers around an imaginary neck. It took a lot of something to choke the life out of a person while you looked them in the eyes. A lot of fear. Or a lot of hate. Or a lot of love. He'd learned early on that the last of those was just as often a reason for killing as the others. And quite possibly the most painful of them all.

He squeezed his hands into fists and dropped them to his sides. He did one more sweep of the entire room and then quietly stepped outside. He locked the door, carefully replaced the crime-scene tape, and trudged up the stairs to the pilothouse. There was nothing there, except Albert's aviator sunglasses, folded neatly in the middle of the well-worn seat of the captain's chair. He sighed, then dug out an evidence bag and put them inside. He took it and the bagged purse and headed down to the dock. Tucker was standing at the gate, waiting.

"You done?" he asked.

"For now," Hank bit out. He didn't bother with a good night as he turned to start the climb up to the road. "What an asshole," he heard Tucker mutter behind him. Hank smiled in the darkness. He'd been thinking exactly the same thing.

CHAPTER

13

Duncan stomped into the kitchen, where Hank and Maggie sat with their coffee. It was just before six and the kids were, remarkably, still asleep. But they wouldn't be for long with all the noise Dunc was making.

"Where is that darned Walkman?" he rummaged through the desk in the corner that was the dumping ground for everything they didn't know what to do with. "I thought I put it . . ."

He looked up and noticed the two of them sitting at the table. "Oh. You two seen my Walkman?"

Maggie shook her head. Dunc grunted and headed toward the living room. Hank turned to his wife. "He doesn't mean an actual Walkman? That plays tapes?"

"Yes," she sighed. "Goodness knows how old it is now. Mom tried to get him to upgrade to a portable CD player about ten years ago. He wouldn't. Said it was too bulky. Said his

Johnny Cash tapes worked just fine, thank you. And even those were a sin against the purity of vinyl."

Hank knew all about his father-in-law's beloved record collection. His back still seized up when he remembered having to move those ridiculously heavy boxes out of the old house and into this one. He curled his fingers around his mug and grinned. "What do you think he'd do with digital? We should get him an iPod."

"An iPod? One of those little glass things? No, thank you," Dunc said as he walked back into the kitchen, triumphantly waving his Walkman in the air. He clipped it on his waistband. "They don't make 'em like this anymore."

"Yeah, there's a reason for that," Hank said. "Tape is about the crappiest way to listen to anything. I can't believe that thing even still works."

"Works fine. The tapes only get gummed up every once in a while." He clamped on the big foam earphones. "Now I'm going for my walk. Got *Everybody Loves a Nut* all cued up."

Well, that is certainly appropriate, Hank thought as he pointed at the frosted-over window. "It's gotta be ten below out there."

"It's only fifteen degrees, you pansy. I checked."

Maggie laid her hand lightly on Hank's sleeve.

"Can't you take a break for another day or two, Dad?"

"No way," Dunc said. "I have to get my miles in. Walkin' the inversion of my age, I am."

They both stared at him in confusion.

"Every week, I walk seventeen miles. I'm seventy-one. Get it? I flip-flop the numbers. If I miss more than a day or two, I can't catch up."

He disappeared into the mudroom, humming as he went. Hank grinned at his wife. "Well, doctor, when he slips on that icy hill at the end of the street and turns into the Wabash Cannonball, at least he won't be my problem."

Maggie smacked him on the shoulder as she stood up. "I don't need any more problems, you wise-ass." Then she kissed the top of his head. "You better get out of here before the kids get up, or they'll want you to stay and do your talking banana."

Hank drained the rest of his coffee. He didn't have time for the talking banana. That was the thing about kids. Do something once on a whim—like sticking Cheerio eyes and a mouth on a half-peeled banana and doing an Adam Sandler impression—and you were stuck doing it every morning for the rest of your life. He hustled out through the garage just as he heard little feet trotting out from the bedrooms.

"All units. Table Rock Lake. East shore. Exact twenty unknown. Witness reports large explosion heard."

"Union-two-oh-four, copy. Is fire responding?"

"Affirmative. Appears to be something behind the trees, possibly out on the lake . . . stand by . . . caller pretty far away from the scene. He states it appears to have come from the same area where the Beauty *came in for emergency docking. Over."*

"Union-two-oh-four, responding. Six twenty-three A.M."

Hank stared in horror at the radio on his dash. What the . . . ? He yanked the wheel, barely making the turn down the state route to the lake. He had been planning to go straight and check in on the Brysons before heading back to the boat, but now . . . The back end of the car fishtailed before he got it back under control, loosening his grip on the wheel only long enough to turn on his emergency lights. He pressed his foot to the floor, and the car shot along the ice-crusted roads toward a horizon that was turning red. And it wasn't the sunrise.

The air reeked of oil and charred wood. The noxious fumes pricked at his eyes and tickled his nose—which had miraculously cleared, so he could smell every horrible scent wafting through the frigid air.

"It looks like it got blown apart pretty good." Larry Alcoate appeared at his side.

Hank didn't look up from the water. "What are you doing here? Nobody was hurt."

"I'm emergency services, and a big-ass explosion qualifies, even if there are no injuries. I wasn't going to pass up seeing this." He gleefully rubbed his hands together. "This has been the best week ever. Rescues and explosions and snowstorms. It's better than KC."

Well, it is certainly different than KC, Hank thought as he turned a full circle on the dock. There was no deputy in sight. No one had been guarding the boat—the crime scene, *his* crime scene—when it exploded. And now it was at the bottom of Table Rock Lake. Fantastic.

He turned away from the polluted water and saw Lovinia standing off to one side, her hands stuffed in her green ski coat. He wondered how long she'd been there. He'd actually gotten to the scene before her, which was rare.

"Hey, Lovinia."

She snuggled deeper in her coat and gave him a sympathetic smile. "Not the best way to start your day, is it?" she said.

He shook his head. "No. It's not." He gave her a rueful grin. "I did beat you, though. That's something."

She chuckled, and her gray curls bounced against the turned-up collar of her jacket."Don't get used to it. I decided to finish reading the newspaper first, otherwise I would have beat you."

Hank turned his back on the oil-slicked water. He knew that wouldn't make it go away, but focusing on something other than a crime scene for a few seconds always helped him clear his head for the investigation to come.

"Six is awfully early to be up reading the paper when you're retired," he said.

"Oh, I don't sleep much anymore. Not since Walter died." She shrugged. "I just try to keep busy."

Hank knew her husband had died shortly before Hank became sheriff. "When did you two move down here?"

Her smile was wistful this time. They'd come to Branson about five years earlier, she said, and bought the house out on Roark Creek just a little northwest of Branson. Walter loved to fish and she loved to hike, and they'd intended to spend their retirement enjoying the beautiful Ozark Mountains and area lakes.

Lakes.

They both turned and stared at the decidedly un-beautiful water in front of them. "When's the state fire marshal going to get here?" she asked.

"Not for a couple of hours. And when he does get here . . ." He swung his arm wide, taking in the black water, the burnt flotsam, and the charred gangplank, which reached out from the dock like a severed limb. "This is what he'll get. One big, wet, inaccessible mess."

"That's for sure." Bill Freedman walked up, pulling gloves out of the pockets of his blue water patrol parka and putting them on. "I don't think we'll be able to get a diver down there. Weather's too iffy." He glanced up at the sky, where a wall of storm clouds was advancing slowly from the south. "And the visibility down there. Awful. No point putting somebody in danger just to confirm that the boat's a goner."

Hank gritted his teeth. "It'd be for a bit more than that, Bill. Why'd it explode all of a sudden?"

Bill shrugged. "Probably something to do with hacking the paddle wheel off. Poor thing couldn't have liked that much." He started to turn toward the water and then stopped. "Actually, you tell me. Didn't you have somebody down here . . . you know, guarding it?"

Hank's scowl deepened. When he got ahold of that fat, insolent Good Ol' Boy . . .

"I don't know what you're talking about." The words were followed by a stream of cigarette smoke as GOB exhaled directly in Hank's face. "I finished my shift and came home. Nobody told me to do no different."

"So you just left the boat unguarded. You left a homicide crime scene unsecured."

GOB shrugged. "It was all taped up. That's secured."

Hank literally counted to ten before speaking again. "You should not have abandoned your post."

GOB crossed his arms over his chest and leaned against the railing of his front porch. "Look, nobody authorized me overtime. I wasn't staying and not getting paid."

"All you had to do was call in and ask." Hank knew he was about to veer into soapbox territory, but he couldn't help himself. "I find it very sad that you put money over the safety of this county's citizens and the sanctity of the investigation."

"Sanctity?" GOB snorted. "This ain't church, boy. This is a job. This is business. You authorize the overtime, I stay. You don't, I go. Seems simple enough that even a city boy could understand."

Hank's fist clenched of its own accord. He forced it to relax. "It ain't church? Funny, it seems to me like it's exactly that. The breaking of one of the Lord's Commandments, isn't it? And we are charged with finding the killer."

GOB shook his head. "Nope. *You* are charged with that, boy. This . . . all this is on you." He jabbed his finger at Hank's chest.

I am very aware of that, Hank thought, but I will not be poked at by a lousy, lazy law-enforcement apostate. He slowly raised his own finger and leveled it at GOB's face. "Because of your devotion to duty, you can report for your next shift at the county jail in Forsyth. That will be your new permanent assignment, one more fitting for someone with your . . . initiative."

The puffs of cigarette smoke stopped coming, and Tucker began to turn purple. Outrage . . . or a heart attack. Hank doubted he'd get that lucky. He slowly lowered his hand and walked away from Tucker's small frame house, leaving his deputy to stew in a preexisting pot of anger that he knew he had just set to boiling.

By the time he got back to the boat, the fire marshal was there, staring at the water much like everyone else. A big, burly man with gray hair, he was even less receptive than the water patrol to Hank's suggestion that a few divers be sent down to look at things. The guy pulled at his mammoth mustache and adopted a look that Hank was sure he used when teaching at whatever fire marshal training school they sent stupid rookies to. There were such things as priorities, Mustachio explained. No one was hurt, no one was killed. The boat had been severely damaged the day before, and it was quite possible—no, quite likely—that as a result, gasoline had leaked and something had ignited it. Did the boat have a generator? That could have malfunctioned. Provided an ignition source.

Hank pointed out—perhaps a little too loudly—that the boat was also "quite likely" insured, and was worth a darn sight more in burnt pieces than it would be moldering in dry dock with an amputated paddle wheel. Mustachio nodded with what Hank took to be feigned sympathy and turned away to ask Freedman how the wife and kids were doing. Hank stood there, alone on the crowded dock, and stared at the water. It was flat and slick and shot through with oily rainbows, and for the moment, completely impenetrable.

CHAPTER

14

Hank rang the doorbell again and waited. The little front porch was swept clean of any blown snow. A fake ficus, all glossy-leafed health, swung in complete incongruity next to the icicles descending from the eaves. He blew on his hands and swung his arms as he waited. Finally, the lace curtain in the front window twitched. He pulled the badge off his coat and waved it at the movement. He heard a heavy scraping, and then the door swung open.

He introduced himself, and the *Beauty*'s private dining room cook led him into a living room full of more ficus plants and way too much flower-print furniture. He sat where instructed, in a huge, overstuffed easy chair with lace doily things on the arms. He avoided them and put his hands in his lap.

"Goodness," Mrs. Pugo puffed as she pulled a wooden dining table chair out of the entryway and sat across from him. "I'm sorry about that. I got no locks, you see. And well, this business . . ."—she dropped her voice to a whisper—". . . *this murder* . . . well, it just has me in a fright. A real fright, I tell you. So I shoved the chair under the doorknob. I didn't know what else to do. That seemed to work. It would work, wouldn't it, Sheriff? It would keep the bad folk out . . . wouldn't it?"

She clasped her hands and turned huge brown eyes toward him. Short and round, she looked exactly like one of those plump, kindhearted housekeeper/nanny/godmothers in Disney films. All she needed was a flouncy little cap and a singing crab. She blinked and waited for his approval. As he was busy sinking ever farther into his excessively cushioned seat, she actually had to look down at him from her perch on the solid wood chair. He felt that the positioning did not do any favors to his authority as he explained that while it had been a very good idea, a chair was no substitute for a good deadbolt and perhaps she should think about going to the hardware store today to get one.

She nodded solemnly and then dived right in. "I expect you're here to talk to me about that sweet young thing?" Hank nodded and asked when she had first seen Mandy on the boat.

"Oh, it was before we launched," she said. "All the sudden, she comes bursting in the kitchen door. She was white and trembling, like a ghost that had gone and scared itself. I sat her at the table and got her a glass of water. She looked like she was going to be sick. I didn't have much to do right then, so I sat with her. Plus, I was worried. I didn't know what was wrong with her."

It had taken Mandy quite a while to tell the good Mrs. Pugo what happened. "Oh, I just felt so bad for her. She was so upset. She didn't want anybody to see her, and I can't say I blamed her. To give that horrible boy the satisfaction of embarrassing her? Not if I had anything to say about it."

She kept Mandy in the kitchen. They were the only two people there, she said, unless you counted Roy Stanton. The way she said it had Hank asking whether he shouldn't count Roy for some reason.

"That man is enough of a hassle on a normal day," she said. "He was beyond that something considerable on Sunday."

Hank began to piece together "Captain" Roy's problem. The people who rented out the private dining room had told him that they did not want his hosting services. In fact, they didn't want him in the room at all. That had led the rejected Roy to spend the cruise sulking in the kitchen, which distracted Mrs. Pugo from the person in the room she felt had a legitimate reason to be upset—Mandy.

"I tell you, Sheriff," she huffed, "I about gave him a piece of my mind. He could plainly see this poor girl was hurting, and he still went on and on about his insulted dignity and whatnot." She paused to puff a bit, and Hank cut her off before she could build up more steam.

"Ma'am," he said, leaning forward in his deep cushions, "I need you to think about this for a minute. Who else came into the kitchen? At any time during the cruise or after the crash—who else besides you and Mr. Stanton?"

Mrs. Pugo's face screwed up in thought. Hank waited.

"Well, Tim, of course. Tim Colard, the waiter. He was in and out. He's the one has to set the table and everything before and then clear it all up after. But he didn't finish with the clearing, actually. That was when the boat crashed. Then

he and Tony Sampson moved all the folks in the dining room
over to the lounge. They all used the hallway, of course. No
one came through the kitchen."

"Nobody else? Just Tim Colard and Roy Stanton? They
were the only other two who would have seen Mandy?"

Mrs. Pugo nodded hesitantly. "I'm pretty sure. After the
crash, it got real crazy, though. All us in the kitchen—well,
not Mandy—ran into the hallway, and all them in the dining
room was running around, too. It was hard to know what was
going on, exactly. I guess somebody could have gone into the
kitchen then, but it would have had to be one of the folks
already there. There weren't nobody unusual on that level of
the boat. And when I went back into the kitchen, Mandy
didn't say if anybody had come in or not. She just asked what
was going on."

People continued to wander around, getting more and
more upset, she said. So that's when all the guests were shown
into the lounge. She made up the coffee, Tim served it, and
then the three of them and Mandy started playing cards. "Just
some go fish, mind you. No gambling or nothing." Hank hid
a grin.

"Mandy started getting restless. All fidgety-like. I didn't
blame her. The poor thing, stuck in a tiny kitchen with three
old fogies. I told her that she should get some air. She didn't
want anybody to see her, so I said she should go up to the
pilothouse. To get there, you turn right down the hallway.
That's past the dining room, which was empty, instead of left
and past the lounge, which had that awful boy in it."

That would leave several hours unaccounted for, Hank
thought. He sighed. Tim had been in and out frequently,

checking on the guests in the lounge. Roy left the kitchen a few times to use the restroom, as did she. And Mandy had not come back.

"Where did you think she was that whole time?" Hank asked. "That was kind of a long time for her to be gone—just to get some air."

Mrs. Pugo flushed. "Well . . . I honestly forgot. Not really, now, but with Roy yammering on about his hurt feelings, and me having to tend the coffee all the time for all them in the lounge . . . I just never got 'round to checking up on her. And then you were there, and we were rescued. I figured she got off the boat in the whole crush of people, and that was why I didn't see her." She started to cry. "I've been praying about that. I feel so guilty. If I'd gone looking for her, would she still be alive? Would she, Sheriff? I feel like I failed her. I failed to do my Christian duty."

Silence. The flames popped in the fireplace. She stared expectantly at Hank, who decided this would be a good time to ask for some tea. He had a feeling that was her beverage of choice, and he was right. She bustled into the kitchen, apologizing profusely for not having offered him something earlier and listing half a dozen different flavors for him to choose. He avoided the fruity ones and picked what sounded like it had the most caffeine.

As she put the kettle on, he steered the conversation into the past. How long had she worked on the *Beauty*? Her mood lifted as she piled a plate with tiny cookies and readied the tea. She had been there from the beginning, she said, ever since Crazy Otis launched the boat back in '83. She was a cook for the main dining room most of that time, until about five years ago, when her bursitis got real bad and Otis moved her up to

the private dining room's kitchen. She didn't have to
cook up there, just make sure the food they brought in
downstairs stayed warm and was served up correctly bef
Tim took it out to the diners.

"It was a much easier job. I didn't have to stand on my
feet so much. That's the kind of boss Otis was, though. He
treated you right. Made sure you were taken care of. Like
when Anna Fenton got her leg chopped off in that car accident. He moved her from waitressing to ticket taking, even
though he already had somebody taking tickets onshore. Built
her a whole special little table and chair so as she could sit and
put her stump up. He could have just fired her and let her go
on the disability, but no, sir. That wasn't the way Otis worked.
You got a job with Otis, and you had a job for life."

But then Otis died. Went and left the boat, and the whole
business, to some no-account nephew who didn't have the
love for it, in her humble opinion. So the no-account sold it to
Henry Gallagher. That was two years ago. He had tried to
shrink the size of the *Beauty* staff, but after he laid off two musicians and Frieda from maintenance, people started talking.
A lot. And it wasn't flattering. No, sir. And then the newspaper
got wind of it and wrote an editorial.

"Yes, they did. About Crazy Otis's legacy and how he was
one of the folks who first put Branson on the map. His dream
to have a big ol' showboat on the lake was one of the first
things that brought people down here. And you can't go
ing the people who worked for him. Well, that just er
Mr. Gallagher right there. The musicians had fuljobs, but Frieda came back, and everything wbe. We all thanked the Lord. A lot of us can't
jobs at our age."

e way she phrased her last comment gave Hank pause. ...idn't know her job had disappeared into the depths of ...le Rock Lake. He gently told her about the fire, handed ...er a large number of tissues from the box next to his chair, drank three cups of tea, and promised that the next time he saw Mr. Gallagher, he would ask about the fate of the *Beauty*'s employees.

That last one is easy, Hank thought as he left Mrs. Pugo's. He definitely planned to have a long and very specific chat with Henry Gallagher about his business and the fact that it was now miraculously rid of the burden of an aging showboat and an even older staff.

CHAPTER

15

The high school office was quiet after the chaos of the halls as what seemed to be hundreds of teenagers elbowed their way to different homerooms. Hank felt like he had barely made it to safety. That is a switch, he thought with silent chuckle. Growing up, he had certainly not considered the high school principal's office a desirable location. He straightened as a large battle-ax of a woman stormed out from the back. She looked at him over a pair of bright blue reading glasses.

"And you are here for . . . ?" she asked.

Hank put the yearbook he'd been carrying on the counter and smiled. "The girls' track team." Nothing like making the secretary think she had a pervert on her hands right before lunchtime. Her eyes widened, but before she could get sharp he put up a hand and explained why he was there.

"Oh," she gasped. "Oh, oh. That poor girl. Suc heart. Oh, goodness. Oh, my. I . . . I'll just, I'll ju: get Mr. Narwall, shall I?"

She retreated and then returned with half a dozen women—who must have made up the entire office staff—and one man. Hank had to guess that he was Mr. Narwall. The women pushed forward to the counter and started peppering him with questions. Now, this is more like a principal's office, he thought.

No, he had not caught the murderer yet. No, he hadn't seen the story in the paper. No, he didn't think there was a serial killer on the loose. Yes, he had spoken with Mandy's parents. No, he was not really qualified to say how they were doing. Yes, he would pass on that they were all praying for the family.

"Now," he said, speaking loudly to be heard over the verbal bombardment, "I need to speak with Danielle Krycenski."

"Oh, yes," the Battle-Ax said briskly. "She was on the track team with Mandy last year. She's in government class right now." She shot a look at one of the women, who immediately trotted off. She showed Hank into an office in the back, and five minutes later the blonde who had so enjoyed the medic's company in the boat lounge walked into the room. She wiped tears off her face as she sat down.

"I didn't even know she was on the boat," she sobbed before Hank said a word. "Why didn't she say hi? Why didn't she . . ."

She dropped her head into her hands and wept. Hank cringed. Comforting teenage girls was not exactly his forte. He opened the door and beckoned in the hovering Battle-Ax. It would be better to have an observer anyway. Could never be too careful these days.

The Battle-Ax was armed with fistfuls of tissue and the

somewhat surprising ability to offer copious amounts of sympathy. Several hugs and murmurs later, Danielle was able to speak again.

"You wanted to ask me some stuff?" She sniffed.

Hank took her through the morning. Her account of the meal and the time in the lounge didn't vary much from everyone else's. She had felt somewhat awkward. The only person she really knew was Ryan, and all his attention was directed at his "college girl." Danielle had assumed Ryan invited her because Mandy would be there—although he had been friendly with her in high school, he knew she and Mandy were very close.

"So you were surprised Mandy wasn't there?" Hank asked. Danielle nodded. "Did you ask Ryan about it?"

"Yeah," Danielle said. "He just blew me off. Said he was with Kelly now. Said he was sure we would be good friends. Me and her? I don't think so. And he wouldn't say anything about Mandy. I kept trying to ask when they'd broken up, but he wouldn't talk about it. He was really being a jerk."

"Do you think Mandy would have come to the party if she'd known Ryan had a new girlfriend?"

"No way," Danielle said. "I know she really liked his grandma and all, but no way. She would not have put up with that. But . . ." She trailed off.

Hank leaned back in his chair and waited.

"She was different, a little. When she was home for Christmas break, she seemed different. She was kinda jumpy and nervous. And she really seemed to cling to Ryan. She never used to do that."

"Did she talk to you about anything? Over the break?"

Danielle looked puzzled. "Nothing special. Just how

college was fun, but really hard, too. And we talked a lot about her track practices and conditioning and stuff. I'm hoping to make it as a walk-on at Mizzou."

"You two ran together last year?"

"Yeah. I did pretty well for being a junior. She was a senior, of course. And so good. She got first in a couple of meets. And our whole team got third at state. Coach Schuster and Coach E. were really proud of us. And especially of her."

She broke into sobs again. The Battle-Ax wrapped her in a hug, patting her head as she aimed a look at Hank that clearly asked whether he was done making her student cry. Hank nodded, and she silently led Danielle from the room. He stared into space for a moment, going over what Mandy's friend had said. By the time he stepped out of the office, the Battle-Ax was back with three other students. Hank frowned.

"Here are the other girls who were on the track team with Mandy last year who are still here at school," she said. "They are all on the team again this year."

He had not needed to talk to anyone else at the school. He frowned again. The three teens looked more excited than upset. He had a feeling they had not been as close to Mandy as Danielle had been. He bit back a sigh and backed into the office. The trio eagerly followed. They plopped down into chairs and stared at him with wide eyes.

"We heard about Mandy," the tall one said breathlessly. The other two nodded. The short one leaned forward. "And you're investigating, right?" Before Hank could answer, she leaned even closer. "Was it vampires?"

Hank stared at her. He could not—for possibly the first time in his adult life—think of a single thing to say.

"Was it?" she repeated.

The three of them stared at him. He began wishing that the Battle-Ax had joined him for this. Were they serious?

"Nooooo," he said, drawing the word out. "It was not vampires."

"How do you know?" asked the tall one. "They're every-where. And they're very sneaky. They're way smarter than cops."

How on earth had he lost control of this conversation—before it even started? And how was he going to get it back? By protesting that no, he was indeed smarter than imaginary monsters who existed only in pulpy teenage crap?

They continued staring at him. Well.

"It has been my experience . . . as a police officer," he said very slowly, "that people who try to redirect the focus of an investigator's interview with silly theories are usually the ones who end up under arrest for murder."

All three jaws dropped. The short one turned very red. No one said a word.

There.

He leaned back in the creaky school-issue desk chair and gave them a good long glower. The one who was neither tall nor short started to fidget. All right, her first. He leaned for-ward quickly.

"What's your name?"

She jumped and gasped at the same time. She had shoulder-length brown hair and pretty brown eyes, but she was dressed in clothes that were just a little too big and a little too out of date. Hand-me-downs. Her chin started to tremble.

"Alyssa . . . Sampson . . . sir," she squeaked.

"And you were on the track team with Mandy last year?"

he asked. She nodded. "Did you talk to her at all after she went away to school? Did any of you?"

"We all saw her during Christmas break. It was a party at Chad's house. Chad Sorenson. For New Year's," Alyssa said.

That name was on the boat manifest. "Who's Chad?" he asked.

They all shrugged and mumbled. Alyssa shifted in her seat.

"Who. Is. Chad?" Hank growled. He had had enough of these three. Maybe they should go over to the Brysons' place, watch Mandy's mother sink into her dining room tablecloth sobbing as she tried to pour a cup of coffee. That was where he had been before coming to the school, and right now, he thought seeing that would be a darn sight better education for these flippant children than whatever they were ignoring in government class. He leaned farther forward and waited.

"Chad's a . . . a friend of Ryan's," Alyssa said finally. "He's new. He didn't go to school here. His family just moved to town. That big house right on the other side of Lake Taney-como."

"And he had a party on New Year's Eve?" Hank asked. All three nodded. He pointed at the tall one. "You—tell me about it. And what's your name?"

"Oh . . . I'm Jennifer Wilson. Um. Yeah. The party. There were a lot of people there. It was pretty cool. In the big house and everything. Chad had it all done up. Black lights and champagne and . . ."

The short one made a small, strangled sound, and Tall Jennifer stopped, apparently realizing what she had said. Hank fought back a smirk.

"So there was alcohol at the party? What else besides champagne?"

Jennifer stared down at her hands. Her friends looked like they wanted to kill her. "That was the one cool thing that's ever happened around here, and now it'll never happen again, because you . . ." hissed the petite one.

Alyssa smacked her quickly on the arm to shut her up. Hank kept staring at Jennifer. Her shoulders slumped, and she said, "There was beer and some kind of shots, but I didn't do those. That's all."

The other two reluctantly nodded their confirmation. "And what happened at the party?"

"Just dancing and hanging out, you know. Nothing else. It was just cool," she said.

"Except for when Mandy freaked out," said Alyssa. "That was just weird."

"What happened?" Hank asked, keeping the interest out of his voice.

"Chad came up behind her while she was talking to Ryan—she didn't see him—and put his arm around her shoulder. He's really tall, so his arm kinda went down her shoulder and around her neck. He was just being friendly, but she totally flipped out. Jumped about ten feet in the air and then turned around and almost punched him, until she saw who it was. She was shaking and almost crying. Spilled her drink all over."

"What did Ryan think about it?" Hank asked.

"He was totally surprised," she said.

The short one chimed in. "I think he was mad, too. His girlfriend starts acting like a spazz on the most important night of the year. And he was mad that it made Chad mad. That wasn't cool, either. You don't want to tick off the guy who's put on this awesome party. It was just a bad deal."

"What did Mandy do after that?"

"Oh, she made Ryan leave pretty soon after that. I think they even left before midnight."

"And how did Chad take all of this?" Hank continued.

All three girls sighed. Apparently Chad was all that and more. Alyssa cleared her throat. "He was great. You could tell he was upset, but he totally brushed it off and was a lot of fun."

"Yeah," Jennifer said. "And with Mandy gone, he paid more attention to the rest of us."

Hank kept his face impassive. "He didn't before that incident?"

"No," she said with a bit of an edge to her voice. "He followed Mandy around. Sure, she's in college and everything, but I can run faster than she can . . ." She trailed off and blushed slightly.

"It wasn't very smart," said the short one whose name Hank still didn't know, "because she made Ryan so mad that he started dating someone else."

Hank was unaware that was common knowledge. "Really?" he said casually.

Shorty nodded. "Yep. We saw him in January up in St. Louis. Jenny and me went up with our moms to use our Christmas gift cards—St. Louis is a lot more fun than Springfield—and we saw him at the Galleria. He had some hot blonde that he was hanging all over. Making out with her in the food court. We told Alyssa as soon as we got back."

All three of them grimaced in disapproval. They clearly expected better from someone now in college.

"Did you say anything to him?"

Shorty shook her head. "He didn't even see us. We had to go, and besides . . ."

There was an exasperated huff from the doorway. The Battle-Ax had returned. "We do not gossip about other people, Melissa Garvey. You ought to be ashamed of yourself. Good Christians never—"

Hank cut her off, although he was tempted to let her have at them. "Ma'am, they are answering my questions. And I'm pretty sure the Lord approves of people who help—with all seriousness—the police and their investigations. Don't you agree, ladies?"

All three nodded quickly. His other questions produced nothing important, so he nodded to the Battle-Ax and the three rose to leave. "Oh, Alyssa," he said. "You said Sampson, right? Are you related to the Tony Sampson who works on the *Beauty*?"

"Yeah, he's my older brother," she said.

"Has he talked to you about all this?" Hank asked.

She shrugged. "Nah. Not really."

"How long has he worked out at the *Beauty*?"

She thought for a moment. "About two years, I guess. He started after he graduated. Now he thinks he could be the captain." She rolled her eyes.

Hank smiled. "Older brothers, huh?"

She grinned. "Yeah. Exactly."

The Battle-Ax marched them from the room. Hank followed a moment later and found no one in the office. He felt odd standing on that side of the counter, so he walked around it to the front. The Battle-Ax came in from the hallway.

"I do hope that helped, Sheriff."

More than you know, ma'am. More than you know. He stuck out his hand. "I hadn't expected that, but it was very valuable, ma'am, and I thank you."

She smiled, which softened her face considerably, turning her into more of a Battle-Spade. She pressed his hand with both of hers. "And please, tell Mr. McCleary for all of us that we pray for him every day. And we miss Marian so much . . ." Her eyes filled. "She was such a good principal. Such a good person. To go like that. At sixty-four, from a heart attack! That shouldn't happen. God forgive me, but it shouldn't. She should have had many more years left in her."

Hank felt his eyes prick. "Yes, ma'am. She should have." He retrieved his hand and moved for the door before his eyes could do more than that. Going the other direction now in the hallway, he noticed the trophy case against the opposite wall. In the middle place of honor was the track team trophy from last season, and next to it, a photo of the long-distance runners. He moved closer. It was a different picture from the one used in the yearbook. Seventeen girls in track uniforms and two men, one of whom had mussed '70s hair and aviator sunglasses. Albert Eberhardt. Coach E. Standing right next to Mandy Bryson.

CHAPTER
16

Hank burst back into the school office and yanked all four girls out of class again. None of them remembered Coach E. being overly affectionate with Mandy, but they said he did pay a lot of attention to her at practices. They all figured it was because she was so good and had the best shot of placing in the state competition. He was apparently a cool, laid-back dude who knew lots about running techniques and training. He had been the assistant coach for five years and had missed the yearbook team photo shoot last year because it was scheduled at the same time as one of the *Beauty*'s luncheon cruises.

Hank wanted to shake the comatose nutjob awake and demand some answers. Albert the Moron was now doubly important, and instead of cooperating with the investigation— or sitting in a cell in the county lockup—he was peacefully snoring away up on the third floor of Branson Valley General. His doctor there—who, Maggie assured Hank, was perfectly competent—said he would need to remain heavily sedated for some time. So no interview, no information, no nothing. But at least he knew where Albert was. He couldn't be sure of that when it came to Chad Sorenson. He hoped Mr. All That was at home in his parents' palatial retreat overlooking Lake Taneycomo.

He was not.

"There was a phone call yesterday, ma'am, from my deputy—asking that Chad remain in town until we spoke with him about his voyage on the *Beauty*." All That's mother looked at him serenely from her seat on a very expensive couch and shrugged delicately.

"I never received any such phone call, Sheriff. And my son is a grown man. He is not obligated to stay here and wait for you." She tucked a bit of her perfectly done blond hair behind her ear, making sure Hank saw the several diamond rings on her hand as she did so. She had not offered him a seat, so he stood in the middle of the large living room, literally with his hat in his hands. He wished he'd left it in the car.

"Actually, ma'am, he is. He is a material witness to a murder investigation. Where is he now?"

Another shrug. "As I said, if he was not told to stay in town, how could he follow your orders?" Her last word was weighted with sarcasm. Hank fought the urge to return it.

"Really?" he said. "According to the nice lady who let me in, 'Mister Chad' took a call from the sheriff's department yesterday morning."

Mrs. Sorenson frowned. Hank hoped he hadn't gotten the woman in trouble. "I will see," she said slowly, "if I can locate him." She stood, effectively dismissing Hank. He didn't think so.

"Good." He smiled. "While I wait, I'll just have a chat

with your help." She froze. "Oh, don't worry," he continued, "I'll make sure I don't keep her long."

Hank found the woman in the kitchen, prepping that night's dinner. Her name was Lupe Gonzales, and she was both the cook and the maid. She had been with the Sorensons for five years and had moved to Branson with them a year ago. They were very good employers, she said with a scared look. Hank had to reassure her that all he cared about was finding Chad. And also a party he threw on New Year's Eve. Señora Gonzales rolled her eyes.

"I was here for that, yes. He made me cook up all kinds of food, without any warning. That morning, he says, 'Lupe, I'm going to throw a big party. Cook this, make that.' Later I find out that he gave the invitations very much before. He could have told me in advance, too. In that way, he is not like his mother."

Mrs. Sorenson, while very demanding (Hank's word, not Señora Gonzales's), had realistic expectations and always gave her plenty of notice before throwing a party or traveling. Actually, Señora Gonzales said, both Mrs. Sorenson and her husband had been out of town over New Year's. Chad had been the only one in the house. She doubted his parents knew he was going to have a party. They did not approve of strangers in their house, especially rowdy teenagers. Chad had told her to be quiet about it, she said, jabbing a finger in the air. And she had, but only because Mr. and Mrs. Sorenson were gone a lot and she was stuck with "Mister Chad." He could make her life very miserable, and she knew it.

"You will not tell them that I say these things?" she asked, her eyes darkening with worry as she realized how much she had told Hank. He shook his head and smiled at her. There was no need to upset her—he had a feeling having a source inside this house could come in very handy. He wasn't quite sure where the Sorensons got their money or why they'd moved to Branson, of all places. But those questions were merely academic at this point. Right now, he needed to know everything he could about Mister Chad, and *la señora* was his best option.

Chad was twenty, quite sociable, had lots of friends, and was kind of a flake (again, Hank's word, not Señora Gonzales's). He had flunked out of a fancy little college in upstate New York just before the Sorensons moved to Branson. Señora Gonzales came with them because it was the only way to keep her job. Finding a new one would be next to impossible with the way things were now. She had to leave her nieces and nephews, who were her only family since her husband had died years ago of the heart disease. And she did not like it here. She was not comfortable. There was no Latino community. Well, she admitted, there might be, but it was small. Nothing like what she was used to in New York. Everyone here seemed to be white. They were not used to seeing people like her. She got stared at in the grocery store. Thank God the Catholic church down by the lake had a Spanish Mass on Saturday nights. That was the only time she felt at home. She wanted the Sorensons to move back to New York, she said. Their older son worked for some big company on Wall Street. She had hoped that would be a strong enough pull, but so far, they had shown no desire to leave this place.

Chad had adjusted well. He had met several local young people—she didn't know how—and started socializing with them. During the summer, he would go out. He would tell her he was going to the water park or the go-karts, but whether that was true . . . She shrugged. He had been happy then, but over the past several months had become mopey and bored. She thought it was because several of his better friends had gone away to college. Most especially some boy named Ryan and a pretty girl named Mandy, whom he talked about all the time. They had both come to the New Year's Eve party. But Señora Gonzales had not stayed, preferring to set out the food and then retreat to her room to watch Univision's coverage of the Times Square ball drop by herself.

If all the good *señora* watched was Spanish-language TV, she probably had not seen coverage of the boat crash, or Mandy's death. Hank really wished he could stop breaking news of a murder to people.

"*Dios mio!* That sweet *niña*? That is why you want to talk with Mister Chad? Did he do it?"

Hank assured her that all he wanted to do was talk to Chad, since he had been on the boat at the time. He needed to do that with everybody.

"He could not have done it. He liked her, very much. You know, like a schoolboy. *Enamorado.*"

And that was what Hank was afraid of.

Chad Sorenson was not in Branson. And Hank doubted Mr. All That was hiding in the surrounding county—he didn't seem the type to have made friends with the more . . . authentic . . . residents of the Ozark area he now called home. He had not left through the small airport south of town, so Hank called an old work buddy in Kansas City and had him start the process of watching the major airlines there and in St. Louis. He took some ribbing when the guy found out Hank did not have the personnel to handle it on his end.

He hung up the phone and scowled at the whiteboard in his office. It was decorated with crossed-out names, arrows, and a few question marks. It looked more like a football playbook than the work schedule for an entire county department. He didn't know who was on overtime, who was still within the number of hours for normal pay, and who needed mandatory rest time by the end of the day.

He did know that he only had one deputy out on routine patrol at the moment. He also knew he should be praying that nothing else happened anywhere in the county, at least until Sheila got back and could fix this mess.

He was so intent on his scowling stint, he did not hear the visitor until . . .

"Hello? Anybody here? Helloooooo . . . ?"

Hank lurched to his feet and quickly took the three strides necessary to go the length of the short hallway and into the waiting room. Standing there was a man of ordinary height and build, with short salt-and-pepper hair sticking out from his head at several random and unflattering angles. His nose was small and a nice shade of Rudolph red. So were his ears.

"Can I help you?" Hank growled. The man's eyes narrowed, and his ears turned a concerning shade of maroon. Hank stared at him impatiently and was about to repeat the question when he realized he was looking at a Branson County Commissioner. One of the ones who had backed him for sheriff six months ago. The guy did not look like he would make the same decision today. Hank braced himself.

"Sir," he said. "My apologies. Please have a seat. Can I—"

"Sheriff," the commissioner cut him off as he pressed a tissue to his nose, "I am not here for small talk. I am here to talk about the awful events that have occurred in our fair county in the last several days. Have you caught the killer yet?"

Hank bit back a sigh. Of course he hadn't. And this guy knew it. And was going to force him to say that, no, he had not caught the killer. So Hank said it. Then he gave a short explanation as to why such things tended to be difficult to do. The commissioner, in between nose blowing and coughing, responded that those folks on the TV didn't seem to have much problem with it.

Hank had been appointed, not elected, he reminded himself in an effort to keep his temper. And so for now, Rudolph here thought he was kind of Hank's boss.

"Do you have suspects? Are you interrogating people?" he asked, wheezing.

Hank explained that at this stage of the investigation, it was called interviewing, and yes, there were several suspects. Rudolph demanded to know who, and when Hank wouldn't say, waved a very full tissue in his face.

"What do you mean, you can't divulge details of the investigation? I'm not a lawyer. Don't use those fancy words on me. You got suspects, you tell me. I'm a county commissioner. I hired you, boy. I set your budget. I can undo anything I want. You hear?"

Hank took a step back to avoid the fluttering tissue. Rudolph took it as capitulation, moving closer and waiting with an expectant and self-satisfied look on his face. Hank gritted his teeth. He'd never been one of those people who could talk without saying anything. And he'd always been proud of that, until now. Now, being able to tell this guy things without actually giving him any information would come in pretty handy. He took a deep breath and launched into what he hoped was a superficial account, explaining that he was canvassing the victim's friends for clues as to her life and relationships. He had determined that she was alive when the *Beauty* ran aground, but had died hours before the rescue, so she had to have been killed by someone stuck on the boat with her. Everyone who had access to the second deck of the boat was being interviewed. His office was knocking on every door, pulling out all the stops, leaving no stone unturned.

Rudolph appeared to be appeased by the clichés and mercifully took his tissue out of Hank's personal space. "Good," he wheezed. "I want you to keep working on this night and day. Mandy Bryson was a track star. She was known throughout the region. Everyone knows she's dead. Even the TV stations in Kansas City and St. Louis have been talking about it."

And there you had it—the distinguished commissioner's true concern. Hank did not respond.

"This murder has the whole county just terrified," Rudolph continued. "I'm leading a prayer vigil Thursday night. It will be at the old Mel Tillis Theatre. It's one of the only ones big enough to hold all the folks I expect to come. And it's got enough parking for the TV trucks, too."

Hank nodded and moved slowly toward the door. He really, really just wanted this guy to leave. Rudolph followed, digging in his pockets for another tissue. He found one just in time to smother a sneeze. Hank yanked open the door and fought the urge to shove him out. Rudolph mopped up his sneeze and then stopped.

"Oh," he said, "and if you happen to see Mr. Gallagher before I do, please let him know that he's got our sympathies for his poor boat, and if there's anything the commission can do to help him out, well, you just let him know that we care."

Excellent. Hank closed the door tightly behind the departing politician, locked it, and put the closed sign in the window. He was walking back down the hallway when he realized he should have asked the jerk to put more overtime money in his budget.

CHAPTER

17

"We're done out there for the night," Sam said. He shrugged out of his parka, sending another wave of fire stink through the office. Mustachio kept his coat on. It did not appear that he would be staying. Hank was both glad and peeved about that.

"I don't think there's much more to do, anyway," Mustachio said. "It'll be ruled an accidental fire likely caused by the damage to the boat sustained during the earlier wreck and subsequent rescue."

"'Likely'?" Hank pounced on the word. "So you aren't sure?"

Mustachio groaned. "Look, that boat was done for. It could have been fuel that leaked after the paddle wheel got hacked off. Or hydraulic fluid. All it needed was an ignition source."

"But was there one—that wasn't supplied by an arsonist?" Hank pressed.

Mustachio glowered at him. "We don't know. The boat, in case you hadn't noticed, is destroyed. *And underwater.* So we have no way of knowing what the ignition source was. We have no way of knowing if someone just left a coffee pot on. Do you know? Did you check the whole boat? Every coffee pot? Every curling iron in the dressing rooms? Was everything off? Did you check the generator? When you went back there last night, did you check? Everything?"

Now Hank glowered back. "No," he spat. "I did not."

Mustachio sniffed, in what Hank considered a very condescending manner. He started to speak again, but Hank cut him off.

"What about the divers? Shouldn't you send down divers?"

"In this weather? The temperature of that water is about forty degrees. There is absolutely no reason to do that—to send men down when there is nothing left to see." Mustachio's glower got worse. "I got a finite number of resources and a huge area to cover, pal. I work for the state, not just your little ol' county. I got three fatal fire investigations going, including one that's two counties over where the parents mysteriously escaped the burning house, but the kids sleeping right by the front door didn't. I think I'll put my time into trying to get them charged with murder, instead of hanging around here, putting divers in danger to chase down your cockamamie theories. If you want to put on a dry suit and take a look down there, be my guest. But it seems to me that you got better things to do, too. You know, with that dead girl of yours and all."

Hank stood there, too furious to speak. The Pup, trying to stay unnoticed, inched toward the back offices. The fire marshal turned on his heel and stomped out of the office, leaving crusty snow footprints and oily smoke smell behind him.

Sam had almost made it to the safety of the hallway. Hank stopped him.

"How long you been on duty?"

The Pup scratched behind his ear as he thought for a minute. It must have been a little after six this morning when he got the call about the fire, he guessed, so coming up on twelve hours now. And yesterday was the same. And the day before that, too. Good, Hank thought, three twelves isn't too bad. Then Sam cleared his throat.

"Um . . . but Sunday, you know, when the murder happened, um . . . that was supposed to be my day off. I'd already worked a full week."

Great. Hank had no idea what that meant as far as overtime. He sighed.

"Uh, Chief . . ." Sam said. "Don't worry about it. I'm not going to just leave. I'm not Gerald Tucker."

Hank raised an eyebrow. "That's getting around, is it?"

A huge grin split Sam's face. "Heck yeah. He's a jerk and—" He stopped short and turned bright red. "What I mean is . . . um . . ."

Hank smiled and was going to drop it, but paused. Getting a read on his deputies might not be a bad idea. He asked how many others weren't fond of Tucker. Sam's grin came back.

"Most of us . . . except some of the older guys. They're his buddies. There were a few of them that were real upset when you got the sheriff job," he said. "Tucker thought it was all his, being so tight with Sheriff Gibbons and all. But it wasn't the sheriff who got to decide, was it?"

No, Hank thought. It was the county commission, for whom he was now no longer the bright, shiny, from-the-big-city upgrade they'd wanted. Sam, who knew nothing of that, kept talking.

". . . so the younger guys, well, we were talking about it. I guess you could say everybody's heard you shoved him off to the jail. Except Sheila. Hooo, boy. When she comes back . . ." He trailed off. They looked at each other and broke into identical grins. That would be fun. Might even put her in a good mood for a while.

Roy Stanton looked like he was in no shape to put on a show. His jowly face hung slack and his glasses sat crookedly on his nose. He hadn't bothered with his comb-over, and the long gray wisps hung along the right side of his head. It was almost eight o'clock in the evening, and he was still in his bathrobe.

"I can't believe it, Sheriff. That sweet girl." He let out a sigh that soaked the air with enough bourbon to make Hank tipsy. "I have thought of nothing else since I heard yesterday. And to think, it happened with all of us on board. Absolutely terrifying. A murderer in our midst. A killer among us. A . . ."

Hank had misjudged. Roy Stanton clearly could not help putting on a show, even while three sheets to the wind. He kept talking as he arranged himself in a large easy chair by the fireplace. It was obviously where he spent most of his time. It had a direct view of the television and was surrounded by piles of books and newspapers. Hank saw several volumes of the collected works of Shakespeare stacked on top of a Neil Simon biography and a copy of *A Streetcar Named Desire*. He waved Hank into the rickety chair opposite and reached for the half-empty bottle of Maker's Mark sitting on *The Plays of Oscar Wilde.*

"I should have known it would be an ill-fated voyage," he said, topping off his glass. "I have never been treated so contemptibly. They did not want my services. My talents. I showed everyone up to the private dining room and was ready to start my act when I was dismissed. Like I was the common help. I . . ." Stanton's jowls trembled, and he steeled himself with a sip of bourbon.

Hank managed to get him to set down the glass as he recounted the reactions of those in attendance when he exited his stage. The biggest crime of all had been that most people did not even notice when the snooty middle-aged lawyer dismissed him. One of the young men did, however. Very tall and wearing an expensive leather coat, he had been hovering around the door into the hallway and had heard the lawyer's rejection. In the throes of his own drama, Stanton had not noticed what the man—who had to have been Chad, Hank thought—was doing, or whether he was waiting for someone.

Stanton had left through the door that led directly into the kitchen. "And there, well, you can imagine my surprise. I found a young lady who had obviously been weeping. Mrs. Pugo was guarding her like a mother bear, which made her all the more unbearable, and I . . ." Stanton broke into giggles as he realized his wordplay. Hank didn't stifle his groan in time, and Roy collected himself, looking hurt. He straightened in his chair and took a moment before continuing.

Yes, he admitted, he did not much like Mrs. Pugo. A flighty, flustered mess, she was. Could barely keep the food warm. There was many a time he'd had to cover for her with the guests, explaining away the cold food as he hosted their private voyages around the lake. She should have retired years ago, but no. Just like half the staff on that boat, she was too old and doddering to be working.

When Hank asked who exactly fit that bill, Roy rattled off a dozen names. None of them worked on the upper deck, though. What about Tim Colard?

"Oh, Tim. He's all right. Whines a lot, thinks he's over-worked. But he does a good job. Looks the part, too. Just like a paddleboat waiter should for the private dining room folks, dapper and dark-haired. Lives up in Ozark, I think. Must be about forty-five. Been with the crew for about twenty years."

"He married? Seeing anybody?" Hank asked. Roy shook his head. "He like younger girls?"

Roy's laugh caught on his swallow of liquor and had him coughing for a solid minute. "Tim? Heavens, no. He's, um, not inclined that way . . . so to speak. Never told me direct like or anything. But females of any age aren't really his thing, if you get my meaning," he said, waggling his eyebrows sug-gestively.

Hank got it. He also doubted that people in this county ever used the word "homosexual," direct like. In his six months here, he'd never heard it uttered. He decided to follow local custom and gloss over it—for now. He moved on to the other boat staff.

"What about Tony Sampson? How long have you known him?"

"Tony? Oh, since he came on as the captain's assistant, about two years ago. He must have been one of Mr. Gallagher's first hires, right after he came to town and bought the *Beauty*. Thought Tony was a bit young for the job, myself. He had just graduated from high school. Very serious young man.

Never cracked a smile. No joie de vivre." Roy punctuated his French with a showy arm wave that sloshed bourbon all over his hand. "Oops," he said, handing his drink to Hank and using the sleeve of his robe to soak it up as he continued talking. "And he's always looking at his phone. One of those new smart things. Never seen him without it. Kids today . . .

"He's nice and polite otherwise, though. And he does know his stuff. Learned all about how the boat works and the staffing and everything. And he knows the routes and the lake and such. Of course, he knew that stuff before. Grew up on the lake. His daddy owns one of the charter fishing companies out there."

Roy finished mopping up his spill and began to look around for the drink he clearly did not remember giving to Hank. Hank, having hidden it behind a stack of books to the right of his chair, waited patiently for the other man to continue.

"Yes . . . well . . . hmm. Where did I . . . ? Huh. Well, anyway . . . where was I? Oh, yes—Tony. He is good at his job. Has been a real help to Albert. Piloting that big old thing across the lake in every kind of weather isn't easy."

Hank nodded encouragingly and asked about Albert. He left out the moron part. Roy's face split into a grin, then just as quickly fell serious. "How is he, Sheriff? Is he up yet? Awake? It's very worrying. The whole thing . . . very worrying."

No kidding. But before he started talking about Albert's current condition, Hank needed a lot more background. The guy had no family, lived alone, and apparently had only one extracurricular activity, which was coaching the girls' track team. A check had turned up no arrest record, one overdue parking ticket out of Kansas City, military service during the

Vietnam War, a Republican voter registration, a thirty-year-old divorce, and ownership of a little two-bedroom place on two acres out on Highway 248.

And the house was just as uninformative. The Pup had searched it yesterday with a warrant and found a treadmill, lots of health food, no alcohol, a desk with only routine bills and paperwork but no computer, two very hungry cats, and several half-finished landscape paintings. Sam had pronounced the cats "pretty mean" and the paintings "pretty good." None of them helped further the investigation.

But then "Captain" Stanton got himself a fresh bourbon and started talking. And he made no attempt to distance himself from the man who'd basically sunk everyone's livelihoods. "Al Eberhardt is one of the best men I've ever served with. And that's the God's honest truth. Crazy Otis hired us both right about the same time . . . within six months of each other. That was back in '95. I called us 'the Two Captains.'" His arm swept dramatically upward again, but this time he managed to hold on to his liquor. "Al didn't, though. He's what you would call understated. No dramatic flair. Can't act worth a can of beans."

Albert kept mostly to himself. He enjoyed his job—the peace of the lake, the moderate challenge of navigating the well-worn paddle-wheel route. He especially liked being able to disappear into the pilothouse without having to interact with the tourists. Roy shook his head sadly—it was obvious that, even after twenty years, he could not relate to such reticence. But that didn't mean, he added quickly, that Albert didn't get along with people. People he knew, well, he got on with them just fine. It just took him a while to warm up, that was all.

Roy wasn't sure his friend had always been that way. He had a feeling that Albert had withdrawn after coming back from Vietnam. His marriage had ended, and he'd bounced around, working in factories mostly, until he came to Branson, where Otis had taken him on. And taken him in. That was how Otis worked. All manner of lost souls. Folks who needed a chance, or just a little bit of help. Otis would reach out a hand. He wouldn't give out handouts, no. He'd give you a job, a way to support yourself.

"And that was how it was with Al. I don't think he ever really shook Vietnam. I don't know for sure what happened to him there, but . . ." He trailed off. "That was how we became friends, you know. I was in 'Nam, too. We were the only two 'Nam vets on the boat. We'd talk about it every once in a while. He didn't like to, actually. Something about what he did over there. Went on a lot of bombing raids. I think he did napalm drops, but the couple times I brought it up, he got up and left the room. But he knew the military, and we'd joke about it sometimes. It's nice to know that someone else gets it, you know?"

None of Albert's habits or routines had changed recently, as far as Roy knew. Work had been normal—excepting Sunday's mishap, of course—and Albert wasn't having any financial problems. The guy never spent money on anything except painting supplies and running shoes. Hank leaned in. About the running . . .

"Oh, goodness. He runs every day. Has ever since I've known him. Absolutely crazy. About ten years ago, he was on a run and met Gene, the high school track coach. Gene talked him into helping out. He didn't want to at first—you know, the whole shy thing. But I told him the opportunity wouldn't have fallen in his lap if he wasn't meant to do it. Plus, it's hard for the school to find folks willing to coach things." He smiled sadly. "Except drama, apparently. They've never needed my help. I offer every year, but they always already have someone." He stared pensively at his stack of plays for a moment before a sip of his drink got him back on track.

So Al had started coaching. Originally, Roy said, he'd helped with both the boys' and girls' teams. But after a few years, he'd realized that the girls were much more open to his suggestions and techniques than the boys, so he began working only with them. And it was no coincidence, Roy said with pride, that now the girls' team was one of the best in the state, and the boys' was not.

"Did he ever talk specifically about Mandy Bryson?" Hank asked.

Roy thought. "I don't know, honestly. He talked about all of them. What their times were, how they'd done at the last track meet. I don't remember him talking specifically about anybody. Oh, except Tony Sampson's sister. Told me he liked her a whole lot better than he did her brother. Said that Tony did his job well, learned the ropes pretty quickly, but Albert just couldn't figure the kid out. Always looking over his shoulder. I teased him, told him it was because Tony wanted his job."

Hank wondered how much pressure Albert's job did put on him. Enough to send him over the edge? That sounded possible. But what was that edge? Running the boat aground? Murdering his track star? Or both? What had happened that day?

Roy hadn't seen Albert before the boat launched that morning, which wasn't unusual. In fact, he hadn't seen him

at all. He'd pondered going up to the pilothouse after the
boat ran into the rocks, but thought better of it. In what Hank
considered an atypical burst of self-awareness, Roy said he
figured Albert didn't need any more drama right then.

The crash had sent everyone, staff and guests, rushing into
the hallway to get a better look out the big windows. Roy
didn't think Mandy had come out, but he was sure everyone
else in the kitchen had. They all milled around in the hallway for maybe ten minutes. Roy supposed someone in the
crowd could have ducked into the kitchen during that time,
but—being focused on the unbelievable sight of the *Beauty*'s
wheel wedged between the rocks—he had not paid any attention to the kitchen door, so he didn't know for sure. He did
know that he hadn't seen anyone new on the deck. The only
passengers there were the rude ones from the private dining
room. And the only other staff member to show up was Tony
Sampson, who appeared a few minutes after the crash. Roy
wasn't sure whether he had come from the main deck below
or the pilothouse above.

Tony and Tim eventually got all the passengers down the
hallway into the lounge and things quieted down. And after
Tim cleaned up the lunch dishes, no one had used the door
between the dining room and the kitchen. He had no idea if
it had been locked at some point or not. Hank did not tell
him it had been.

Tim had served the coffee, which ran out way too soon.
He had told Mrs. Pugo to water it down, but did she listen?
No. Irritating woman.

"So I—not unlike the poor *Beauty*—was stuck between
a rock and a hard place. I could go into the lounge with those
ungracious people, or I could stay in the kitchen with silly

Mrs. Pugo and a weepy teenager." Roy sighed. "I chose to stay. At least Mrs. Pugo had not insulted my professional capabilities. We played cards for some time, and then Mandy wanted to get some air."

He had also stepped out, to use the facilities, and last saw Mandy walking past the dining room and toward the stairs to the pilothouse.

"I'll be honest," Roy said, leaning forward and grasping his drink with both hands. "I didn't think about her again. Now I look back and know I should have wondered where she'd gone off to, but there was so much going on once you and the Coast Guard came aboard. I didn't hear anything in the dining room. I wish I had. That poor thing."

Now Hank leaned forward.

"Do you think Al did it?"

"He loved those track girls of his," Roy said. "Why would he kill one of them?"

"That's what I'm asking you," Hank said. "Would he have killed her?"

Roy thought for a long moment. "I don't think so. . . . He has some demons, though . . . so I don't know."

"What about you," Hank asked. "Did you kill her?"

The "captain" stared at Hank for a long moment. He'd expected the question about Albert. He wasn't expecting one about himself. Hank watched him very carefully.

"No, I did not," Roy said slowly. "I'd never met her before. I watched her walk off, and that was the last I saw of her." He raised the glass to his lips with a steady hand. Innocence or good acting? Hank wished he knew.

CHAPTER

18

"Yeah," Hank said. "The whole thing stinks."

His wife took a step back. "No. Not the case. You. You stink. Dear God, where have you been? You smell like an ashtray that caught on fire and was put out by a bottle of whiskey."

Hank glared at her. "You can't put a fire out with alcohol." He started to shrug out of his coat, which seemed to have absorbed most of the fuel and smoke smell from the boat explosion site.

"Wait a minute," Maggie said. "Go take everything off out in the garage. You do that in here and you'll stink up the whole house."

Hank had no intention of stripping in the freezing garage. And Maggie apparently had no intention of letting him traipse through the house radiating toxic fumes. They stood there in the kitchen staring at each other until Duncan came shuffling in from the living room. "I'm off to bed—oh, you're home.

Finally." He put his empty cocoa mug in the sink. "Your wife only beat you by half an hour. Make sure both of you busy people go in and kiss your children. It was the last thing they asked for before they went to sleep."

The sound of his slippers scuffing on the carpet faded away as Duncan walked down the hallway. Maggie gave Hank a once-over that ended in a resigned glare. "At least go down to the basement and take them off by the washer. I'll go check on the kids."

"Oh, man. You stink."

Hank was getting more than a little tired of hearing that. Especially from the deputy he had hoped would have more to offer than obvious statements of fact. Sheila wrinkled her nose—the exact same way Maggie had the night before—and stepped back. Hank scowled at her.

"It's nice to see you, too. I'm looking forward to hearing your report. Why don't you have a seat?"

She eyed him as she slowly sat in the chair in front of his desk. "I thought the boat fire was yesterday."

"It was," Hank growled. "But I only have one winter coat. And it was either wear it—even though it smells, um, pungent—or leave the house in only a sweatshirt. Since it's about ten degrees out there, I was not going to do that—even though it managed to stink up the rest of my clothes just in the couple of minutes I had it on."

Sheila chortled. "It's not that cold. Jeez, a person would think you'd never been through a Missouri winter before."

"I've been through quite a few," Hank protested. "Never gotten used to them, though."

Sheila gave him a dismissive sniff—which, Hank happily

noted, she paid for with a large noseful of smoke stench. When she finished coughing, he said, "I know you've sent in a couple of updates, but why don't you lay out everything you learned all at once. That'll be the most helpful to me and Sam." Hank looked at the chair Sam had been sitting in seconds ago. "Where'd he go, anyway?"

The Pup trotted back into Hank's office. "Just taking care of something, Chief." Sheila didn't seem at all annoyed about being made to wait, which was strange. Then Hank noticed that his coat no longer hung on the rack by the door. Sam sat down with an excess of nonchalance and readied his pen and notepad. Well, Hank thought, at least I don't have a problem with these two showing initiative. He sat back and let Sheila report on her trip.

She reached into the large reusable grocery bag at her feet and pulled out several sheets of paper, each one in a plastic sleeve. "I found two more letters. So that's a total of five, including the ones I read you over the phone. I went through every piece of paper in that dorm room, and that's all I found. When you read them, it does sound like there's at least one missing, though."

The first new letter seemed to come before the one where the writer had obviously seen Mandy and wrote that he wanted her to stop wearing ponytails:

My Mandy,
I hope to be able to see you soon. I want to know what your world is like although I know that it is incomplete without me. I miss you every day. I will come, just to watch you. Soon my love.

The other letter Hank hadn't yet heard came after Mandy had been home during the holidays.

Mandy,

You have not been a good girl. To be with other men when you know you are mine is a sin. I had hoped we could be together over Christmas, but you kept looking at other men. You had no time for me. That hurt me. You need to know that. You need to be better. You need to be mine only.

The first letter was signed with the same squiggle as the others. The second was not signed at all.

"You think he was losing patience with her?" Sam asked. Hank nodded.

"And then the extraordinary luck . . ." Sheila stopped herself. "That's a bad word . . . the extraordinary *coincidence* that he happened to be on the *Beauty* that morning. The only person who knew she was coming was Mrs. Honneffer, right?"

Hank nodded again. "Mrs. Honneffer. And her son. They both made the arrangements with the boat staff for the party. She said she didn't tell Ryan, because she assumed he already knew."

"But these notes aren't from Ryan. He had dumped her," Sam said.

"Yeah, he isn't the stalker," Hank agreed. "But that doesn't mean he isn't the killer. He clearly wanted to be rid of her. If he discovered her on the boat, who knows?" He turned to Sheila. "What did people down there know about him?"

All Mandy's college friends knew about Ryan was what

she told them, Sheila said. He was smart, funny, and cute. They all thought the two were still dating. Mandy's roommate, an eighteen-year-old from Tulsa, did say that she thought he had gradually stopped calling as often. It was difficult to say for sure, though, because of course Mandy had her own cell phone and could have taken his calls anywhere.

Sam broke in. "I went back through her phone's history. He only called her twice after Christmas break. She had"—he flipped through his notebook—"twenty-four outgoing calls to his cell number in that time period. All but three were about ninety seconds to two minutes long, so I'm assuming she was leaving voice mails most of the time."

Her other phone calls and texts were fairly routine, he said, and most corresponded to the cell numbers Sheila had gotten from college friends. Many track team–related calls. Her parents, at least once every couple of days. Repeated calls right before Christmas break to a number that came back as the listing for Calfort's Firing Range and Gun Shop. Hank nodded.

"And then," Sam said, "there's one I don't know about. It's a New York area code and comes up as a cell phone. I've got a call into the phone carrier to try to get a name with it, but that's slow going. I was going to just call it directly, but I thought I'd ask you first."

Hank, who had been leaning his office chair back on its rear legs, banged down on all four. "New York? Well, now. When?"

Sam flipped his pages. "Three before Christmas, including one when she was back in Branson for break. All incoming. Then one outgoing one the afternoon of New Year's Eve. Then two more incoming, one in January and one last week."

Now, that was interesting. Chad had wanted to talk to Mandy, had he? "Don't call it right now. It's got to be the Sorenson kid's number. Any call from us would probably spook him even more. Let me have the number . . . I have an idea."

Sam scribbled it down, and Hank put the piece of paper in his pocket. He turned back to Sheila. "Anything else? What about the track thing Saturday night?"

She shook her head. Nothing out of the ordinary. Her teammates said she was excited to go home to see her "grandma friend" and her folks, but that she was not looking forward to getting up so early to make the drive.

Her coach had noticed she was jumpier and more anxious than most of his kids during the fall semester, but he'd attributed it to simple freshman jitters. He said she'd calmed down after Christmas, but joked that she still must have needed a grown-up version of a security blanket. She never went anywhere—even practice—without her purse.

"Now, of course, that makes sense," she said. "And we still haven't found the gun?"

"No." Hank scowled.

"Are you sure it wasn't on the boat?"

Sam cringed. Hank's scowl got worse.

"Yes. I am sure it was not on the boat. I searched the whole damn thing. Again. And now it's at the bottom of the lake. And the fire marshal isn't—"

Sheila cut him off. "I heard. And it does make sense, actually. C'mon, dead kids? You can't argue that isn't more important than mucking around on the bottom of Table Rock Lake when you know no one was on the boat. What'd the posted guard deputy see?"

Hank's ire returned tenfold. "Nothing," he spat, "because

he'd gone home. The minute his shift was over. Even though no one had arrived to relieve him. Didn't call in, didn't do a damn thing except leave a crime scene unattended."

Sheila's mouth dropped open. "That's . . . that's . . . who would do that? Who would—" She stopped. "Oh . . ."

Hank nodded.

"You never should have assigned him that," she said. "The man is a—"

"You assigned him that," Hank snapped. "Plus, everyone else was either ending shifts with tons of overtime already, or patrolling this ice rink of a county, or investigating a homicide, or—"

"Well, if you would listen when I talk about the scheduling, then—"

"Really? You briefed me on what to do when every deputy in this damn department is on overtime? You went into your contingency plan for when there's a huge snowstorm, a murder, and a big-ass fire all at the same time? Somehow I don't remember you getting into—"

Sam cleared his throat and looked at them with a mixture of sheer terror and exasperated gumption. "I think . . . that we should get back to the case . . . here . . . now," he said, his eyes wide as he looked from Hank to Sheila. He cleared his throat again. "Alice is trying to get prints off the purse. There were none but Mandy's on the phone. I had her do that before I started going through it.

"Now." He took a deep breath, sat up a little straighter, and shifted subjects. "I got the autopsy report, and it was definitely manual strangulation. No sexual assault. No assailant DNA. Nothing under her fingernails or anything like that." He laid the report on Hank's desk and slapped his hand down on top of it. Sheila gave him a puzzled look, but Hank just raised an eyebrow. Less Pup, more Dog. Good.

Hank walked back into the lobby and reflexively looked up at the clock. It was still broken. He dug his cell out of his pocket. 10:02 A.M. Icy snow crunched in the parking lot as a car slowly rolled in. Hank straightened and put down his coffee.

A tall, stocky older man with very polished gray hair and wearing a dark suit pushed open the door. The bell above tinkled unnecessarily. Hank waited, but there was no sign of Gallagher following. He picked up his coffee and took a deliberate sip. The dark suit frowned.

"I'm here to meet with Sheriff Worth," he said in a clipped tone.

Hank looked at him over the brim of his mug as he continued drinking. He finally lowered it and said, "Are you? You don't look like Henry Gallagher to me."

The suit's eyebrows rose. "I am Mr. Gallagher's attorney. Mr. Gallagher could not attend and so asked me to come. I represent his interests."

Hank took another drink and sized the guy up. He was definitely not local. Probably not Springfield, either.

"Where you from?"

The suit straightened. "St. Louis."

"Huh." Hank would have bet money that he actually lived in the ritzy suburb of Ladue. Self-satisfied confidence, expensive tailor, Catholic school ring on his hand.

"And your name?" he asked.

"Richard Clancy."

Marvelous. He had to be the Clancy in Wikson & Clancy. They had an office in Kansas City, but they were based in

St. Louis. He knew this because their fingers were everywhere. And now they were reaching into his little corner of the
state.

"You ever been to Branson before?"

"Yes, actually. We've vacationed here several times.
Beautiful lakes."

"Mmmm," Hank said. He had used vacation as a verb.
Definitely Ladue. "See any shows?"

The suit shook his head. "Only once. My mother-in-law
insisted on seeing Andy Williams . . . that was the only time she
came with us."

Hank wondered where the mother-in-law was now. So
he asked. Then he asked where they'd stayed, what they'd
done, how long the drive had taken. He asked when the suit
had left St. Louis that morning and whether he'd stopped at
Russell Stover on the way down. He asked if the roads were
clear and what kind of car he drove. And he carefully watched
the vein in the man's forehead get more and more prominent
with every question. Right before Hank figured it was about
to burst, the suit said, "Really, I think we should get on with
business. I am not here to chat. Can I see the sheriff, please?"

Hank smiled and put down his coffee cup. "I am the sheriff. And you are not here for business, because you did not
even bother to bring in a briefcase. I'm sure you are a very
good lawyer, but I doubt you have the details of Gallagher
Enterprises committed to memory. And you did not bring
your client, per my very explicit instructions. So until you
show up at this office with Mr. Gallagher, you are just wast-
ing my time."

He picked his mug up again and stared at his visitor, who
clearly was of the opinion that it was *his* time that had been

wasted. The suit's nostrils curled, and he straightened again. He spun on the heel of a shoe buffed almost to the same high sheen as his hair and marched out the door. Hank broke into a genuine grin. He hadn't gotten a single scintilla of usable information—unless the guy's "Moon River"–loving mother-in-law turned out to be the killer—but he'd certainly had some fun. His smile widened. If nothing else, the little encounter had cost Gallagher an arm and a leg in legal fees.

The Krycenski family stared at him across their kitchen table. Mother, father, and sweet Danielle, whose face was still splotched from crying. She clutched her mother's hand.

"Are you sure this is necessary? Why can't *you* find him?" Mr. Krycenski asked.

"If we could find him," Hank explained with much more patience than he was actually feeling, "we would." Deep breath. "But Chad Sorenson has disappeared. Having your daughter call him from a trusted phone number is by far the quickest way to get him to come out of hiding. If we go through the cell phone company, we need to get a warrant and then track down his signal. That takes a lot of time that I do not have."

He turned to Danielle. "You want to catch whoever did this to Mandy, don't you?" She nodded. "I don't know if Chad did it," Hank continued, "but I do know that I need to find him. Now. You remember what to say?" She nodded again and picked up her cell phone with a trembling hand. She scrolled to his number, her other hand clutching her mother's. The only sound was the dog panting under the table and then the ring coming over the speaker phone as the call went through.

One. Two. Three. It was going to go to voice mail. Hank
sighed. He'd have to jump through all the legal hoops after
all. Four— "Hello? Danielle? What's up?"

All three adults leaned forward. Danielle's whole body
shook. "Hey. How . . . how are you?"

"I'm fine. Just hanging out. You know."

"Yeah. Me, too. I guess. Um, I . . . I can't believe it about
Mandy. . . ."

A pause. The adults leaned closer. "Um, Mandy. I can't
believe it, either. It's totally nuts. Right on the boat like that."

"Yeah, I know. I . . . I'm really, um, really freaked-out
about it. Is there any way we could meet up? You know, like,
to talk? I could really use a friend."

Another pause. "Can't you talk to those other chicks at
school?"

Danielle started to cry. "They don't know. They weren't
there. They weren't friends with Mandy like we were. Nobody was. And . . ." She stopped, sobbing. "Please . . ."

A very long pause. Even the dog had stopped panting.

"Okay. Sure. How about Battlefield Coffee up in Springfield?"

"That's fine," Danielle said.

"In an hour. I, uh . . . I got somewhere to be after that."

"That's fine. I'll be there." She hung up and looked over
at Hank. "He didn't even ask me how I was doing." She put
down the phone and let go of her mother.

"What do you want me to do now?"

The caravan slowed as it approached the busy intersection of
Glenstone and Battlefield. Danielle led in her father's Toyota

Camry. Then came Hank, following discreetly behind in Maggie's minivan, which he had not told her he'd taken from the hospital parking lot. And behind him were Danielle's parents in their other car, a Chevy Tahoe. They had insisted on coming. Hank had been about to say no, but then he put himself in their position. There was no way—absolutely no way—he would let Maribel trot off to meet a possible murderer without him hovering as closely as possible. So he had looked at Danielle's distressed parents and relented. But he had insisted they park across the street, stay in their car, and under no circumstances call or text their daughter.

Now Danielle was pulling into the far end of a strip mall's parking lot. She and Chad had arranged to meet at a coffee shop across from the Battlefield Mall. Hank took a different entrance and parked behind the long building, where his car couldn't be seen. He peeked around the corner as she walked into the shop, then nonchalantly entered the end store. Conveniently, it was a convenience store, so he stood near the front window, browsing the candy bars as he watched. Five minutes later, a Lexus SUV pulled in and a very tall young man in a leather jacket strode into the coffee shop. Hank put down the Snickers and followed.

He pulled his wool hat down farther on his head. At the strong suggestion of both Sam and Sheila, he'd borrowed the extra St. Louis Cardinals windbreaker Sam had in his trunk, so he was not in the cop-looking—and still smelly—winter coat he had been wearing at the boat fire. He hoped he looked different enough that Chad would not recognize him the minute he walked in. The bell jingled.

The place was almost deserted. Chad was folding his tall

frame into a chair opposite Danielle, who did not look nearly as teary as she had earlier. Hank grabbed a newspaper from the recycle bin and sat behind Chad.

"Do you know anything about it?" Danielle was asking.

"No way," Chad said. "I didn't even know about it until I saw it on the news."

"Wow," Danielle said. "Nobody called you or anything? The cops came to school to see me."

"They did?" Chad sounded worried. "Why would they do that?"

Hank could see a sliver of Danielle's face from behind his newspaper. She looked as if she was going to smack Mr. All That.

"They're trying to figure out who did it. Duh. They need to talk to all her friends to find out everything they can . . . you know, about Mandy. I can't believe they didn't want to talk to you."

The leather-clad shoulders lifted in a shrug. "Maybe they did. I don't know." He pulled his phone out of his pocket and glanced at the time. "Look, Danielle. I gotta go."

Over the top of the newspaper, Hank could see her trying not to look toward him as she thought about what to say to keep Chad talking. With effort, she focused on Chad and suddenly burst into tears. Brilliant.

"Where are you going? What's so important?" she sobbed.

Chad started to fidget. Apparently, Mr. All That wasn't used to his young honeys throwing tearful fastballs at him. He took a sip of his drink, looked at his phone again, and then glanced worriedly around the shop. The four other customers and two baristas were all staring at him as Danielle's sobbing grew louder. Hank, while enjoying the jerk's discomfort immensely, just wished he'd answer the damn question.

"Where are you going?" Danielle asked again, reaching across the little table to clutch Chad's jacket sleeve.

"Somewhere. Doesn't matter." He tried to dislodge Danielle's hand from his arm. "I've gotta go. I'm gonna be late."

Late for what? Danielle upped her crying a notch to near-wail. Everyone in the shop had stopped even pretending to do anything but watch the production. Chad, looking around frantically, turned a little too far around in his chair and met Hank's gaze over the newspaper's edge. His jaw dropped for a split second and then he ripped his arm away from Danielle's grasp and bolted for the door.

Well, that is certainly the sign of a guilty mind, Hank thought as he tossed away the newspaper and lunged after him. Friends of a dead girl with nothing to hide did not take off at the sight of a cop.

Chad pushed chairs into Hank's path as he made for the door. Wood clattered against the hard linoleum floor, and Danielle let out a genuine shriek. Hank jumped over one up-ended chair but got the next one directly in the shins as Chad heaved it back toward him. Swearing, Hank shoved it aside and kept after his quarry, who had made it to the door.

They went through it seconds apart, ripping off the jingle bell as they burst out of the coffee shop. Hank reached out, his hand millimeters from the leather jacket. Then Chad turned on the speed. His long legs stretched out, seemingly covering yards with each stride. Hank dug in. He was not going to let someone outrun him. Not on this case.

Chad sprinted around piles of snow in the parking lot and onto busy Glenstone Avenue. Tires started squealing as drivers slammed on their brakes. Hank plunged into the traffic, right in front of a sedan that swerved to miss him and crashed into the curb. A quick running burst got him across a lane just in front of a delivery truck. The wash tugged on his windbreaker and almost broke his stride. He paid no attention, all of his focus on putting one foot in front of the other as quickly as possible. The cold air refused to travel very far into his lungs. All he could hear were the rasping gasps in his throat. And all he could see was the black jacket in front of him.

Chad made it across the street and looked to be heading for the mall. Hank knew he had only the nice flat parking lot left to catch him. If the jerk got into the mall crowded with shoppers, Hank would never find him. He lengthened his stride, and the overtime schedules, the insubordinate employees, the political pressure—they all fell away. And the jacket got closer.

Chad reached the doors. He shoved a guy out of the way, yanked one open, and slipped inside. By nothing but luck, it happened to be a disabled power-assist door. Triggered by Chad's yank, it swung wide open, and Hank tore right through. The seconds gained were all he needed. He launched himself at Chad.

He got his arms around those long legs and they both hit the ground. Chad smacked against the shiny floor, and Hank could hear the wind knock out of him with an explosive sigh.

"Chad Sorenson, you are under arrest." The last word caught in his raspy throat and he gasped for a minute before he was able to get his breathing under control. He used the time to dig his knee into his suspect's back and admire the scuffs now decorating the leather jacket. He shifted in order to get the handcuffs out of the holster on his belt and stopped at the collective gasp that arose.

He looked up for the first time and saw that he was surrounded. About a hundred people stood around him, many balancing packages, all of them staring at his right arm. He realized that the windbreaker had ridden up as he reached for his cuffs, making his gun visible.

And then he realized that he was a wheezy, unshaven guy wearing an old wool hat and a crappy windbreaker. And he was sitting on a well-groomed, expensively clothed kid with movie-star looks, who was beginning to moan theatrically. And since he was in southern Missouri, he'd put money on the fact that he wasn't the only one here with a gun. Odds were that at least two or three concealed carries stood in his audience. He saw a guy to his left reach toward his waistband, and Hank quickly raised both of his arms out to the sides. He identified himself and said—looking directly at the guy to his left—that he was going to slowly pull out his identification. Once he did, the crowd began to mutter excitedly. The guy to the left stepped forward and examined his badge closely. He gave a nod, and Hank got a spontaneous smattering of applause. That's a new one, he thought as he was finally able to cuff Chad and haul him to his feet.

It took twenty minutes to get back to his car, between explaining everything to mall security and walking all the way back across the parking lot. This time, he used the cross-walk.

Chad said nothing until Hank guided him head down into the backseat.

"What am I under arrest for?"

Hank smiled as he leaned down toward the car so they were at the same eye level.

"Resisting arrest."

"You were going to arrest me before?"

"Well, no. Not until you ran." Before he'd run, Hank had nothing solid enough to connect him with Mandy's murder. He still didn't, but now he could keep Chad in one of his nice, new jail cells until he found something.

"So . . ." The kid interrupted his thoughts. "How could I be resisting an arrest that wasn't going to happen?"

Hank grinned. "I've always liked the lack of logic, myself. Never seems to faze a judge, though. So you might as well get comfy. You're going to be my guest for a while. Now," he said as he slammed the door in Chad's face and turned toward the strip mall, "I'm going to get some coffee."

CHAPTER
19

Hank's main office voice mail had four calls from different TV stations and two from the kid at the *Daily What's-It*, which didn't even come out every day, so how was Hank supposed to take it seriously? He paused for a moment, then wrote down the kid's callback number. He at least had made an effort to cultivate Hank as a source after the county commission had appointed him sheriff. He showed up at the Forsyth office pretty regularly, and he handled the police blotter with more flair than Hank would have expected of somebody so young at such a rinky-dink paper.

Hank didn't like him enough to give out his cell number, though. That was sacrosanct, and that was why the kid had been forced to leave a voice mail just like the yahoos from TV. Now, Hank knew those people didn't care about you at all until something big happened. Then they were in your face with their highlighted hair and their Channel Twelve windbreakers. Gave him indigestion. Up in KC, the policy had been to avoid antagonizing them, then politely pawn them off on the public information officer. As the Branson County Sheriff's Department had no PIO—heck, there weren't even enough deputies to adequately staff a murder investigation—he had no one he could pass them to. But, he thought with a smile, as I am now the boss, I can make my own rules. And, he decided as he walked down the hall to the break room and poured the first cup of coffee from the fresh pot, his first revised media relations directive would be that he was allowed to blithely ignore anyone with a satellite truck.

He walked to the interview room where he'd left Chad Sorenson and considered him from behind the two-way mirror. The kid sprawled casually in the hard plastic chair, one arm thrown over the back and his legs stretched out in front of him. But his right heel was doing a quick tap on the floor, and his jaw was clenched so tightly that Hank could see the muscles quivering.

Good.

He went in and sat down at the table across from the kid. And waited. Chad started to sit up straight, but then thought better of it and forced himself into nonchalance again.

"What do you want with me, man?"

Hank took a sip of coffee and just stared at him.

"What? I didn't do anything wrong. I want a lawyer."

"If you didn't do anything wrong, why do you want a lawyer?"

Chad glared at him. "I'm not some country bumpkin idiot. That shit won't work on me. I have the right to a lawyer."

Hank took another sip of coffee. Chad shifted in his seat. Apparently appearing so relaxed took a lot of effort. His jaw muscles trembled. Hank waited.

"What do I tell him—when I call? I'm charged with resisting arrest?"

Sip. "Yep."

"That's it?"

"Yep."

Chad really did relax at that. His foot stopped tapping and his jaw slackened. Hank put down his coffee cup.

"For now."

Chad's eyes widened.

"I'm not done with you." Hank leaned forward over the table. "You were running for a reason, and I think it has to do with a dead girl on a boat."

Chad recoiled in shock, which was exactly Hank's intent. He couldn't ask the punk any questions, but he could ensure that the time he spent waiting for his lawyer was passed in a state of extreme agitation. He stood.

"Someone will come and escort you to your jail cell. You will stay there until you see a judge about bail. And since it's five P.M., that won't be until tomorrow. So sleep tight."

He walked out without a backward glance.

Hank's legs and his feet hurt like hell, and he was pretty sure blisters were starting to form on his heels. He stuck them even closer to the fire and wiggled his toes. That prompted a giggle from behind his easy chair. Maribel poked her head around and grinned at him. "Hi," she said, as she crawled into his lap. "Mommy said you were tired, and I should come check on you." She eyed him critically. "You do look tired. Did you take your nap today? Benny didn't. That's why he had to go to bed early. Grandpop said he was almost as grouchy as you've been lately."

Nice. Thanks, Dunc. Hank leaned back as his daughter chattered away about her day, and looked around the room. His easy chair on one side of the fireplace, and Dunc's on the other. The couch positioned against the far wall and his beloved stereo system along the opposite one. He'd bought it back when it made sense to pay good money for good speakers, when bigger was better. And back when he was single—when deciding what to spend good money on was still his decision. He'd never admit it out loud, but that was why he'd fought to put it here in the main room. A little declaration of independence.

The built-in bookshelves were packed with Dunc's albums. He'd been delighted when he figured out that his record player would hook into Hank's system, and Hank had to admit, Johnny Cash did sound pretty good coming out of his speakers.

But right now, it became blissfully quiet. Maribel, worn-out from her busy four-year-old's day, had fallen asleep on his chest. He looked into the fire, burning briskly in the huge river rock fireplace. It took up the entire back wall, except for the tall windows on either side looking out into the woods that made up his backyard. Hand-built out of local stone by the original owner, it was a one-of-a-kind. It was what had sold him on the house.

Well, that and the separate bed and bath for Duncan, tucked far away down in the basement. Maggie had been worried it would be too isolated, that it would send the wrong message. Hank had pointed out that they were both giving up jobs in Kansas City and moving down here in order to take her father in, and if he didn't get that message, they might as well forget the whole thing.

Of course, they were also sending a message to themselves, and they both knew it. What they had been doing was not working. A police detective and a surgeon did not lead calm, scheduled lives. They got home late, they got called out in the middle of the night, they forgot to pick up the groceries. And they couldn't find child care that was able to handle that. No one could. Unless you had a live-in grandparent who doted on the two children you didn't have enough time for. So they moved. And they didn't talk about it.

Maribel shifted on Hank's chest, and he wrapped his arms around her, resting his still-unshaven cheek on the top of her head. Maggie tiptoed out from the kitchen and waved his cell phone at him, mouthing "Sheila." He thought for a moment and then shook his head. He pointed down at Maribel and then toward the bedrooms. She nodded and took the phone back into the kitchen. Just as quietly, he rose from the easy chair and carried his girl to bed.

"Well, I've finally sorted out the mess you made of the schedule," Sheila said.

Hank thanked her and moved to hang up the phone.

"Not so fast," she said, even though she obviously could not see him reaching for the end button. "Most everybody's back where they're supposed to be, although you're going to have to find an extra twenty grand out of the budget somewhere to pay for all the overtime you've already done."

That meant going to the county commission. Hank felt sick.

"So, everybody's back on regular shifts, except we're short one deputy for tonight's graveyard. I haven't been home in three days, and Tyrone can't survive more than two by

himself. He's probably eaten nothing but cereal since I left."
That didn't sound like a bad thing to Hank, and he doubted
that Tyrone much minded, either. But his wife obviously did.
"So I'm going home. And that means you're going to have to
do it."

Hank stood there on his aching feet and looked around
his nice cozy kitchen. Then he did hit the end button.

He took two-lane Highway 248 north out of town, into one
of his favorite parts of the county. All sorts of hilly forest, and
once he got past the Ozark Mountain Highroad and onto
160, well, that was when it got entertaining. Turn down one
side road and you were in a community of huge new man-
sions, with broad lawns, three-car garages, and elegant brick
façades. Turn down another one and you were in the middle
of a mobile home park, with junk cars, metal awnings, and
the only bricks around propping up the sagging corners of the
double-wides.

He cruised through a neighborhood of McMansions, most
of which had their security lights blazing. It certainly helped
in a neighborhood with no streetlights. The new version of
country living, he supposed. He turned the squad car around
in a cul-de-sac and was heading out when something darted
across the road. He slammed on the brakes and slid across the
road, plowing into a snowbank on the opposite side. If he'd
been going just a little bit faster, he might have managed to do
a complete 360, which would have been fun. As it was, he
forced open his door against the snow and got out to survey
the damage. The bank had actually cushioned the blow—only
the left front had really hit the snow. He was contemplating
whether he would need to push it out, or if he could get away

with just putting the car in reverse, when he sensed something behind him, watching.

He slowly reached for his gun as he began to turn. He got about halfway around, hand on his gun, before he realized it was only a dog. About the stupidest-looking dog he'd ever seen. It sat in the middle of the road, its head tilted to the side and an extremely long tongue lolling in the same direction. It appeared to have the body of a basset hound and the head of, well, the head of something else. It was too small for the body, with a squat snout and mismatched ears. One was the loose, floppy ear of a Lab, but the other stuck straight up, cropped and pointy.

They looked at each other for a minute. Then Ugly got up, trotted over to the snowbank, and lifted his leg. As he was doing his business, Hank saw the collar and sighed. Now he'd have to find the stupid dog's stupid owners. He whistled and Ugly obediently loped on over. Hank caught his collar and then had to take the flashlight off his belt in order to read the tag. He gave thanks that along with the required rabies tag, there was a cute bone-shaped one with a name and address. Two streets over. He moved to get the dog into the backseat of the squad car, but that only got Ugly excited, and he started piddling all over. Fantastic. That meant a two-block walk hunched down to keep a hand on the collar of a wiggly, bladder-challenged, mutt-tastic monstrosity. Oh, and he nipped, too. Hank was about out of swear words.

Fifteen minutes later, he pounded on Ugly's door. Eventually, the lights inside came on and a beefy guy with blond hair sticking out in all directions came to the door. He saw Ugly and turned purple. "How . . ." He sputtered. "How . . . did you get out again?" Hank let go of the collar and shoved the dog across the threshold with his foot. Ugly disappeared inside just before his owner's own foot connected with the dog's backside. The man turned back to Hank.

"I'm sorry. He was locked in the kitchen. He must have gotten the dog door undone. He's . . . he's absolutely impossible. He was supposed to be a purebred Lab. We ordered him from a breeder. And we got . . . that." Hank had spent the walk over getting as ticked off at the owner as he was with the dog, but now he had to admit the guy deserved some sympathy. He bet that breeder had charged a pretty penny, too.

"Well, sir, just make sure you always keep that collar on him. Maybe get him microchipped, too."

The man's eyebrows raised. "That would imply that I want him back." He sighed. "But thank you, Officer, for your help. It is nice to know that you guys patrol out here. You're with animal control?"

Hank, who was wearing his uniform, pointed to the sheriff's star on his chest and bit back a sigh. "No. Sir. I am the Branson County Sheriff. 'Working for your safety and security.' Sir."

The guy looked sheepish as he apologized and shook Hank's hand. Then a crash and a howl from inside had him turning purple again. Hank headed back to his car, glad—for once—to be the one out in the cold.

Pleased that his Ugly skid had resulted in only a slight dent to the front left fender, Hank decided to head farther north and cruise the country lanes. He had dubbed this homestead country—old houses on several acres. Many were completely tucked out of sight at the end of long, winding driveways. This drove him crazy. How was he supposed to keep an eye on things if he couldn't see what was going on? He had always been a firm believer in the broken windows approach—crack down on the people committing minor crimes, and they wouldn't progress to the big stuff. But then, he'd always worked in cities, where broken windows were a lot easier to spot. Out here, you couldn't see a damn thing.

He completed a very boring loop and started to head back south. By now it was about three o'clock, and he was starting to crash. He decided to head out east, maybe check out near the county line. And that would take him past Lakefront Manors, which—naturally—had no lake, and no manners. Instead, it had a ramshackle accumulation of mobile homes that made the term "trailer park" seem upscale.

He drove at almost a walking pace through the middle of the park, avoiding the bigger ruts in the road, which was just dirt covered with snow. His headlights were the only illumination, except for one light nailed halfway up a power pole. And it kept flickering on and off, like the bulb couldn't decide whether it was ready to just give up.

Everything else in the place seemed to have already made that decision. Trailers tilted on sinking supports. Several windows were broken. One had a hole stuffed with what looked like socks. One set of steps up to a front door had been re-placed by an overturned five-gallon bucket. Another place had an end that looked as if it had blown out and someone had tried to seal it up with plywood.

Hank stopped the car. That had to have been quite an explosion. He was mighty curious about what that resident had been cooking to cause such a blast. He got out of the car to take a look around, and then he heard it. Much farther down, two from the end. One hell of a fight. At least two people screaming and then glass shattering. Hank took off at a flat run.

The woman's screams got louder and longer as he neared the trailer. Another crash. He leapt over the rotten bottom step, hit the top one, and threw his shoulder into the door. It flew open, he skidded to a halt in the middle of someone's living room, and the screaming stopped.

The three of them stood there. The silence felt like the instant before a static electricity shock. Crackling, and sure to be painful. The man's grip on a chair leg tightened. The woman had a knife in her right hand and a plate in her left. Hank had a stitch in his side and a hand moving toward his gun.

The place was completely torn apart. The couch sat on its side in the middle of the narrow room, half of it knifed and in shreds. Dinner dripped down the far wall. Broken dishes carpeted the floor. There was an enormous dent in the refrigerator and a chunk taken out of the Formica bar. The chair with the missing leg lay at the guy's feet.

The woman had a huge red welt on her cheek and an eye starting to swell shut. The man, a wiry little guy, had a torn sleeve and nasty red slice down his arm. Hank honestly wasn't quite sure who was winning. But he couldn't very well call it a draw and just leave. He held out his left hand, keeping his right one on his gun. He slowly identified himself and asked them to put down what they were holding. Nobody moved.

"You in my house," the man growled. The chair leg inched higher.

"Yeah, and I'm here to stop an assault," Hank said.

"You trespassin'." The woman this time.

So *now* they were in agreement? Apparently so, because

they both started to advance. The woman began to swear at him.

"This *my* job, bitch," the man snarled as he took a step closer to Hank. "I'm the man. This my house, I defend it."

"Fuck you," the woman screamed, and she let loose the plate. Hank dropped to the floor as it cut through the air just where his head had been. It stabbed right into the middle of the flat-screen TV, the one previously undamaged thing in the whole trailer, and the front cracked into a hundred pieces.

The man hesitated, unsure of who he should take his rage out on. He chose Hank. The chair leg whizzed past his ear as he rolled to the side, praying that the woman and her knife would not be waiting when he popped up onto his feet. She wasn't, and he dodged to the right as the chair leg came at him again. It hit him in the left shoulder and knocked him into the trailer wall next to the sagging front door. He grabbed the door, yanked it the rest of the way off its hinges, and got it in front of him just in time for the man's next swing. The chair leg hit the door and splintered in half. Less reach, more sharpness.

Hank held the door like a shield as he unholstered his gun. He steadied his hand, pushed away the door, and aimed for the spaghetti on the wall. The shot tore easily through the ridiculously thin shell of the trailer. And froze its occupants. The woman gawked at him from behind the Formica bar. The man stared at Hank with his jaw hanging open. Hank moved the gun until it was pointed quite clearly at his pasty face.

"The next one gets you in the head."

CHAPTER

20

Apparently, the law in these parts did not typically open fire. No deputy in his department had discharged his or her weapon in six years—in a county that included places like Lakefront Manors. Hank, after experiencing that neighborhood's particular charms firsthand, found this very hard to believe until he reviewed enough patrol records and dispatch logs to figure out that the law rarely left the squad car. There was a lot to patrol, and not a lot of deputies to do it. Heck, he almost hadn't gotten out of the car, either.

But every once in a while, it did seem that deputies stumbled upon some law-breaking in their cruises through Lakefront Manors. They had to find it themselves, though. All of the incident reports Hank sat looking at before dawn that morning were deputy-initiated. No one in that trailer park ever called the police. For anything. One man there had shot his wife to death in their trailer several years before. With a shotgun. A big, loud, twelve-gauge. And no one had called it in. It wasn't until the woman's employer reported her missing that the sheriff's office knew anything was wrong. They'd found her buried five feet from the back door.

Certainly no one had bothered to call in the Mocklers and their volcanic fight. No one had even come out of their trailers to see them taken away in handcuffs. In Hank's experience, that action always drew a crowd, even if it was only to jeer the cops. But not here. There were absolutely no signs of life as he drove away. But they were there. He could feel the eyes on him as he backed slowly down the one road out of there.

Now Jay and Jean Mockler sat in separate sections of the county jail. He filled up his travel mug—there were still several hours to go on his patrol shift—and decided to make a pass through the jail on his way out. He regretted it as soon as he stepped into the women's section. The Lady Mockler's screeching bounced off the walls and pierced the sides of his skull. Man, could that woman yell. And she had the whole wing yelling back as Hank walked down to her cell.

"Shut her up, will ya, Sheriff?"

"That man of hers shoulda finished her off."

"Lemme out. I'll do it."

That one drew laughter from the others. Hank hid a smile and stopped in front of Jean's cell. Her screeching hit new highs.

"You can't hold me. I ain't pressing charges. You hear? You got to let me out. I ain't gonna press charges and neither is he."

Her eye was now completely swollen shut. Stringy hair that might have been blond when clean hung over her face. She was as little and wiry as her husband. But he doubted they were evenly matched as he caught a glimpse of the cauliflower ear underneath her dirty hair. The holes in her sweatpants showed bruises in various stages of healing. And the fingers she was currently using for obscene gestures were twisted in the kinds of positions that only came from broken bones that hadn't been set properly.

"I don't care if you don't want to press charges," he said, leaning toward her cell door and speaking softly, which forced her to stop yelling so she could hear him. "In the morning, I'm going to put you in touch with the domestic violence crisis center. You'll have to at least listen to them, because they're going to visit you here in jail. And this is where you're going to be for a very long time. You tried to assault a police officer." He smiled. "And I do press charges."

He left her screaming after him and walked out and over to the men's side, which was delightfully quiet. Jay Mockler was passed out in his cell, snoring away the drunkenness that had become obvious once Hank had gotten him handcuffed in the trailer. He stared at Mockler and rotated his left shoulder. The pain was really starting to kick in, and he could feel the welt rising in a straight line where the chair leg had landed. It was going to be a monster of a bruise. The only good thing, he supposed, was that it certainly took the focus off his aching feet.

He left the snoring drunk and walked two cells down the row. Chad Sorenson had fallen asleep sitting up. He slumped against the wall, looking quite uncomfortable and out of place. He'd have to have a bail hearing in the morning. Hank had initially been worried about that. Judges usually let nice well-off boys like that out on bail, but the airplane ticket the jail search had found in the inside pocket of that nice leather jacket—Springfield to New York's LaGuardia via Dallas–Fort Worth—would go a long way toward proving that Chad was a flight risk.

He purposefully left through the jail lobby. His feet hurt, his shoulder hurt, his tired eyes hurt, and he felt like picking a fight. The intake desk was empty. He walked outside. Gerald Tucker was standing with his back to the wind, trying to light a cigarette with a match.

"Hello." GOB spun around. The match went out. Hank smiled. "I'd like a rundown of the inmate roster."

GOB struck another match, slowly lit his cigarette, and shrugged. "It's inside."

"You should be, too," Hank said. "You seem to have a habit of abandoning your post."

GOB glared at him. Hank looked at the book of matches in his hand. "No lighter?"

"I lost it," GOB growled. He stuffed the matches in his breast pocket. "And I got a right to a smoke break."

Hank held open the door into the jail lobby.

"Break's over."

GOB didn't move. The two men stared at each other. Hank could practically see the guy's thought process play across his face, trying to decide whether it was worth challenging his new boss. He looked Hank, who was almost a head taller, up and down. Hank waited patiently with a blank look on his face. After about thirty very chilly seconds, Tucker grunted and walked inside. Hank smiled as he let the door slam shut behind him.

He had come into Forsyth, a town of about 2,500 people about fourteen miles east of Branson, from the north. As he left, he

decided to head south, taking Highway 76 over Bull Shoals
Lake and then looping west through tiny Kirbyville to Branson.
It wasn't the patrol area assigned to his shift, but at this point, he
didn't care. He was patrolling, and that was good enough.
And since he was now the boss, he could make that call without
having to justify it to anybody. That was nice.

He cruised into Branson at about 5:00 A.M. and stayed on
76 as it hooked left and headed up the steep hill from the Taney-
como shoreline, past the electric company and then the
Steak 'n Shake. He crossed over the freeway as the road curved
to the south and then back around. That was where it turned
into the Strip. Technically, it was Country Music Boulevard,
but he'd found out quickly that everyone local called it the
Strip. And everyone local tried to avoid it. Stoplight after stoplight. Tourists unsure of where they were going. Cars competing for space in the middle turn lane. Median driver age
seventy-five. But apparently 5:00 A.M. was too early even for
the early breakfast specials. No one was out. The entire stretch
was quiet. Piles of dirty black snow lined the roadsides, hiding many of the theater parking lots, but not the signs. They
stood tall and clean, advertising everything from the Boxcar
Willie Theatre to an auto museum to go-kart rides.

Hank smiled. Maribel had been crushed to learn when
they first moved down here that she wasn't tall enough to ride
one by herself. Little Miss Independent had no interest in rid-
ing one with a grown-up. They'd told her she only had to
wait until the spring before she would probably be the right
height. She'd made them measure her every week since then.
Kids.

He paused, then tapped the brakes and turned right. A
few miles and he was at the Brysons' house. The kitchen light

was on. He pulled into the driveway. Mrs. Bryson met him at the door.

Neither one said a word until she had poured Hank a generous cup of fresh coffee and they were seated across from each other at the kitchen table. He took a grateful sip and said, "I just wanted to stop by and see how you were doing. I'm afraid I don't have any news, though. I'm sorry." He wasn't sure whether it was a condolence or an apology.

She tried to smile. She succeeded in turning one side of her mouth upward, but that was as far as she could get. The tears in her eyes made them look a brighter blue than normal. He wondered if Mandy's had done the same thing.

"Thank you, Sheriff. I . . . I appreciate it. More than you know. It's nice to have my thoughts interrupted. All I do is sit here and think. About who. And why. Why? Why would anyone do that? How could someone hate that much? How could someone hate Mandy that much? My Mandy? She was so good. So good . . ."

The tears spilled over. She reached for a tissue from the box on the table. The motion was fluid and automatic. She'd probably done it hundreds of times in the last three days.

Hank asked after her husband, who she said had finally been able to fall asleep tonight. She had not.

"I've been sitting here all night. Safe and warm. Not like my Mandy." She didn't bother with a tissue this time. The tears fell unimpeded. They and the steam rising from Hank's coffee were the only movements in the room.

"What am I going to do?" The question was so quiet Hank thought he'd imagined it. "What am I going to do now? How am I a person anymore? I'm not a mother. That's what I've been. For eighteen years. That's what I've always wanted to be. I waited so long. We tried and we tried, and we prayed and we prayed. For years. And then—Mandy. This beautiful perfect being"—her hands went out, as if she were presenting her infant daughter for christening—"this blessing. This gift from God.

"And she was so much better than either of us. In every-thing. A better athlete, a better student, a better person. She was the greatest thing I've ever done. That I've ever even had a small part in. She was my baby . . . my baby . . ."

She dissolved, slowly, right in front of him, like salt into water, blending with the grief, becoming a new solution altogether, unpalatable. Hank's coffee grew cold on the table between them.

CHAPTER

21

He rolled over, still mostly asleep, and then sensed something. Someone in the room, at the foot of the bed. He sprang out of bed and into a defensive crouch.

"Good grief," Duncan said. "I just said, 'Wake up.'"

Hank swore and slowly stood up, his heart pounding, semi-dizzy from the quick movements.

"What the hell are you doing in here?"

"What? You told me to wake you up at eleven. It's eleven. Wake up."

"I didn't tell you to sneak into my bedroom. You could have just knocked."

"Oh. I didn't think of that. Hmm."

Hank sagged against the bed as his father-in-law shuffled out of the room. He was pretty sure that was not the most healthy way to wake up after only three hours of sleep. He almost wished it had been an intruder. At least then he could have gotten a few punches in. He staggered off to the shower.

. . .

The hot water hadn't helped his bruised shoulder at all, which hurt like hell whenever he moved. And his shins were almost as purple from the chair Chad Sorenson had thrown at him in the coffee shop. He sat, slouched and sullen, at his desk, occasionally stabbing at the keyboard as he searched the internet for information. The only good thing going on was the Pecan Delight that Sheila had left for him. Apparently getting attacked during a patrol shift was what it took to get any sympathy from her. Good to know.

Gallagher Enterprises had a very snazzy website, but it told him nothing about the actual state of the company's finances. It was not a publicly traded company, so it did not have to file with the SEC or anything like that. As far as he could tell, it was strictly a family business. He clicked on a few newspaper articles.

Gallagher had made his money in real estate. He told reporters he'd visited Branson on vacation and fallen in love with the area. The first thing he bought was the *Beauty*—which Crazy Otis's nephew was trying to unload—for dirt cheap. After that came two different hotels on the Strip, the nice resort a little ways out into the country, and one of the outlet malls in town. Hank wondered why he'd bothered when most of the stores in it had shut down after the economy tanked. Apparently a reporter had asked the same thing, but Gallagher batted the question away. "I am confident that the market will rebound. Branson is a well-known and prized tourist destination, and I am investing in its long-term future."

Hank rolled his eyes. He drove past that place all the time, and he guessed there were ten or twelve stores hanging on in a development built for sixty. But, on the other hand, even if all those businesses went under, Gallagher would still own the land and would only have to pay a couple of guys to maintain the buildings so they didn't fall into too much disrepair. Maybe that wasn't such a bad deal after all.

Not like the *Beauty*. Unlike the mall, the boat had some significant local sentiment attached to it. Maybe those feelings hadn't been clear to Gallagher until he tried firing the very old, unproductive, and expensive staff. He had done a pretty quick about-face on that one. Hank wondered why public opinion was so important to Gallagher. It was after that backlash that he'd funded the new county animal shelter, which had worked like only cute kittens could. Gallagher had been named Citizen of the Year by the *Daily What's-It* and gotten an honorable mention of some kind in the bigger Springfield paper.

That reminded him. He dug around on his desk until he found the kid's number and dialed.

"Good afternoon, *Branson Daily Herald*, this is Jadhur. How may I help you?"

Hank identified himself and answered a few questions about the status of the murder investigation. Then he asked if Jadhur was going to have anything on the boat fire in Friday's edition of the paper.

"Yeah, we'll have that. It'll be short. There's no new art—uh, I mean pictures—to go with it, cuz we couldn't get down to the dock after the fire, so it won't be on the front page. I talked to the fire marshal, so we'll have the cause and everything."

Hank counted to ten. "Really? The cause, huh? What'd the marshal say?"

"Oh, same thing he told you, I'm sure. That due to the damage caused by removing the paddlewheel, fluid leaked and ignited, starting the fire. That is what he told you, right?"

Hank gripped the phone tightly. "That is what the fire marshal thinks, yes."

Jadhur was no dummy. "So, what do *you* think?"

Hank decided not to think, and spoke instead. "It's awfully coincidental that an old boat, badly in need of updating and with significant personnel expenses, suddenly caught fire in such a way that no real investigation of it can take place."

Jadhur pounced. "So you're saying it wasn't an accident?"

"I'm saying I don't know what it was, and I don't think they do, either."

After a few more questions, Hank hung up the phone. He swiveled in his chair and caught a glimpse of his computer screen, which still showed the web page with Gallagher's Citizen of the Year article. He smiled and bit into his candy bar.

"We're coming to you live from the Branson Events Center, where the grieving small-town community has gathered for a prayer vigil after the shocking murder of homecoming queen Amanda Bryson. The eighteen-year-old was found strangled to death Sunday on the showboat the *Branson Beauty*. Police have not made an arrest."

The Springfield Channel Twelve reporter cut to video of a group of middle-aged women, hands clasped in prayer as a portly man in a clergy collar railed against the encroachment of evil. Then came a shot of a bunch of teenagers holding candles and singing. Then it was back to the reporter, strategically positioned in front of the building, so that the emotional crowd was clearly visible in the background.

So far, Hank hadn't seen anyone actually connected with the case—except a plain-clothed Sam, at the corner of his TV screen, trying to nonchalantly circle the crowd. He wasn't doing a very good job, slouching quickly from person to person and constantly swiveling his head from side to side. Fortunately, it didn't appear anyone was paying any attention to him. He'd told Hank that he'd never "gone undercover" in all his years with the department. Hank hadn't pointed out that the kid had only been a deputy for four years or that actual undercover work involved a lot more than not wearing a uniform. He hadn't wanted to quash Sam's enthusiasm, which had been considerable. So instead he'd just said yes, he knew Sam would do fine and no, it wasn't a good idea to wear a fake mustache.

Hank was glad to see Sam had listened and was his normal clean-shaven self. He grinned and put his feet up on the coffee table as the reporter interviewed a sobbing teen who said she'd been in Mandy's algebra class two years ago and was "totally freaked-out" by the killing. Hank took a sip of his beer. And then sat up straight, adjusting the ice pack on his swollen shoulder.

"Also with me tonight is Branson County Commissioner Edrick Fizzel. Commissioner, you are the one who organized this vigil, correct?"

Fizzel's nose was not nearly as red as it had been when he visited Hank on Tuesday. And he'd obviously anticipated a TV appearance—his porcupine hair had been tamed with enough gel to nicely reflect the camera's spotlight. Since Rudolph's nose could no longer guide the sleigh home, his hair apparently was picking up the slack. Hank leaned toward the TV.

"Why, yes, Tom, it was my idea. I thought it was important to allow the community a chance to grieve. And," he added, turning from the reporter to face the camera directly, "I want to assure y'all watchin' tonight that Branson is perfectly safe and you should keep comin' on down here. We are the Ozarks' vacation destination." His smile oozed snake oil and backwoods smarm. Hank was pretty sure he saw hair gel dripping onto his collar.

"I also want to take the opportunity to assure everyone that we are doing all we can to find the murderer. This was not a random act. Poor Amanda Bryson was being stalked. She was targeted, hunted down. You can be sure, Tom, that we will hunt down her killer. I have been told that there will be an arrest very soon."

Hank's jaw dropped. He hadn't told Fizzel that Mandy had a stalker. And he certainly hadn't said he was close to making an arrest. He glared at the TV.

"And," Fizzel said, twisting his face into an expression of almost comic concern, "anyone with any questions or concerns about this can call the new sheriff. After all, protecting us is his job."

Hank almost threw his beer at the television. That pompous jerk. That was all he needed—a swarm of freaked-out, candle-waving vigil-goers hounding him about the case.

His cell rang. He snatched it off the coffee table and saw it was Sam.

"Please tell me you have something good."

"Uh, not really," Sam said. "There was nobody important here—no suspects, I mean. The only person I recognized from the boat was Tony Sampson. He was with a group of girls that I think are from the track team." Hank heard Sam flipping pages. He'd sent the Pup with last year's BVHS yearbook.

"It was just here . . ." Sam muttered. "Aha. Okay, yeah. That one, that's his sister. Alyssa Sampson. Her and two others, a tall one and a short one. They were all here. Just saw them drive off in a newer Ford Fusion. Black. My bet is it's the tall one's mom's car. She was driving."

"What'd they do while they were there?"

Sam thought for a moment. "The girls were into it. Went right up front, got their candles, did the prayer circle, everything. Tony stayed in the back. Kept taking his phone out, fiddling with it. Didn't really seem like he wanted to be there."

Hank heard the yearbook close.

"Oh, and Chief?"

"Yeah?"

"I just think you should know that the commissioner dude was going around to everyone and handing out business cards. At first, I thought they were his business cards, which would have been weird. This isn't a business meeting, right? Why would . . ."

"What's the point, Sam?"

"Oh, yeah. Anyway, they weren't his cards. They were yours. Or at least ones with your name and phone number on them."

"What?"

Sam chuckled, not noticing Hank's tone. "It was pretty funny. He gave me one. Said I should 'Let the sheriff know we're all concerned.' I told him I'd be sure and report in." He laughed again. Hank just glowered some more at the TV news, which had moved on to the weather.

"Huh . . . What's he doing? He . . ."

Hank pulled his attention back to Sam. "What's who doing?"

"Well, people are starting to leave, and I'm sitting here in my car—you know, my car, not the squad car—and the commissioner is standing over on the side of the building talking to somebody. They just walked behind the building, like they didn't want anybody else around. I can't see the other guy very well. They look like they're having quite a conversation, though. The other dude is waving his arms all around. Looks pretty upset. I'm going to go see . . . ah, shoot. They're leaving. The commissioner's going back to the crowd. And the other one is walking toward the parking lot . . . toward me." Hank heard some loud shuffling and a thud, followed by a mumbled curse.

"I'm ducking down, so as he doesn't see me," Sam whispered loudly.

"Why?" Hank was not sure that kind of stealth was necessary. "How would he know you're a deputy?"

"Cuz we've met. It's Terry Cummings."

"Who?" Hank said.

"You know, the guy who works for Mr. Gallagher. The one who was out at the boat with him."

The Company Man.

"Follow him."

"Yes, sir."

Sam's beloved 1983 Bronco coughed to life. Hank heard the phlegm clear from the engine—Sam had been trying his hand lately at tuning the thing himself—and then more excited shuffling. "He's getting into a red Ford Explorer. I'll call you when we get wherever he's going." The Pup hung up.

Hank sat there in his cozy living room and envied the kid's energy. Envied it like he was an old man muttering into his sweet tea as he sat on the nursing home porch. But he wasn't old—thirty-seven wasn't old. Then why did he feel like it? Lately, especially, he'd taken to looking around and wondering how he'd gotten here. To this point. Kids. And a mortgage. And a father-in-law. And an entire law enforcement department. For which he was solely responsible. It was just yesterday that he had been in college, hanging out with his roommates, dating a beautiful girl named Maggie. Just yesterday, dammit. He dragged his busted frame off the couch and toward the kitchen. He needed another beer.

CHAPTER

22

Sam's phone kept going straight to voice mail. And since he was out of uniform and not driving a squad car, he didn't have a police radio. Where the hell was he? It was past eleven, so it had been almost five hours since Sam had followed the Company Man from the church. That was more than enough time to make several trips to Springfield and back. Hell, that was enough time to drive the 250 miles to St. Louis. And there was nothing stopping Sam from calling with an update while on the road. But he had not.

Hank slammed his own cell down on the kitchen counter, then picked it up again. Enough. He had pulled Cummings's address, which was up near Springfield. He stared at the scratch paper he'd scrawled it on and shook his head. He just didn't think that was right. Cummings had not been at that vigil on his own behalf. And if he had left with something to report, it was likely he had not gone straight home. Hank went back to the laptop on the kitchen table. Perhaps it was Henry Gallagher's address that needed visiting.

An hour later, after sifting through way too many databases to figure out which of Gallagher's numerous properties he actually lived in, Hank silently coasted to a stop about twenty yards from a nondescript wooden gate at a curve in a quiet country lane that had, mercifully, been plowed. The shortleaf pine trees rose tall and thin on each side and cut the moonlight into jagged slivers that bounced off the piles of snow. He couldn't tell if Sam had come this way or not.

And he couldn't tell if Gallagher had surveillance cameras mounted on or near the gate. It was safer to assume the guy did, though. All he needed was Gallagher giving Fizzel a still video shot of the county sheriff climbing over his estate gate in the middle of the night.

Hank stayed out of sight of the possible cameras and turned his car around, rolling back the way he came as he looked closely at the estate fence. It finally ended about half a mile away from the gate. He eyed the closest trees and could see no cameras, so he climbed out of his car and walked along the fence as it turned away from the road and into the woods.

The snow, hard now after days in the sun, cracked and split under his boots. The clear cold numbed his cheeks and felt like shards of ice as it passed through his sinuses. He moved carefully, avoiding snow drifts and staying several feet away from the fence. He was about thirty yards from the road and contemplating going back and just banging on the gate when he saw them. Footprints, coming from the east, perpendicular to his own trail and the fence. They then continued along the property line and out of sight. They were fresh, and they were huge. Only one person could have left such size-fifteen gouges in the snow. Hank smiled in relief and set off to track down the Pup.

He found Sam lying full out behind a small knoll about a hundred yards behind the main house. He had on a camou-flaged coat and snow pants and was looking through a huge pair of binoculars. Hank, also shielded by the hill, crawled up behind him and then paused. He did not need to draw attention to them by scaring the bejeezus out of the kid. He was pondering how not to do this when Sam—without moving a millimeter—said, "Hi, Chief. Could you be a little more quiet, please? And get down."

He obviously needed to redefine his notion of stealthy movement. He flopped onto his belly, slid up next to Sam, and peered over the knoll at the house. No wonder Sam was hid-ing. There were enough windows in that thing to see into the next county. The entire back was made up of nothing but huge panes of glass and the occasional oakbeam. Gallagher must have quite the view during the day, looking out over acres of hills and rolling forest. But at night, the view turned inward, and the brightly lit interior became the show. At least it had tonight. Hank hoped Sam had seen all of it. He could make out two figures standing near what looked like the entry foyer. It appeared that the shorter one was leaving. That must be the Company Man, although Hank couldn't positively identify him from this distance. He didn't need to be close to recognize the taller one with the snooty, upright posture, however.

"Uh, sir?" Sam still hadn't moved. "Where'd you park your car?" Hank watched Gallagher swing open his front door.

"Out on the road. Why—?" Hank stopped and then swore. It was out on the road, where the Company Man would drive right past it on his way out. A solitary Crown Victoria half-blocking an otherwise deserted country lane. No, that wouldn't give away their presence at all.

Hank slithered back down the knoll, stumbled to his feet, and took off toward the hole in the fence that Sam had found earlier. The force of his sprint caused his boots to sink deeply into the snow. He lifted his legs higher with each step, plowing his way back toward the road and praying that no one from the estate would have occasion to walk out this way before the snow melted.

By the time he reached the road, his lungs felt frozen solid from the huge gulps of cold air he was downing. The stitch in his right side made him double over as he stumbled over to his car. He collapsed behind the wheel and said yet another prayer that the damn thing would start as he turned the key. The car chugged awake and he sped toward the main road, coughing uncontrollably as his abused airways protested their treatment.

He had no idea if he'd made it in time—there was no way to tell whether the Company Man had already driven past. He made it to the intersection with Highway 176 and yanked the car hard to the right. The back wheels slipped and then caught as he made the turn. He knew there were a few driveways close by. He found the nearest and again yanked the steering wheel to the right. He slid the car in behind someone's battered Chrysler minivan and killed the engine, hoping it looked like an ordinary car parked for the night. He crouched behind the seat and peered out the back window, trying to regain his breath.

Two minutes later, a red Ford Explorer drove past at a high rate of speed. Hank slumped against his seat in relief. He'd made it. He stiffly turned himself around and started the car again. He was pretty sure the guy was just headed home to Springfield—it was almost one in the morning—but he had to make sure. He pointed the Crown Victoria north and hoped his coughing stopped before he got there.

"He said what?"

Sam, who had been fairly definitive two seconds earlier, began to back off.

"Well, I can't be sure. I was lip-reading. You know, through the binoculars. But it looked like he said, 'You're on your own.'"

"Then what?"

"Then the suspect . . . er, Cummings, he said something like, 'I did what you—' and then he turned, so I couldn't see any more. Then they were both so hot, they were moving around a lot and I couldn't do any more lip-reading."

After what seemed like an eternity of yelling, arm-waving, and finger-pointing, Gallagher had disappeared down a hallway. Cummings sat and waited.

"But how did he wait?" Hank asked. "How did he sit? What was he doing?"

The Pup stared at him with late-night exasperation he didn't even bother to try to conceal. "He sat. On a couch. You know, like people do. Sit on couches. With their butts."

Hank shifted in his own seat, the lumpy, listing desk chair in his office at the Branson substation. The heat had been off for hours, and both of them still wore their coats.

"Watch." He leaned back, casually linking his hands

behind his head and stretching his feet out in front of him. "Or this." He sat up straight, shoulders back, feet flat on the floor, hands in his lap. "Or—"

"Oh, I get it." Sam paused, then carefully arranged his gangly limbs. When he was done, Hank smiled. "Good. Our Company Man is in trouble. Then what happened?"

Sam—who had positioned himself slumped forward, with his elbows on his knees and his head in his hands—straightened. "Gallagher came back after about fifteen or twenty minutes. And then you showed up."

Hank nodded. Cummings hadn't done anything else interesting, just driven home to Springfield and disappeared inside his house, which was a standard brick Tudor-type thing on the south side of town. Hank had a feeling the guy hadn't gone right to sleep. But it was about time Hank did. He stood up and was about to dismiss the Pup when he stopped.

"You mind telling me why you got a full camouflage outfit with you? And high-powered binoculars?"

"Oh, that's my hunting gear. It was still in my trunk from when I went out with my dad last month. I usually leave it in there. You never know when you'll need it." He grinned. "I never thought I'd use it for work, though, that's for sure."

"I didn't know you hunted." They were both up and moving toward the front door.

"Oh, yeah. Ever since I was little. You should come sometime. Give it a try."

"How do you know I don't hunt?"

Sam burst out laughing. Apparently his deference to superiors expired at midnight. "You sound like a freight train, for one thing. I could hear you coming the minute you left

the road. You probably scared off any game from here to
Arkansas."

"Well . . . I tracked you, didn't I?"

Sam did not look nearly as impressed by this as Hank was.
"Uh, I guess . . . I wasn't trying to cover my tracks, though.
Pretty easy to see, in the moonlight and all. I did get rid of
everything on my way out. No one'll know we were there."

Hank was grateful and irritated at the same time, a combi-
nation he hated. He stomped—loudly—out the door, Sam's
chuckles still chafing his ears.

CHAPTER

23

"And now, let us pray."

The pews creaked and clothes rustled as everyone in the church bowed their heads. Except Hank. He remained straight, studying the congregation from his seat in the last row. About two dozen high school students occupied the several rows in front of him, with the girls bunched together and the boys sitting solo, uncomfortable in their special-occasion ties. In front of them, Hank recognized several of the school office staff and the mousy principal. Next to him was the head track coach, whose name Hank couldn't remember. The next pew held Tony Sampson, who kept wiping his eyes with a shaking hand, and at the other end of the row, the Company Man. In between sat boat cook Mrs. Pugo and her co-worker, Roy Stanton. Stanton kept inching away from the sobbing Mrs. Pugo.

Then there were older folks who he guessed from their comfortable postures were church friends of the Brysons, and two rows of crimson—Mandy's Sooner Track teammates in full school colors. That's nice, he thought.

In front of them, two rows from the altar and the coffin in front of it, sat Ryan Nelson, who kept tugging on his tie even in prayer. His mother, who appeared to have fresh hair highlights, sat next to him. Her brother, Jeffrey Honneffer, and his family filled the other end of the pew, with the matriarch Frances in the middle, probably serving as a kind of buffer. Hank stared at Ryan for a long time, and then Jeffrey.

Bill and Gina Bryson huddled together in the front. Next to her sat her brother, who had the same thin, sharp looks and had delivered the eulogy a few minutes earlier. Next to him sat a very old man whose head bobbled constantly and whose attention span seemed just as shaky. At the end of the pew sat the Krycenskis, with Danielle protectively bookended by her parents.

"And now," intoned the pastor, "Sister Danielle has a few things she would like to share."

Hank was surprised. She had not been listed in the program. Danielle rose and walked, slowly but steadily, to the podium at the side of the altar. She placed a paper in front of her and smoothed it very deliberately.

"Mandy was my best friend. We knew each other forever, ever since she was five and I was four. We met here in Sunday school, when there was a mix-up in the classes and I got put with the older kids. She didn't let them put me back. She made them let me stay, so we could be together. She was like that. Always loyal and always your best defender. Even when she was five, she stood up to the grown-ups and got them to back down. She was like that.

"And if she couldn't convince you she was right, well,

then she'd just take off. She'd run. But it wasn't running away. She never ran away or anything. It was more like she was running toward something. Toward her future, maybe. At least that's what I always thought . . . before." She stopped and gripped the podium. The church was completely silent except for her shaky breathing into the microphone. She inhaled deeply and found her place on the smoothed paper.

"Her future . . . her future was running. She was so excited to go to OU. She was so excited to run at that level, maybe even more than that. She knew she could do it. Heck, everybody knew she could do it. After last year, after she won state. She was incredible. She made us all better. It was like a dream, running with her. My best friend.

"And she was more than just fast. She was kind. She was friendly to everyone. It didn't matter who you were. If she thought you were a good person, then Mandy liked you. She'd help you. She'd stick up for you. There was this girl in her English class one year who didn't really have any friends. She was kind of shy and lived outside of town, so she didn't really do much. Mandy wanted to invite this girl to her birthday party, but she knew the girl wouldn't come to something with a lot of people. So she threw a second birthday party, and that girl was the only one she invited. I think they just hung out, but that next Monday at school—you could tell. That girl was *so* happy.

"That's why . . ." Danielle stifled a sob. "That's why I don't understand . . . I don't understand this. Why Mandy? Good people aren't supposed to be murd— This isn't supposed to happen to good people. And Mandy . . ." Her voice was barely audible, even with the microphone. "Mandy was the best. And she always will be."

No one heard what the minister said next. There was really no way to follow that. People were sobbing in their seats—women clutching each other, men trying to compose themselves so as not to have to meet anyone's gaze with teary eyes.

Ryan dabbed at his eyes. So did Tony, as he kept tugging at his tie with shaking hands. Jeffrey's eyes he couldn't see. The attorney was hugging his daughter, who had collapsed against him in the pew. Hank watched carefully, then slipped from the church and posted himself just outside the door, where he could see everyone as they made their way out into the clear, cold afternoon.

First came the high school classmates. Alyssa Sampson and Tall Jennifer stopped when they saw him.

"You arrested Chad." It was an accusation, and Jennifer then looked surprised, as if she hadn't thought the words before she spoke them.

"Yeah, I did. He resisted arrest. And impeded a murder investigation. And was attempting to flee the jurisdiction." The two girls' eyes widened in unison—he doubted they thought Mr. All That capable of such delinquencies. Hank now knew better. "How close is he to his brother, do you know?"

Alyssa frowned. "I'm not sure. He would talk about him sometimes, like he looked up to him, but was also kinda jealous, you know? Of all his brother's success, being a big-time player in New York."

"Do you know what his brother does—what his job is?" Hank asked. "Did Chad talk about that?"

"He works for a bank or something, doesn't he? Some kind of stockbroker, maybe?" Alyssa said.

It was a hedge fund, actually, a very large one from which the elder Sorenson brother had transferred large sums of money that were not his. He had then hedged his own bets by leaving the country on a flight from LaGuardia to Grand Cayman and then disappearing.

When Hank had spoken to him that morning, the U.S. Attorney for the Southern District of New York had no idea where the Sorenson brother had gone after that. And Hank was pretty sure from the timing of his flight that Chad—whose plane from Springfield, by way of Dallas–Fort Worth, landed at LaGuardia two hours before Big Bro took off for the Caribbean—was supposed to have joined him. But whether Chad's plan was merely to enjoy the spoils of his brother's theft, or to flee the country after committing a murder—that was something Hank was still working on.

"Will Chad get out?" Jennifer asked. "Don't you have to give him bail?"

Hank smiled. "That decision is up to a judge, actually. And the one yesterday didn't believe that Chad will stick around, so he decided not to let him out." Throwing phrases like "Wall Street" and "corporate raider" and "one percenter" at a country judge from the Ozarks had that effect. It had been one of the more enjoyable bail hearings of Hank's career.

The girls looked disappointed. They were starting to move away as more people came out of the church when Hank caught a glimpse of Alyssa's brother still sitting in his pew inside.

"What's up with Tony? Why didn't he sit with you guys?"

Alyssa shrugged impatiently. "He's all upset. Been that way since the boat crash, but he's gotten real bad since it burned up. It means he has no job, so he might have to give up on his dream of moving out. And that's made him all moody. He said after the vigil that we had all just jumped on the bandwagon. That we liked the attention." She sniffed dismissively. "He can be a tool. I'm glad he drove himself."

Hank looked back in at Tony, who had gotten up and was walking toward the door. Hank turned as someone tugged his sleeve.

"Thank you, Sheriff, for sending that young man over to put a lock on my door," said Mrs. Pugo. The showboat's cook clutched a large handkerchief and wore a dress that looked to be made out of the same material as her flowered armchair. He asked why she had wanted to come to the service.

"Well, now . . . I am still having a hard time with myself. For not going after her. For forgetting. I thought the least I could do was come and pay my respects before the Lord." She swiped her nose with the handkerchief. "I got atoning to do. And so does he." She pointed at Roy Stanton, who was trying to inch behind her and get out of the cluster of people in the doorway. "I had to convince him to come. Told him that he needed to do some praying for that poor child, too. He done forgot her, too."

Hank turned and said hello, loudly, as Stanton started down the steps. The actor stopped and gave him a nod.

"Why, hello, Sheriff. Of course I was going to come and pay my respects to that dear girl." Mrs. Pugo rolled her eyes. "She was just lovely," he continued. "All dressed up for the day, with her fancy dress and her hair done and that bright red lipstick. Such a tragedy."

He bobbed his head again and continued down the stairs and away from Mrs. Pugo's fluttering—and well-used—handkerchief. Hank tried to do the same, gently prying her hand off his arm. He spotted the Honneffer family coming out of the church and gestured toward them. "You understand . . ."

"Oh, yes, yes." Mrs. Pugo bobbed politely in Mrs. Honneffer's direction and moved away as they approached.

"How do you do, Sheriff?" said Frances Honneffer, who seemed to have shrunk into a state of even greater fragility than she'd been in earlier in the week. She held her granddaughter Ashley's hand. Michelle stood on her left. "Are you any further along in . . . in finding . . ."

He glanced behind her to Patricia Honneffer, whose look told him she was remembering his Presidents' Day promise to her. He answered them both. "I'm getting closer. Definitely closer."

Mrs. Honneffer nodded, and they all moved away, headed for the fellowship hall and the reception of tea and cookies. Jeffrey shook his hand as he moved past. Strong handshake, strong hand. Hank sighed. Jeffrey could theoretically have killed Mandy, but Hank was now giving him only ten-to-one odds. Sheila had done some digging into his background, and the guy didn't seem to be a womanizer. All he did was work. He had shown no particular interest in Mandy. As far as Sheila could determine, he had never even been alone with her—he'd always just seen her at family gatherings, surrounded by plenty of other people. He wasn't known to drink, didn't have money problems, and was mentally stable, at least according to friends and legal clients. He was, essentially, a very boring man. Now, very boring men often made fantastic killers, but Hank wasn't feeling it this time. Maybe even twelve-to-one.

Ah, but the odds significantly improve with this one, he

thought as he turned back toward the church doors. Ryan
was trying to slip through unnoticed. Hank stepped in front
of him.

"Hello there."

Ryan's smile was forced. "Hi."

"It's good to see you here. I wasn't sure you would come.
You know, having moved on and all. Where's Kelly?"

Ryan swallowed noisily. "She, ah . . . she had to go back
to St. Louis." He bit his bottom lip.

"Really? Huh. How does that make you feel?" Hank
leaned in just a little. Ryan dug deeper into his lip and glared
at Hank.

"How d'ya think? Lousy. The whole thing is lousy. She's
talking about it all over the place. You should see her Insta-
gram page. I'll never be able to get a date now."

"Will you talk to her when you get back? Tell her how it
makes you feel?"

Ryan let go of his lip and curled it into a sneer. "What's
the point? She doesn't care how I feel."

Hank stifled a chuckle. The irony of that was obviously
lost on young Ryan. "Can you do anything to get her to stop?"
he asked.

Ryan shoved his hands into the pockets of his coat. "I've
been thinking about it, and I maybe could put the heat on—"
He stopped short, and his eyes widened. "I don't think I should
be talking to you anymore."

"Why not? Kelly doesn't have anything to do with
Mandy, with her murder. Right?" He had continued to lean
slightly closer throughout their conversation—by now, he
hung so far over the shorter Ryan that the kid was forced to
angle his whole torso back to look up at him—because he'd

refused to shift his feet and take a step back. Interesting. "Does she?"

"No!" He spat the word in Hank's face. "No, she doesn't. Cuz I don't. I didn't want to kill her . . . I just didn't want to be with her anymore. I didn't do it."

Ryan finally broke position, stepping back and spinning quickly away. He took the steps down two at a time, his hands still crammed in his pockets as he hurried to catch up with the rest of his family. Hank pulled himself out of his lean and realized Ryan was one of the last ones out of the church. A few older women who had to be parishioners stood just inside the doorway talking to the pastor. But Tony was no longer there. Neither were the Brysons, but Hank didn't necessarily need to talk to them. The *Beauty*'s second-in-command, however . . .

He ducked back inside and saw a side door, up near the altar. He jogged down the side aisle, hoping he wasn't violating some kind of Baptist pew decorum rule, and pushed open the door. A narrow walkway led toward another building and then branched off toward the parking lot. He saw Tony headed toward the back and either a beat-up Chevy sedan or an even more rusted pickup of indeterminate make.

"Hey there," he called. Tony came to a slow-motion stop and turned around.

"Oh, hello, sir. Can I help you with something?"

"Yeah, I thought since you were here, I'd clear up a few things," Hank said. "Whose idea was it to move all the folks from the private dining room into the lounge after the crash?"

Tony stopped dabbing at his bloodshot eyes and stared at the ground. "I don't know." He shrugged. "Could have been either one of them—Tim or Roy. Wouldn't have been

Mrs. Pugo. She, um, she doesn't really take the lead on stuff." He looked up at Hank with now-dry eyes. "Anything else, sir?"

"Yeah," said Hank. "When did you go to the second level? How soon after the crash?"

Tony thought for a moment. "A few minutes after, I guess."

"And where were you when the crash happened?"

"I was down on the main level. Just here and there. It wasn't a very important part of the route—for me, I mean. I didn't have much to do."

"So you came upstairs after the crash? Why? Weren't there more people to take care of down on the main level?"

Tony nodded slowly. "Yeah, I guess so. I just thought about how ticked off the private party would be. And I wanted to get up to the pilothouse, too. To see what had happened."

"And what did you see up there?"

"Just Captain Eberhardt. Sitting stone still. Like he'd been frozen. I couldn't get him to move, or even look at me. I didn't know what to do, so that's when I went back down to check on the folks on the second level."

"And was the dining room locked?"

"I don't know." Tony ground the toe of his shoe into the snow on the sidewalk. "I went straight to the lounge. Look, I got to go, okay? I have an interview at a theater. I got to find a new job."

"Yeah," Hank said. "You sure do. What kind of job are you interviewing for?"

"Assistant stage manager," he said. "Can I go now?"

Hank nodded and watched as Tony walked quickly down the snowy sidewalk to the beat-up Chevy. That kid is becoming more and more interesting, he thought as he headed back around to the front of the church. The loud roar of an engine stopped him. He turned to see the derelict pickup pulling out at a distance behind Tony's Chevy. The driver appeared to have long, light brown hair.

CHAPTER
24

"Hello, Callie."

He had bolted for his car and managed to get to it in time to cut off the pickup as it started down the long driveway out of the church parking lot.

"How am I supposed to follow him if you do that?" she snapped as he walked up to her truck door.

"It's nice to see you again, too," he said. "Why didn't you come in to the funeral?"

She glared at him. "I was here to see who came. And he was the one who didn't go into the fellowship hall. So he's the one who needs to be followed." She jabbed a finger in the direction Tony's Chevy had taken.

"Relax," Hank said. "I know where he's going. What do you know about him?"

Another glare.

"Come on, Callie . . ."

"Don't talk to me like some grown-up that thinks I'm just some stupid teenager," she snarled. "You're no better than I am. You don't know who did it, either."

Well, that was true. He tried again.

"Okay, look. I'm interested in what you know about him. Do you know him from school?"

She eyed him, and he knew she was wishing they were back in her woods with her rifle pointed at him.

"Yeah," she said after what felt like several minutes. "He was two years ahead of me. Me and Mandy. He didn't really do much. No sports or clubs or anything, I don't think. I never even talked to him. I know he hung around with them, though. The track girls, cuz his sister was one of them. So he knew Mandy."

"That gun of yours turn up? The one you lent Mandy?"

She shook her head.

"If it does—and I am very serious about this, Callie—you need to tell me immediately. I won't concern myself with any other guns you got—you understand me?" Callie nodded slowly. "But that one could be the key to solving Mandy's murder," he continued, "so you tell me. Got it?"

She nodded again. He stuck out his hand. "Don't push it," she said, and threw the truck into reverse, backing away toward the other exit out of the parking lot. Hank grinned and went to move his own car out of the way for the people just starting to leave the fellowship hall.

Rudolph was shaking. Standing in front of him and shaking so much that the newspaper rattled in his hands as he waved it in Hank's face.

"Do you have any idea . . . ?" Rudolph sputtered. "That you would slander this town's most respected citizen . . . to even suggest . . ."

Hank plucked the paper from the county commissioner's hand and smoothed it out. It appeared that Jadhur had taken full advantage of the sheriff's quote for the boat fire story. And moved it to the front page.

SHERIFF QUESTIONS
ACCIDENTAL FIRE

TABLE ROCK LAKE—Authorities continued this week to investigate the cause of the fire that sank the *Branson Beauty* on Tuesday. State fire officials are calling the blaze an accident, but County Sheriff Hank Worth thinks otherwise.

"It's awfully coincidental that an old boat, badly in need of updating and with significant personnel expenses, suddenly caught fire in such a way that no real investigation of it can take place," Worth said earlier this week.

The *Beauty*, one of Branson's oldest and most beloved tourist attractions, has been navigating the waters of Table Rock Lake for three decades. Originally owned by "Crazy" Otis Schornberger, the boat was purchased after his death by Gallagher Enterprises, which has run the operation for the past two years. It employed more than 100 people, many of whom started with Schornberger in the 1980s. There are no records of it being retrofitted at any point in its existence.

"We kept the *Beauty* meticulously maintained.

It received a yearly bow-to-stern inspection and daily upkeep," said Henry Gallagher, president of Gallagher Enterprises. "It was the crown jewel of our business here in Branson County, and I am devastated by its loss."

The *Beauty* ran aground Sunday morning during a routine cruise. The showboat's paddlewheel wedged between boulders south of Poverty Point and had to be removed in order for the boat to be towed to shore. The cause of that incident is still under investigation, Worth said.

The hasty amputation of the paddlewheel likely led to fuel or hydraulic fluid leaking and caused the fire, according to fire investigator supervisor Mike Salvatore of the Office of the State Fire Marshal. The entire boat is now underwater, and the wreckage is too dangerous to send down divers, he added.

According to sources, Gallagher Enterprises had insured the boat and accompanying business for $20 million. With the fire officially ruled an accident, that payout should not be questioned, industry experts said.

Hank stopped reading. Twenty million. Interesting. Jadhur apparently had better sources than Sheila did, because she'd been trying to get that figure ever since she got back from Oklahoma. He was wondering how soon Gallagher would get the money when the paper was snatched from his hands, forcing him to return his attention to the irate politician standing in his substation lobby.

"You can't operate like this!" Rudolph was almost yelling

now. "He is the most important businessman in the county, he—"

"He certainly is," Hank cut in. "But do you want to tell me why you were chatting with his flunky at the vigil yesterday?"

Rudolph looked as though Hank had hit him with a two-by-four. He clamped his slack jaw closed and glared up at him.

"How do you know that? You weren't there." He looked as if he regretted the words the second he uttered them. "What I mean is . . . I don't know what you mean. I spoke only to the concerned citizens who attended the vigil. And the pastor. Yes, yes. The pastor. We prayed together. Yes, yes . . . when was the last time you prayed, Worth?"

Hank couldn't help laughing. "Nice try. I'm not asking you about the pastor, or your religious pedigree. I'm asking you about Terry Cummings. What were the two of you talking about behind the church as the vigil let out?"

Rudolph took a step back and began to look a bit wary. His gaze darted around the lobby as if he were looking for hidden cameras. *He should know I don't have the money for those,* Hank thought. He crossed his arms and waited as Fizzel, now a decidedly un-Rudolph-like shade of white, shifted from foot to foot in front of him.

"I was . . . I was offering my condolences . . . about the *Beauty.* That's all."

"Really? Then why was Cummings so upset? What did you do to make him mad . . . Commissioner?" Hank drew out the last word with a mix of contempt and distaste that he had honed in KC interrogating gangbangers whose drive-bys shot up uninvolved bystanders. He'd never gotten to use it on a politician before. Fizzel blanched and took another step back.

Hank took a shot in the dark. "Were you talking about me?"

Fizzel got even more pale, which Hank hadn't thought was possible. His Adam's apple bobbed up and down. "Why would we be doing that?" he asked in a shaky tone that confirmed Hank had scored a direct hit.

"Well . . ." Hank was coming up with this on the fly. "You already gave me a warning. Then I tried to get Gallagher in here to explain his holdings and the state of his showboat business. Then his chief assistant was seen yelling at you. And now, you're awfully upset about an observation I made in the newspaper. You're not doing a very good job of keeping me in check, are you?"

Fizzel flushed, his face regaining its standard red hue. "I was the chief supporter of your appointment as sheriff. You wouldn't be here if it weren't for me. You should . . . you should . . . act as if you appreciate that fact."

Hank raised his eyebrows in mock surprise. "Oh, but I do. I very much appreciate my job and the responsibilities that come with it. But here's the thing *you* need to appreciate. You might have hired me, but you can't order me around. I am not your employee. I am the law." He couldn't believe he'd just said that. In Kansas City, that would have gotten him laughed off the streets. Down here, though, it fit. So he said it again. "I am the law. And I will uphold it. And if anyone broke the law, or thinks they can cash in by committing fraud, I'm going to stop it. And then I'm going to arrest them. And anyone who might be helping them." He paused. "So, what do you know about the boat fire?"

Fizzel's throat convulsed again. Hank's eyebrows climbed even higher as he waited. And waited. This guy was not quick on his feet. Hank sighed. "Who have you talked to at Gallagher Enterprises since the fire?"

"Uh . . . Mr. Cummings, at the vigil. And . . . uh . . . that's all."

"Bullshit," Hank said. "You told me when you came here Tuesday afternoon that you'd already spoken to someone there. So you at least did that."

Hank slowly pulled out of the commissioner that he'd spoken to Cummings a few hours after the Tuesday morning fire. And then every day after that. Rudolph insisted that the conversations were only about his concerns for the welfare of the *Beauty*'s employees—"my people," he called them—and that they had nothing to do with keeping Hank in line.

"Yeah. Just like handing out my name and number to all of those people at the vigil had nothing to do with keeping me in line. My phone in Forsyth has been ringing off the hook with people freaked out about the murder. Like that's not going to cause me to spend less time investigating the boat fire."

A smirk flashed across Fizzel's face and was just as quickly gone. Hank wanted to punch him in his red nose. He took a step back instead. "The law" would lose a lot of his moral high ground if he hauled off and hit somebody—even if it was a politician.

"I really think—" Hank started, when the bell on the lobby door jangled loudly and the one person with even less restraint than he had burst in.

"I knew it. And I'd be able to say 'I told you so' if you'd just answer your damn cell phone and listen to my suspicions,"

Sheila said as she bent down to brush crusty snow off her boots. "That little weasel took a boatload of cash—hah, boatload—from Gallagher during the last elect—" She straightened up and noticed the weasel standing next to Hank. "Well, what do we have here? It's nice to see you, Commissioner. It'll save me a phone call to ask you about these campaign contributions from the last election. Seems you took the maximum amount from Gallagher Enterprises, along with the maximum amount from Gallagher personally, and his wife, and that Cummings guy. I seem to remember you being pretty far behind Percy Wilcott. 'Fizzel has fizzled out. Vote for someone new.' Heh, that was good. But then you started running TV commercials. Commercials. Nobody's got the money to do that. But you suddenly did. Said all kind of nasty things about poor Percy." She dug a sheaf of papers out of her marshmallow penguin parka and waved it in the air. "And I'll bet these donations don't even come close to paying for all that airtime. What'd you take under the table?"

Hank turned to see that Fizzel had gone white again. He took the papers from Sheila and began to casually flip through them. "What else did Cummings tell you, Commissioner? Or do you want me to do this with your bank statements, too?"

Fizzel's shoulders slumped. "He told me that I'd better get you to shut up about the *Beauty* sinking. That you were creating problems and that it was my job to protect this county's most important business. That was why they were so generous when I ran for re-election."

Hank pounced. "They—they who?"

"Well, Gallagher Enterprises, of course."

Sheila snatched back the campaign finance papers. "These list a lot of money, but everything complies with the law.

Where'd all the extra money come from—the money for all of those commercials?"

Fizzel scowled. "I don't have to say anything. We're not involved in this, and—"

Both Hank and Sheila leaned forward until Fizzel was forced to take a step back. His red-faced belligerence had turned into ashen fear. Hank felt as if he was finally getting somewhere.

"Who's 'we,' Commissioner?" Sheila asked. Then she smiled. "Wait a minute. Didn't your son get hired by Gallagher Enterprises? Before the election? I remember that was one of your pro-business things. That you were supporting jobs—and just look at the opportunities for young people around here now. And then you'd talk about your son."

"So?" Fizzel said. "This area needs jobs. Everybody knows that."

"And wasn't it nice that your son got one of them," Sheila said. "Especially considering that he still lives at home and doesn't have to pay rent. Tyrone sees him while he's doing his mail route, and—"

Fizzel cut her off. "Oh, he pays rent." Then he stopped and his face got even more red. Hank stood back in silent enjoyment and watched Sheila go in for the kill.

"Really?" she said. "How much, exactly? How much does he get paid and then how much does he give you for rent?" She started listing figures as Fizzel stood there mute. She stopped when she got to three grand a month and the veins in his neck bulged. He would not make a good poker player, Hank thought.

"And now we know," Sheila said. "That kind of money month after month would buy a lot of TV commercials."

Fizzel spun on his heel and marched out the door. Hank turned to Sheila.

"Get those bank statements," Hank said. "Oh, and nice work."

Sheila smiled, patted her already immaculate ebony hair into place, and headed to the phone.

CHAPTER

25

Dunc was laughing over the *Daily What's-It* when Hank got home that evening.

"Well, son, that's one way to do it," Dunc said, waving the newspaper at him. "Poke the tiger right in the eye. You're not trying to make any friends in this job, are you?"

"Nope," Hank said. "At least not a friend like Gallagher. Any dinner left?"

"Yeah, there's casserole in the fridge. This one actually came out pretty good. Well, better than usual, at least."

Hank pulled it out of the fridge and sniffed at it hesitantly. Duncan grumbled from his seat at the kitchen table. "You'll take a risk like ticking off Henry Gallagher, but you won't take a risk on my casserole? You are a pansy."

"My odds are better with Gallagher," Hank said as he put the dish back in the refrigerator. He pulled a jar of peanut butter out of the cupboard and started hunting around for the bread. Duncan finished with the newspaper and got up from the table.

"Oh, I almost forgot. I need you to figure this out for me." Dunc pulled something out of his pocket that looked suspiciously like a piece of glass. Hank, his peanut butter sandwich halfway to his mouth, started laughing.

"Is that twenty-first-century technology I see you holding?" he asked. "Where the heck did you get an iPhone?"

Duncan snorted. "Your wife. Ordered it for me without even asking. Came in the mail yesterday. I've been poking at it and now all these little squares here on the screen are shaking, and I can't get 'em to stop."

Hank put down his sandwich, took the phone from his father-in-law, and explained how pushing the device's one button would stop the shaking. "I thought all you had to do was touch the screen," Dunc said. "Maggie didn't say anything about the button."

Hank picked up his sandwich again and wished Maggie were home from the hospital so she could explain elegant technological design to a man who was jabbing at the thing like it had just bitten him.

"Now you got to put some music on here for me," Dunc said in between jabs.

Hank opened the fridge and reached for the milk. "Maybe you should have waited to call me a pansy until after you asked for my help," he said.

Dunc grinned. "Got me there."

Hank's phone interrupted his next sandwich bite. He didn't recognize the number.

"Sir? Sir? It's Duane Shrum. I thought calling was better

than the radio this time of night. Sir, he just woke up. Mr. Eberhardt did, sir. He's awake."

Albert Eberhardt looked very tired and thoroughly confused as he sat, propped up by pillows, in the hospital bed that had been his home for the past five days. He blinked and tried to focus on Hank, who leaned forward and asked again.

"Do you remember your Sunday voyage?"

Blink.

"Al. What happened on your Sunday brunch cruise?"

"I don't know. I'm trying to think. Man, my head hurts. Um, let's see. We started off, same as always. We rounded Poverty Point, and brunch was over. The show in the main dining room had started—Tony told me that—and then . . . then my head started to hurt. The noises were so loud. The bombs were so loud . . . the bombs . . . and the screaming . . . I couldn't get away from it . . . I tried to leave . . ."

"What do you mean, Al? Tried to leave where? The pilothouse?"

The door had been locked from the outside, Albert said. He'd tried and tried the knob and then looked for his keys so he could open it from the inside. He had keys for everything on the boat, but they weren't in their usual spot up by the window. He'd started to search, but the bombs kept going off. And he could hear the villagers screaming. Over and over. The screaming. Then the room started to spin. His head felt like it was cracking open. The bombs got louder, and the helicopter started to go down. The crew chief grabbed him and shoved him away from the door. And then they crashed.

"I don't remember anything after that," he said, slumping against the bed pillows and closing his eyes.

What the hell? A helicopter? A crew chief? Hank sat back in his seat and stared at the ceiling. His own head felt as if it were going to split open.

"Al," he said, slowly bringing his gaze back down to the man lying in front of him. "Were you in a helicopter crash in Vietnam?"

Al did not open his eyes. "Yes."

"And have you had flashbacks before?"

"Yes."

"How often?"

"Not in years. I've been doing pretty good. I run, you know. Every morning. I go for a run. That's helped a lot."

"Did you run on Sunday?"

Albert opened his eyes. "No. Actually, no. I didn't. I couldn't find my running shoes. And I woke up late. There was a dog barking all night long, it seemed like, which was weird, because I didn't think any of my neighbors had dogs. So I slept awful. And I didn't have time. I figured I'd run after I got back from work and had time to look for my shoes."

That would have made him plenty frazzled, Hank thought. Albert had apparently arrived at the same conclusion, because he turned to look Hank directly in the eye. "I know that makes it sound like I just fell apart. Just went nuts or something. But I didn't. It was real. Those bombs weren't just in my head. I swear, Sheriff. It was real."

The result of his flip-out was certainly real. "Would you have any reason to want to not have to work on the *Beauty* anymore?" Hank asked.

"Huh? No. I like my job. Why would you ask that?"

"Would you have any reason to want to harm the *Beauty*? Any reason to destroy it?"

Albert sat up straight in bed. "What happened to my boat? Did something happen to my boat?"

"How do you feel about Gallagher Enterprises?"

Albert clutched the bed sheets. "What happened to my boat?" he shouted.

Hank watched him very carefully. "It ran aground. Two and a third hours into your cruise. They had to hack the paddlewheel off to get it unstuck and then tow it back to shore."

Albert looked shocked. "Oh, God. Did I do that? How could I have done that? I didn't touch the wheel. . . . Is she okay? They'll be able to fix her, won't they?"

"No," Hank said. "The boat caught fire more than three days ago. Sank to the bottom of the lake. Total loss."

Albert slumped back onto his pillows.

"Did you leave the pilothouse at all? At any time?"

Albert shook his head. "Not at all. I went straight up there when I came aboard. Never left."

"Did you know Mandy Bryson was on the boat?"

Now Albert went from shocked to puzzled. His hands still clutched the bed sheets. "Who? Mandy? From my track team? Why would she be on board? Isn't she away at school? She was on the boat?"

"You sure you didn't leave the pilothouse?"

"Why the hell is that important? No. I didn't. What, did Mandy get hurt or something? She didn't get hurt during the crash, did she?"

Go for broke, Hank thought. He made sure Albert was looking directly at him.

"Mandy was murdered in the private dining room. She was strangled to death. Did you kill her?"

Albert's throat made a kind of rattling sound as he sucked

in all of the surrounding air. He opened and closed his mouth several times before he spoke.

"Who would do that? Do you know who did it? My God. Mandy."

Hank watched him carefully. He just couldn't get a handle on this guy. He looked to be telling the gospel truth. But he could so easily be saying everything he thought Hank wanted to hear. Everything to give himself an alibi—for the boat, and for Mandy.

"How are her friends taking it? All the other girls on the track team?" Albert rattled on. "Her boyfriend—didn't she have a boyfriend? And Tony? I always suspected he had a little bit of a crush on those track girls. And her parents? Oh, Lord, her poor parents . . ."

Hank stopped him there. A bit of a crush? On all of them? Well, Albert said, not really. There was his sister, of course. Tony'd always acted as though that was why he was there—to pick up Alyssa or some such thing. He'd arrive early and sit and watch, trying not to let on that he was focused on Mandy. He'd never said anything to Tony, Albert went on, because—well, heck, he had been a teenager once, too, and weren't we all supposed to have impossible crushes at that age? Tony had never said anything to him about Mandy, and he hadn't been around nearly as much this past fall for the cross-country season. Of course, Mandy was off at college then.

Tony had been a pretty good employee. He'd worked on the boat for about two years. Very conscientious, obedient. But anytime he had a spare minute, he'd pull out his phone and start fiddling with it.

"Wait . . . I thought there was no cell service along stretches of the *Beauty*'s route?" Hank said.

"Oh, there's not. He could download stuff to the phone, like a TV show or something, at home and then play it back on the boat. He was showing Roy and me how to do it. Had one of those *Hangover* movies on there. I don't know how he could see anything—it was all way too small for me to focus on."

Hank leaned forward. "Tell me about Roy. He said you two were friends."

"We are, I guess. I'm not, you know, a real friendly guy. But Roy sure is persistent. He just wore me out with all his talking. So eventually, I had to start talking back, you know? He'd been in 'Nam, too, so that made it easier. Not that we talked about that much, just a couple of times. Told him things I hadn't talked about in years . . . decades, really. But mostly we just shot the shit. And boy, is Roy full of it." Albert shook his head. "Very dramatic. Always full of plans about how he is going to break out, become a 'true star.' He has this idea for a huge stage show on the Strip. It would be patriotic and salute the veterans and have magic acts for the kids and be full of country music and maybe a little bit of Shakespeare or somebody like that. And he would be the star—the one who takes the audience on its 'transforming journey.' He repeats that description a lot. I just nod and listen. Listening's a lot easier than talking, you know."

Actually, Hank had found that for most people, the opposite was true.

"He'll talk and talk," Albert continued. "That's all he's ever been able to do. He's gotten turned down by just about everybody in town. Poor guy. And he says he won't go to New York and try out there because they don't have the proper respect for veterans. I think it's because big cities scare him. Don't blame him on that score. Damn frightening, those places."

Hank was about to reply when a doctor walked in and immediately told him to get out. Unless his patient was under arrest, the law had no business being there for a physical exam. He sighed and was halfway to the door when Albert spoke again.

"You know, I wasn't really a believer before. But I've been living down here for a while now, and I've done a bit of thinking. You kind of have to, surrounded by these hills. So I run, and I paint, and it's quiet. Makes you think there might be a God out there. And my boat, too, on the lake. You wouldn't think that would be a blessing—such a silly thing as the quiet—but it is. Quiet, like you're being granted a bit of peace you don't quite deserve. I know I don't. I did things over there. I followed orders like a good soldier. I did it to stay alive, and I've wished I were dead ever since. So I know what you're thinking, and I know it makes sense to you in your investigation, but there is no way that I would ever cause anyone harm ever again. And I would never . . . never have hurt Mandy Bryson."

CHAPTER
26

The house was completely dark. Hank drove by twice, but there was no sign that the Brysons were up again at this late hour. He turned the car around and started down the winding road out of the development, back to his own house. He drove slowly, cautious of the probable black ice that had formed on the insides of the curves. He rounded one and his headlights bounced off a ghost.

All white, it staggered along the edge of the road like an exhausted marathon runner. He was so tired he was starting to see things.

He shook his head, but the apparition continued along with its half jog–half stumble. He carefully pulled up alongside and realized the white was a nightgown and it was occupied by an almost-as-pale Gina Bryson. Jesus. He slammed the car into park and leapt out, calling her name. She turned to look and stumbled. Hank barely reached her in time to keep her from falling into the snow.

"What are you doing? Good God, are you all right?"

She clutched his arms to keep herself upright as her knees started to buckle. She had no coat, no gloves, no hat. Just the nightgown. And running shoes.

"Mrs. Bryson," he said very quietly, "I'm going to take you home now."

She shook her head frantically. "No, no. I'm going for a run. A run. It will help. It will help. It will make me feel free. I've never run, but that's what she always said. 'It makes me feel free.' I don't know why I didn't think of it before. It's so simple, really. Just go for a run. So I need to finish my run."

She sank lower as her knees gave out. Hank scooped her up and carried her to the car. She weighed next to nothing and shook as if the cold originated deep inside her bones rather than from the outside air. "No. Please. I have to finish my run. Please . . ."

Hank arrived at the office the next morning to find that Gallagher had canceled his rescheduled appointment.

"Why do you look like that makes you happy?" Sheila asked him.

"Because now I get to be impolite," he said. "Let's get a warrant for his business records. But first, you want to come with me? I'm going to haul that Cummings guy in for questioning."

Sheila chortled. "Your timing might end up being perfect. The reason that damn lawyer gave me when he called to cancel was that Gallagher had to 'work through the weekend' on very pressing business matters. I heard a couple other voices in the background. Might be Cummings. It'd be damn fun to take him in front of his boss."

"You are a cop after my own heart," Hank said.

They took a squad car over to the glittering new offices of Gallagher Enterprises, a big building of rock and glass off Roark Valley Road that had to have been designed by the same nouveau-Ozark firm that had done Gallagher's mansion. Surprisingly for a Saturday morning, the front door was unlocked. Hank bet that was an oversight that wouldn't be repeated. They walked right in and up to the second floor, where the back of the building overlooked an undeveloped swath of trees. They could hear movement inside the main office.

Sheila strode forward and moved to plow through the half-open door. Hank stopped her and held his finger to his lips. He slowly swung the door open and stood there, arms folded across his chest, and waited to be noticed. In front of him was a very large desk and, behind it, an enormous window that took up the entire wall. No one sat at the desk. The noise was coming from a corner of the office, where the Company Man was hunched over a shredder, pulling tangles of paper out of its nether regions. He gave one last fierce yank, stood up with a fist full of strips, and froze when he saw Hank. He let out a squeak as Hank sauntered into the room.

He walked to the wall perpendicular to the window. It was covered with several poster boards that depicted what he assumed were various Gallagher Enterprises proposed projects. One looked like an addition to the resort outside of town. Another seemed to have something to do with the mostly vacant outlet mall east of the Strip. There were a few more smaller boards, and then a blank spot on the wall. Hank perused them all.

"Wow," he said. "Gallagher Enterprises is in full expansion mode. Where're you getting the money for all of these?"

"What are you . . . you doing here?" the Company Man said. The hand holding the paper strips trembled slightly. "You . . . you can't be here. You don't have permission . . . you're trespassing."

"What're you going to do," Sheila said smoothly, "call the police?" Hank was frankly surprised she'd managed to stay quiet for as long as she had.

He finally turned away from the wall and toward the Company Man, who still stood by the shredder. Behind him sat a large trash can overflowing with paper strips. A broken piece of poster board stuck up like a sail from the top of the pile. He walked forward until he was a foot away from Cummings, who finally moved just in time to reach up and stop his glasses from slipping off his nose. The dude was starting to sweat heavily, even though the office was not well heated, what with the system probably being on a weekend timer.

"So tell me," Hank said. "What is so urgent that you need to be working so hard on a Saturday morning? What are you shredding?"

"Oh, just junk. Old forms and such."

"Anything regarding the *Beauty*?"

Cummings stared down at his fistful of strips.

"I suggest you tell me," Hank said, crossing his arms again. "We're about to get a warrant for this whole place as it is."

Cummings sighed. "Yes, some *Beauty* records. Just confidential employment documents. Since those people are no longer employed with us, I'm just correctly disposing of their records."

"So it's only been four days, and you've already decided you're not giving these people jobs somewhere else in the company?"

"There are . . . there are no open positions right now," he said.

"How much payroll will you get rid of?"

That took Cummings just a second. "Only two hundred and seventy-five thousand dollars a year. See, we're not saving that much."

Hank thought about Anna Fenton and her stump, and Mrs. Pugo and her bursitis, and all the other now-elderly leftovers from Crazy Otis's day. "And what about the health insurance? What were their premiums costing you? You're self-insured, right? You gotta cover all those bills yourselves."

Cummings pushed his glasses back up his nose again. Then he stared at his feet. Then the ceiling.

"You know the numbers for everything," Hank said. "Don't stand there and act like you don't. I'm getting warrants, remember? How much?"

The glasses again. "Two point three million last year."

Sheila let out a low whistle. "And that would only go up as those folks got older," she said.

Cummings's grip on the strips tightened, and he tried to glance nonchalantly out the window behind the desk. The trembling and sweating didn't do much to help him achieve that. Hank bet his next look would be to the clock hanging above all of those planning poster boards. He was right. It was 8:02, and the Company Man was expecting someone. Someone who was now late. He and Sheila both heard the downstairs front door open at the same time. She smoothly moved to the side of the office door and up against the wall. Hank took one step back from Cummings so the little guy would have a clear view of his boss coming into the room. He had been so busy trying to casually get a glimpse of the parking lot through the big window that he hadn't heard the outer door. That meant another squeak was coming.

"What on earth?" Gallagher stopped in the doorway. "What are you doing here, Terry?"

Squeak.

"I don't . . . Oh, my. Worth. Goodness. What are you doing here?" Gallagher stared at Hank. Hank stared back, silently. "Really," Gallagher said, "I don't believe this. Terry, what are you doing with those papers? Why are you shredding them?"

The color drained from Cummings's face. He started to speak, but then closed his mouth, slowly, as if he'd decided there was nothing worth saying. His fist dropped to his side.

"Terry, did you and Mr. Gallagher have an appointment to meet here at this time?" Hank asked.

Cummings didn't speak, didn't move, didn't blink. Gallagher snorted.

"No, we did not. I came to get some paperwork I left by mistake. No one is supposed to be here. I really don't know . . . Terry, what have you done? Is this about the boat? What did you do to my boat?"

Terry stayed silent.

"What do you know about the boat?" Hank asked, turning toward Gallagher. The question gave him the pinched-nose look Hank had seen often on the day of the *Beauty*'s grounding.

"I know that it was my most prized business. That I entrusted it to an incompetent captain. That it is now a total loss—for everyone in town," Gallagher said.

"For everyone except you," Hank said. "You get twenty

million out of it. Everyone else just gets to apply for unem-
ployment."

Gallagher stiffened. "I am getting tired of you slandering
me, Worth. I know nothing about any plan to sabotage the
Beauty."

Cummings took a hesitant step and managed to bump
the overflowing trash can. Strips of paper tumbled out, and
the broken poster board crashed down flat on the floor. Hank
swooped down, snatched it off the carpet, and turned it right
side up. It was the left half of the layout for a theater, with
circular rows of seats radiating outward and stage parts labeled
with terms he didn't know. The heading that remained read:
The Branson Sta— And in smaller print below it: *Coming to
the Stri—*

He raised an eyebrow. "What's this?"

"Nothing," Cummings said.

"Then why do you look even more worried than you did
two seconds ago?" Hank asked.

Cummings shrugged.

"You're coming down to the station with us—voluntarily,
of course," Hank said. "You're not under arrest." Hank did
not want Cummings clamming up and demanding a lawyer.
"But some interesting issues have been raised here, and we
need to talk about them some more."

Sheila escorted the Company Man out of the room.
Hank, still holding the broken poster board, turned to Gallagher.

"How'd you get him to burn down the boat?" he asked.

Gallagher looked at him calmly. "*I* didn't get him to burn
down the boat. I didn't get him to do anything. I can't believe he has done this to my company. I'm heartbroken."

Hank's eyebrows climbed in disbelief.

"Yeah, right," he said. "It's still your show. You're running it. You're running everything. You ordered that boat sunk."

"Well," Gallagher said, smoothing the front of his wool coat, "I look forward to you trying to prove that, Worth. But you won't be able to. Because I didn't order anything done, and I will swear to that in a court of law. I'm just a local business-man, trying to do my best for the community."

He reached out and plucked the poster board out of Hank's hand. "I believe you have a suspect to interrogate, so I'll bid you good day."

Hank let Sheila drive over to the main station in Forsyth. He stared out the passenger window at the snow-spackled trees lining the roadway. He had just heard an awful lot of non-swearing for a situation that called for a lot of it. Everything had sounded rehearsed. From Gallagher, anyway. Cummings's reaction had most definitely not been. The guy had been com-pletely blindsided. Hank's plan had been to turn the Company Man against his boss, but now he wasn't so sure that would work. Even right there, in the moment, Cummings had kept his mouth shut.

But why would Gallagher have chosen to hang Cum-mings out to dry now? He had been blaming the grounding on Albert, and the burning on accidental ignition. And it was working—with the fire marshal and with the insurance com-pany. Why switch tactics now? By setting up Cummings to take the fall, he was almost certainly sacrificing the twenty mil-lion dollars. No insurance company would pay out if a high-ranking employee was convicted of purposefully destroying the boat.

The sun bounced off the melting snow on the side of the road. Hank closed his eyes against the blinding glare. Only one thing would be serious enough for Gallagher to throw away that kind of money. Murder. Felony murder. A killing committed during the course of a different felony—say, insurance fraud—could make the defrauders guilty of homicide, too, even if they weren't on the boat at the time. And a man with a fancy Ladue lawyer would certainly have had that explained to him.

But what would link Gallagher to the murder? Thanks to that idiot Fizzel, it was public knowledge that Mandy had a stalker. And a stalker would have been after just Mandy, not the boat. Gallagher could have easily avoided involvement in that. So what had changed so quickly? Hank's eyes snapped open. Albert had changed. He'd woken up.

But nobody knew Albert was awake. Except the people at the hospital. So of course Gallagher knew. He obviously had sources in the hospital. But just knowing that wouldn't be enough to throw away his currently ironclad strategy. To be really sure that his blame-the-captain strategy wouldn't work, Gallagher had to know what Albert had said last night. And there was no way— Oh, God. Duane.

"Stop the car."

"What?" Sheila said. "Are you kidding me?"

"Stop the car. Now."

Swearing under her breath, Sheila pulled as far off the two-lane road as she could, driving the car half onto a snow-bank to get it out of the path of traffic. Hank climbed out onto the snow and slammed the door. He did not want Cummings to hear this conversation. He whipped out his cell phone and scrolled to Duane's number as he walked as far from the car as he could across the snowbank. He was pretty sure the kid was off duty. Duane picked up on the third ring, his voice shaking. Hank swore to himself. He really liked the kid.

"What'd you do, Duane?"

"I'm sorry, sir. I'm so sorry. He said I needed to call in when Mr. Eberhardt woke up. And that I needed to listen in on what you and Mr. Eberhardt talked about and then call that in. Or my mom would lose her job."

And Hank had let him stay in the hospital room during the interview, so Duane had gotten to listen to the entire thing. He swore again.

"Who's *he*, Duane? Who told you to do this?"

"Mr. Cummings. The guy with the glasses and the nice shoes."

"And who did you 'call in' to?"

Duane paused. "I guess it was him. It was a cell phone number with one of those electronic voice messages. I just left a message about everything."

"So you didn't actually speak with anybody?"

"No, I guess I didn't." Duane's voice was still shaking. "Sir . . . sir, I'm so—"

"Gimme the phone number." Hank fished a pen out of his breast pocket and wrote it on his hand. Odds were that it was a disposable cell and couldn't be linked back to Gallagher.

"Duane . . ." Hank stared at the trees. He thought briefly about doing some kind of job probation for the kid, but if it got around that that was the only penalty for such a huge violation, he'd have no authority left at all. This sheriff job sucked just about every way it could at the moment. He fired Duane and got back in the car.

Sheila glared at him and pulled back onto the road. Hank

turned around and stared at Cummings. "So you threatened my deputy and his mother."

Cummings nodded.

"Who does the phone he left the message on belong to?" Hank asked.

The briefest of pauses. "Me."

"Really? Then what did his message say?"

A slightly longer pause. "He . . . he recounted Albert Eberhardt's interview with you."

"No shit," Hank said. "What exactly did Deputy Shrum say?"

Cummings turned away and stared out the window. "I think I want a lawyer."

Marvelous. Hank spent the rest of the ride trying to figure out what the hell Albert had told him last night that had Gallagher throwing away twenty million dollars. And who the hell had sabotaged the *Beauty* and killed Mandy Bryson in the process.

CHAPTER

27

No one was home.

Ryan Nelson was on his way back to school in St. Louis, Michelle informed Hank before slamming the door in his face. And Roy Stanton had left that morning, according to the neighbor who had thankfully not slammed the door, but actually invited Hank in. For coffee, thank God.

"I guess it finally sank in for the poor guy. He looked down in the dumps." The neighbor's name was Alan. He was tall and wiry and looked as if he hadn't shaved in days. And he made his coffee strong enough to double as an industrial-strength solvent. Hank liked him immediately.

"What do you mean, 'finally'?" Hank asked.

Alan rubbed at his bristly chin. "Well, after the boat sank, it seemed he didn't really mind. He'd come out whistlin', give me a big wave, the couple times I saw him. Didn't seem much like a guy who'd just lost his job." He shrugged. "But this morning, no sirree. He comes out all slumped over. Barely made it to his car. Didn't even say hi to Moses."

"I'm sorry—who?"

"Oh—Moses. My dog. I was out walking him when Roy left." Alan leaned back in his chair and snapped his fingers. A large beagle bounded into the kitchen and skidded to a halt in front of his master. "You like Roy, don't ya, boy?"

Moses wagged in what appeared to be agreement and then went over to his empty food bowl, snuffling around the floor for any fallen bits he might have missed the first time. He should be extra fond of Roy now, Alan said. A few days ago, the back gate had somehow come open and Moses got out. Alan searched the whole neighborhood with no luck. Moses was gone all night.

"Thank the good Lord that Roy found him. Said the silly thing showed up on his back porch looking for food. Roy brought him straight on over." He turned toward his dog, who was now shoving the food bowl across the floor. "You'd better not ever do that again."

Alan filled Hank's travel mug before seeing him to the door. Moses got past them both and ran out into the snow, baying in delight. The barking bounced off the frozen ground and made Alan grin. "The only thing worse is when he gets scared. Then he starts howling. Won't stop for nothing until you get him nice and safe and warm somewhere."

Hank dusted off the snow that Moses' run had flung onto his pants and headed toward his car. He opened his door and stopped.

"What night was it that Moses got out?"

Alan scratched his bristles again. "Let's see, it was the long weekend. One of those days. All that stuff hadn't happened yet, so it must have been Saturday night. And Roy found him early Sunday morning. That was it."

Hank raised his mug in thanks and left Alan trying to get his dog back in the house.

He pounded on the door again. This time, he heard feet shuffling toward it. Alyssa Sampson swung it open and stared up at him in surprise. He asked where her brother was. His car was not in the driveway.

"Tony left," she said.

No kidding. Hank tried not to show his exasperation.

She didn't know where he'd gone. He'd sulked around all day yesterday after the funeral and then this morning moped around a little bit more before finally stomping out to the garage. He threw things around out there and then got in his car and drove off. Their parents were both at work, so he didn't have to explain anything to them, and he'd told her to mind her own business. "Jerk."

"Did you follow him into the garage?"

"No way," she said. "He was *really* pissed."

Hank slumped against the hospital wall. He was so tired, and he could just feel this slipping away. Where the hell was Tony, and where the hell was Roy? And why the hell was Albert asleep again? The doctors weren't sure—perhaps it was "recuperative," they had just told him. But the captain wasn't waking up, and so the questions Hank had hoped to ask were still nothing more than unsolved problems pinging around in his brain.

He pushed himself off the corridor wall and made his way downstairs. He had double-parked in the main circular drive—nobody was going to tow his squad car—so he went out through the main lobby.

"Daddy!" He heard it at the same moment the small form plowed into him, wrapping its arms around his leg. A slightly bigger form was right behind.

"Benny. Good grief. Let go of my leg. Maribel, sweetie, what are you doing here?"

"We're going to eat lunch with Mommy." She bounced up and down and clapped her hands. "Are you here to eat with us? Grandpop said we can have Jell-O!"

Hank turned to see Duncan hoisting himself out of an armchair. "I don't know what they'll have in the cafeteria, but I figured it'd be safe to promise them Jell-O."

Hank detached Benny from his leg and reflexively swung him up on his shoulders. He immediately yanked Hank's hat off and threw it at his sister, who paid no attention and kept staring up at her father.

"Can you come? Please, please, please?" She bounced with each "please," her dark hair swinging around her shoulders and the ball on the top of her snow hat bobbing every which way. "It's a restaurant. You love restaurants. And we'll behave. We already promised Grandpop. Please?"

"You haven't seen them in almost three days," Duncan pointed out. Hank glared at him.

"I know that. I haven't exactly been out partying it up, you know."

"You can spare a half an hour."

No. He couldn't. In a half an hour, Stanton could be across state lines. Sampson could be holed up in a mountain shack somewhere, never to be seen again. He had to go. He gently swung Benny off his shoulders and set him next to

Maribel. He crouched down so he was at their eye level—their enormous, long-lashed, chocolate-brown eye level. And then he broke their hearts.

"I can't. Daddy has to go. I have to go catch the bad guys. They're going to get away if I don't go right now."

Their eyes filled with tears. "When are the bad guys done? When will they go away?" Maribel whispered. "When can you come home?"

"Soon," he said, praying it would turn out to be the truth as he hugged his kids. "Very, very soon."

Childhood was an accumulation of little moments in the memory, his grandmother had told him once. You stack them all up and at the end you have a foundation that holds or that doesn't, because some of those memories become cracks that widen and deepen and eventually break apart. Hank prayed he wasn't creating one right then.

He stood up. Duncan was still glaring at him.

"I already feel bad enough," Hank snapped. "I don't need a guilt trip from you."

Duncan snorted. "I don't have enough to go around." He pulled his new phone out of his pocket and waved it in the air with the time displayed. "She's late. Again. It's a wonder you two ever made time to conceive kids in the first place."

Hank decided that leaving was wiser than responding and turned to go. A loud boom and gunfire stopped him.

The two men stared at each other, and then looked up at the lobby TV, which was tuned to a twenty-four-hour news channel reporting on fighting somewhere, complete with footage of explosions and clattering machine guns. An elderly hospital volunteer, blushing furiously, was struggling with the remote.

She finally turned the volume down, and the sound of war faded into the background once again.

"Sounded like a bomb went off," Duncan said.

"Yeah . . ." Hank stared at the TV and then at his father-in-law. And then at the smartphone in Dunc's hand. "Yeah . . ."

He pivoted and ran through the lobby doors and out to the squad car, leaving his family staring after him.

CHAPTER

28

He stomped through the woods behind Albert Eberhardt's house. The snow was crusty and made for hard going. He stopped at every tree in a hundred-foot radius until he found what he was looking for—a rope, half buried in snow, but still tied tightly to a hickory tree about seventy-five feet from the captain's back door.

He snapped photos with his phone and was heading back to his car when it rang in his hand.

"It's Stanton," said Sheila.

"I know . . . wait, how do *you* know?"

She had taken several pictures of Gallagher's office when they took Terry Cummings into custody.

"I didn't know you'd done that."

"'Course not. I'm good."

One of the photos was a shot of the broken poster board Hank had picked up off the floor. She had just spent the better part of an hour staring at it.

"The full thing has to read *The Branson Stanton Theater. Coming to the Strip*, and then probably a date of some kind," she said. "They promised him his own show."

That made sense. He'd sabotaged the boat in exchange for his own theater. And he'd had to kill to make it happen. But now his dream was in the trash. So where was he?

"Is there anything else on that poster board, Sheila? Anything about a location?"

"Nope. I've enlarged it until I can see the dots from the damn printer, but there's no other text on it . . . wait. Does Gallagher own property on the Strip? I'll call you right back."

Hank jumped in his car and was going sixty down the winding rural road near Eberhardt's place when Sheila called back. Gallagher Enterprises did not own any property on the Strip, but there was one place currently up for sale, something called the Country Song Theater. Slick Billy Tuner had to sell it in his divorce settlement three years ago, and it had been vacant ever since, she said.

He came at the Strip from the north and slowed down once he hit the water slide amusement park. It was still frigid, so traffic was almost nonexistent, but he eased off the gas anyway. The Country Song Theater was almost at the end, on the south side of the street. The big landscaped island along the curb was overgrown and blocked much of the building from view. He pulled around it and into the unplowed parking lot. He was hoping to see one car. He got two.

The theater was a medium-sized rectangular box of a building, with nothing to distinguish it from an industrial warehouse except for the twenty-foot plywood guitar attached to the front façade. Well, semi-attached. Hank doubted it was meant to point neck down and block access to the two front doors, which were secured with a very large padlock and decorated with various code enforcement warnings.

Roy's old Toyota Camry was parked halfway to the theater's big front doors, right about where the snow got too deep to drive any farther. Hank could see Roy's footprints going up to the entrance, then turning and going around toward the back of the building.

Behind the Camry, angled to block it in, sat a beat-up Chevy. Tony had beaten him here. And his tracks didn't bother with the guitar entrance. He had gone straight around the back.

Well, that upped the ante.

Hank followed. He tried for stealth, but he couldn't keep the snow from crunching under his boots. He took his gloves off and stuffed them in his jacket pockets. He wanted to have his fingers ready to fire his gun, just in case.

He edged along the side of the building and stopped at the corner. Both sets of tracks went that way, but he heard nothing. He held his breath so it wouldn't billow up into the air and give him away, and peered around the corner.

Nothing. Except tracks that led from a locked back door into the woods behind the theater. Why couldn't they have just broken into the damn building? Hank groaned, which sent a huge smoke signal of a breath into the air above his head. More kept coming as he pushed himself off the building and started after the tracks in the snow.

As he walked into the woods, the stink of the cold got stronger. It was a peculiar mixture he was becoming too familiar with—the scent of vegetation and animal piss trapped under old snow and inhaled through his snot-filled nostrils.

His nose was in better shape than his ears, however. He suspected his hat was still on the hospital lobby floor where Benny had thrown it.

As he entered the trees, the ground began to slope downward. His feet broke the icy crust of the snow and had trouble coming out again with each step. From the tracks, it looked as if both Roy and Tony had the same problem. He made it about another hundred yards, and then the footprints changed. The ones he assumed were Tony's—lighter step, smaller foot—suddenly broke into a run. He looked ahead and saw that, twenty feet up, Roy's did the same. Must have been where Roy figured out he was being followed and took off. As quickly as a fifty-six-year-old, 270-pound man with a bourbon habit could manage. And Tony was in pursuit.

Hank stepped up his pace. The terrain got steeper, and he slipped and fell, landing hard on his right side. He stumbled to his feet and shook his arm in pain. Ten feet on, he saw where Roy must have done the same thing. A big, churned-up thrashing of snow and ice. But he had made it back on his feet. Both sets of tracks kept heading down.

Hank was practically at a run by now. To add to the difficulty level, the sun was setting to his right and scattering long, perpendicular tree shadows in his path. Both his nose and his ears had lost all feeling. His fingers were close behind.

He tripped again but managed to stay on his feet by skidding forward and catching a tree branch—one of the last tree branches there were before the narrow open strip at the water's edge. He hadn't realized they were so close to Lake Taneycomo. It stretched along the south side of the Strip for a bit as it curled past town. Hank had always thought of it more as a river than a lake as it ran east, thin and long, down from Table Rock Dam.

Right now, though, it was just the end of the line. Roy stood on the shoreline to Hank's left, and Tony stood to his right. Tony was yelling. Hank managed to force the numb fingers of his left hand into his pocket and pull out his phone. He hit the recording function and moved closer.

". . . the best thing to ever happen to me," Tony shouted. "She was everything. She was perfect. And you killed her."

Roy had his hands out in front of him. "Look, kid. She was the one who got in the way. She wasn't even supposed to be there. Definitely not. Not part of the plan. She interfered. It had to happen that day. That was the deal, and—"

"No," Tony shouted, even louder this time. Hank started looking around for a place to stash his phone so it would continue to record clearly. "You took her away from me. I should have protected her."

Well, that was rich, Hank thought as he wedged the phone into the fork of a tree. He crept closer, staying in the cover of the trees and their still-lengthening shadows.

Roy started shouting, too. He took a few steps forward and waved his hands in the air.

"You'll see what I can do," he snarled, and dug in the pocket of his voluminous parka. *The gun.* Hank jumped out from the cover of the trees and swung toward Roy, yelling for him to keep his hands raised. Instead, he stared slack-jawed at Hank, his hand still in his pocket.

"Hands where I can see them, Stanton." Hank slowly reached for his holster and rested his hand on the grip of his Glock. The pain in his shoulder was getting worse, and he hoped he would be able to draw the damn thing if he had to.

The two men stared at each other for what seemed like a very long time, until Roy slowly withdrew his hand from his coat.

There was a snort of laughter. "Yeah, Stanton, get those hands up in the air." Hank swung around to look at Tony. And the .357 Ruger he was holding. Pointed straight at Roy.

Shit.

His own gun felt as if it had been kept in a sub-zero freezer as he pulled it out and leveled it at Tony.

"Poetic justice, huh?" Tony said. "Her gun, to kill her killer."

"She got it to protect herself from you," Hank said, taking a step closer to Tony. Roy hadn't moved since his hand came out of his pocket. His breath was coming in decidedly quicker puffs, however.

"No." Tony shook his head without taking his eyes off Roy. "She didn't need to protect herself from me. She wanted to be with me. That's why she was back in Branson."

Roy sneered at him. "She had bad timing. It's all about the timing. Always is. And she didn't have it. Exit stage left."

Tony's jaw muscles clenched, and the arm holding Mandy's gun trembled. Just a little, mostly in the wrist. The shake right before an inexperienced shooter fires a gun. Hank had seen it many times—in rookie officers on the firing range, in newly minted gangbangers on the street.

Tony moved forward. Hank moved forward. Roy didn't move at all. Then he seemed to make a decision. He drew himself up and threw his arms wide, just as Tony fired.

At the same instant, Hank launched himself across the open snow and tackled Tony, knocking the gun out of his hand. They went rolling toward the shoreline, Tony screaming and swearing and thrashing all the way. Hank finally pinned him to the ground inches from the water. Out of the corner of his eye, he could see Roy flat on his back in the snow. Tony would not stop struggling long enough for Hank to reach for his handcuffs, and he'd dropped his own gun sometime during the wrestling match. Fine. He pulled his right arm back and came forward with all his weight behind his fist. The crunch when it hit Tony's jaw was mighty satisfying.

Hank stumbled to his feet and quickly found his gun. He pointed it in the direction of Tony, who was now making a pathetic kind of moaning sound and clutching his face, and staggered toward Roy.

The guy looked as if he were about to make a snow angel. He lay completely still, with his arms outstretched and a smile on his face. He was breathing. When Hank saw where the bullet hole was, he wasn't surprised. The left sleeve of Roy's parka was punctured just above the elbow. Bits of down stuffing floated through the air.

Hank bent down, grabbed Roy's parka collar with his free left hand, and hauled him to his feet.

"No theatrical death for you," he said.

CHAPTER

29

"Will you hold still?"

"No. That hurts. Stop poking at me."

The doctor glared at him and kept pressing into his shoulder. "Of course it hurts. You tore your rotator cuff. Going to have one hell of a bruise, too. What'd you land on, rocks?"

"I don't know. Probably. I was too busy chasing *a murderer* to notice." Here he sat, getting his T-shirt cut off in a cold ER exam alcove, and he couldn't even get any sympathy. "Ow."

His torturer finally stopped and gave him the smile that always made his breath catch. "I'm sorry, babe," she said. "We're going to have to do an MRI to confirm it. You're going to have really limited range of motion for a while."

Hank used his still-working left arm and pulled his wife close. She leaned down and kissed him. The chill was finally beginning to leave his bones when the curtain was yanked back.

"Oh, for heaven's sake."

Hank buried his face in Maggie's shoulder as she turned. "Hi, Sheila," she said.

Sheila cleared her throat. "Sorry. Didn't realize . . . well, anyway. Alice is still out at the scene, but it looks like there's only the one bullet fired."

"I told you that," Hank said.

"Yeah, well, we still got to do it right. You know that."

Hank nodded and sat up straighter. "What else?"

"They've arrived at the jail in Forsyth with Stanton. And the kid could be moaning for a reason. You might have broken his jaw. They've got him in X-ray now."

Hank nodded again, this time with more energy. Sheila rolled her eyes. "Wouldn't have even needed to tackle him if you'd called for backup in the first place," she said.

Maggie stepped away from him. "You didn't call for backup?" He was always amazed at how instantaneously her sympathetic gaze could turn into a stony glare. She straightened her doctor's coat and turned to Sheila.

"He's lucky I'm not going to give him a Toradol shot in his ass," she said. "I'm going to check on my other patients." She stomped out of the alcove.

Hank shifted uncomfortably on the exam table. "Thanks, Sheila."

She cringed. "I'm sorry. I didn't mean to get you in trouble. But that was a damn fool stupid thing to do."

Hank bristled. "Even if I had called it in, no one would have been there by the time it all went down."

Sheila eyed him. He could see her doing land-speed calculations in her head. "Maybe. Close call. It'd be hard to say, definitively."

"Well, how about you mention that to my wife, okay? I do not need to get in trouble with her for this again."

Sheila raised an eyebrow and considered him for a long minute. Then she sighed, bent down to the duffel bag she had put on the floor, and pulled out a clear evidence bag.

"This is what was in his pocket."

Hank flattened the bag on the exam table and stared down at a blueprint of *The Branson Stanton Theater. Coming to the Strip This Summer.* It looked like a complete version of the broken poster board in Gallagher's office. It was heavily creased, and the paper was worn to a shine in several spots.

"I wonder if he had this with him when he killed her?"

Sheila reached over and put her hand flat over the center of the theater. "I would guess so," she said. "Doesn't look like he went anywhere without it." She slowly put it back in the duffel. "But if the deal was that he crashed the boat in exchange, how the hell did he manage to do it?" she asked.

"That," Hank said, pointing to the open duffel bag and Roy's phone, visible inside in its own evidence bag.

Sheila looked at him skeptically, her eyebrow rising toward her hairline again. "What, he called it in?"

"No," Hank said. "He downloaded it. He downloaded a nervous breakdown."

Hank placed the phone gently on the table, halfway between him and Roy Stanton, who sat straight in his chair with his hands clasped in front of him on the tabletop. Ready for his scene to begin.

He looked at the phone with mild interest. But his hands held each other a little tighter.

"What movie was it? Or was it a TV show? Or news footage? What did you use?"

Roy looked at him and shrugged. "Does it matter?"

"Not really. We'll get a warrant to search the phone and your records. See what you downloaded that would have produced the sounds to send your friend over the edge."

Hank spun the phone around on the table with his left hand. "This model's got pretty good sound. Must have come through loud and clear. That's probably why you bought the phone in the first place, isn't it?"

Roy nodded.

"How loud did you need to play it?"

Roy put out one hand toward the phone, but then thought better of it and pulled it back to rejoin the other one.

"Very loud. It had to be realistic. I bought a speaker. A little one that connected right to it. It fit in my pocket." He shrugged. "I knew it would just make him shut down. Then I could nudge the wheel any direction I wanted, walk back downstairs, and let the lake do the rest. It had to look like an accident, like recklessness or stupidity."

The weather had been perfect. Temperature dropping, storm on the way. He said he'd been watching the forecasts for weeks. Finally, the weathermen said what he needed to hear. So the night before, he'd taken his neighbor's dog and tied the annoying thing up in the woods behind Albert's house. He knew it would bark all night long and keep Albert awake. Prime the pump, so to speak. He smiled. Hank didn't.

"Did you take his shoes?"

"What? Oh, yeah. I'd forgotten about that. I knew he

always left his back porch door unlocked. Snagged those after I tied up the dog."

He sighed again. "It was the perfect plan. The boat gets scrapped, they get their insurance money, and I get my theater."

Hank leaned forward. "Who's 'they'?"

Roy blinked at him. Slowly, like the pet turtle he'd had as a kid used to do.

"Terry Cummings, that's who," he said.

And that was the only name he would give. Cummings was the only person he talked to. Cummings was the one who had the idea to run the boat aground. Cummings was the one who gave him the blueprints. Cummings was the one who showed him the beautiful poster board of his dream theater.

At Gallagher's office?

No, he'd come over to Roy's house. Had a fancy easel, done a whole presentation about how he planned to promote it, how it would be the crowning jewel of the Strip. He, Roy, had finally felt that someone had seen his greatness. Had understood that he needed the proper venue, the proper funding, to bring that greatness to the world. So the money would come from that decrepit old boat. That floating money pit. It was a public service, really, getting that thing off the lake.

And what about all the people it employed?

Roy shrugged. Every man must make his own way in the world. Must seize his own moment. Like he had.

Hank slowly counted to ten.

"Did Cummings mention Henry Gallagher at all?"

Roy thought. No, he didn't. Not once. They went around and around for half an hour, and Roy never deviated. There was never any mention of Gallagher. There was never any mention of Cummings following orders from anyone. Nothing. Nothing but an assumption on Roy's part that Gallagher Enterprises was backing the whole thing. But no proof.

And no, he hadn't started the fire. He didn't know who had. It certainly hadn't been part of the plan he'd cooked up with Cummings. He had done what he was supposed to do: disable the boat without hurting anyone.

"Well . . . almost no one." He gave a fatalistic little smile.

Hank wasn't even angry anymore. Just sad. Sad and tired. And a little bit sick as he sat across from this man. He picked up Roy's phone, left its owner sitting at the table, and went into the adjoining room, where Sheila and Sam had been watching through the two-way mirror.

"Did you get them?" he asked Sheila.

She held up a large envelope.

"Hey . . ." Sam said cautiously. "Why . . . um, why haven't you asked about Mandy Bryson yet?"

Hank took the envelope from Sheila. "Because I wanted these first."

He walked back into the interrogation room, pulled a stack of photos out of the envelope, and laid them one at a time in front of Stanton.

The first showed Mandy Bryson on the blue dining room carpet. The second showed her on the table at the morgue. The third was a close-up of the strangulation bruises on her neck. The fourth had her cut open, mid-autopsy.

"I'd really rather not see these." Roy was starting to look a little green.

"Why not? This is your handiwork. This is your plan in action."

Roy's jowls trembled. He pulled his hands out of sight under the table.

"She was not part of the plan. She was a surprise. How was I supposed to know that some kid would be on board and refuse to be part of the birthday party? And that she'd want to say hi to Albert? What are the chances of that? *What are the chances?*" His shoulders pitched forward and his eyes turned imploring.

"You could have called it off."

Roy's gaze turned to exasperation. "Really? After all that? It had to be that day. The theater deal wouldn't have been there forever."

"Roy, the theater deal wasn't there at all."

He stared at Hank. Hank stared back as his look of puzzlement slowly, incrementally, dissolved into slack-jawed understanding.

"No . . ." Roy muttered. "He wouldn't have. There were blueprints. There was the Country Song. The sale was in the works."

"It was all just a drawing. That's it," Hank said. "No one has looked at the Country Song building in two years. They were not going to give you a theater. They were going to take their insurance money and boot you out with the rest of the unemployed crew."

Roy swung his head from side to side, swaying a little in his seat. "No, no, no, no . . ."

Hank leaned forward and pushed the pictures closer to Roy.

"Now tell me what happened."

Roy stood outside the dining room and smiled. That tall lawyer had escorted him to the door and said they didn't want him around, that their party had no need of his services. Just as he had hoped. They were local, and they were snobs, so it had seemed a good bet that they wouldn't be interested in his folksy historical spiel. He strolled along the walkway toward the kitchen. The sun was out, but the temperature had fallen since the morning. He had faith that the clouds were just over the horizon.

He walked up and down for a bit. He was in no hurry, you see, to go into the kitchen and be subjected to Mrs. Pugo. But he did need that irritating woman to be able to say how disappointed he was to have been kicked out of the luncheon. He put on his best dejected look and went into the kitchen, and, well, that was when things got complicated.

That girl was sitting at the little table, crying and getting comforted by Mrs. Pugo. His exceptional actor's training was all that saved him from showing how shocked he was. And then, neither one of them would tell him why she was there. He calmed down, however, when it became apparent that she did not want to be seen and was not going to leave the kitchen. He began to relax.

He took a few more strolls on the walkway, making sure Tim saw him out and about—so that if anyone asked afterward, Tim would be able to say that he had seen the captain just minding his own business. On his last one, he made sure Tim was nowhere in sight and went up the stairs to the pilothouse. Albert was surprised to see him, but he explained that the luncheon group hadn't wanted to see his show. Then he got out his phone.

He'd also brought a portable speaker. That was in his other pocket. Albert asked what the hell he was doing as he dug them out. He ignored him, plugged the speaker into the phone, and hit play. At first, the guy just froze. Got white as a sheet, then started to sweat and shake. Roy grabbed Al's set of keys, stepped outside, and locked the door. He stood there for just a minute, until he didn't hear Al stumbling around anymore. Then he went back into the pilothouse and made sure Al was seated in his chair, then took the wheel and steered toward the boulders—slowly. It wouldn't do to alert anyone and have them come investigate before the actual crash. He set the proper course, then swiveled the captain's chair back around so it faced forward. The whole time, bombs were exploding, children were screaming, guns were firing. He waited until Albert stopped shaking and then checked his eyes. They were completely glazed over, and he didn't respond to any commands.

He shut off his phone and opened the door to the pilothouse, only to see the quickly retreating figure of that girl just reaching the bottom of the stairs. She had obviously heard the noises, and she might have seen him standing outside as well. He waited until she disappeared back into the kitchen, then left the pilothouse. He locked the door behind him with Albert's keys.

He descended quickly and managed to make it far enough down the walkway to where he could turn and pretend to be coming from the opposite direction as Tim came out with a tray, complaining that the door between the dining room and the kitchen was sticking shut. They commiserated about the sorry state of the boat and went into the kitchen together.

Five minutes later, the crash. Perfection. The screeching of the bottom hitting the rocks. The splintering of wood. The shuddering as it settled between boulders. It was exactly as he had hoped. Except for one thing. And she sat across the kitchen table from him.

When the crash was investigated, as it surely would be,

he couldn't have someone saying they heard sounds of bombing coming from the pilothouse. That would cast doubt on the whole thing—that Al had gone nuts all by himself and was the only one responsible for the crash. And if she'd actually seen him up there, well, that was simply untenable.

His concern continued to grow as the initial shock from the crash gradually wore off, and they got all of the stuck-up locals moved up into the lounge. Tim needed help getting them drinks quickly, and that horrible Pugo woman couldn't carry a tray more than three feet, so he was forced into service.

He came back into the kitchen at one point to find that girl gone. He seized the moment and went to find her, ducking out before Pugo saw him. He put on his concerned face and waited until she came out of the ladies' room. Patted her on the hand. Steered her into the empty dining room. Said she would be more comfortable in there, with the blinds closed, of course, so that no one could see her.

He thought of the years and years he'd spent doing horrible community plays and dinner shows and the stupid boat job. And how he was finally, mercifully, beyond that. And he hit her from behind, with the edge of the heavy metal tray he was holding.

It didn't work. She swayed and stumbled as she turned around to look at him. So he strangled her. It took longer than he would have thought. Much harder work than he expected. She clawed at him, but he still had on the gloves that went with his captain's costume and his heavy coat. When he was done, he had to pick up the contents of her purse, which had scattered all over when she dropped it during the struggle.

He left the purse near her body, turned down the thermostat, and locked the door to the kitchen with Albert's keys. He let himself out the main door, still carrying his tray, and locked that, too. There was no one in the hallway as he walked back to the kitchen, where he calmly wiped off the tray and then took his coat and gloves off. He had gotten quite hot.

Roy sat quietly after he finished. His hands, which he had waved around to illustrate his story, sat clasped in front of him again.

" 'That girl' had a name, you know." Hank slid the fifth photo out of the envelope and across the table. It was another full-length shot, this time of her sewn back together on the steel morgue table. Her limbs were slack, and the thick black suture thread appeared to stitch her limp form together like a rag doll.

The sixth was a close-up after she had won the state championship her senior year. Long brown hair high in a pony-tail. Skin sparkling with sweat and youth and potential.

"Please . . ." Roy was barely able to get the word out.

Hank reached in for the last one and laid it gently in front of the row of photos, closest to Roy. The edges had curled a little with age, and the color had faded slightly, as if it had once hung in a sunny place. Her hair was a lighter brown, cut in a bob with bangs. A light band of freckles crossed her nose, and the corners of her blue eyes crinkled from the width of her smile. She was missing a front tooth. Along the bottom of the picture, in neat adult script, was written:

Amanda Grace, First Grade.

Hank left Roy sitting slack in his chair, his hands in his lap, the pictures staring up at him.

CHAPTER
30

Sheila handed Hank a cup of coffee without saying a word. The three of them stood in the little room and turned away from Stanton, still visible through the two-way mirror. Hank was heading for the door when Sam cleared his throat. Then he squared his shoulders and pulled out his notebook.

"What'd you do, Sammy?" Hank said slowly.

"I interviewed Tony. At the hospital. Before they started working on his jaw. He told me everything. I wrote it up, just to be sure I understood his mumbles, and I had him sign it." He held up his notebook. "I know you said nobody was supposed to talk to him, but I figured if I got to him before he got all doped up, that would be better. . . ." He trailed off and stood there, looking determined and apprehensive at the same time.

"You have a signed confession?" Hank started to smile.

"Well, hot damn," said Sheila. "Good going, kid."

Tony had seen Mandy's purse partially covered by the

long tablecloth in the boat's dining room just after Hank discovered her body. He'd grabbed it while Hank's back was turned and taken it into the kitchen, which was empty. It had obviously been rifled through before he had gotten to it. He quickly arranged everything neatly, just as he thought she would have wanted it. He noticed the wrapped gift, and a tube of new, unopened lipstick. And he noticed the gun, still zipped in the side pocket.

He took her packet of tissues, because he was crying uncontrollably at this point. He took the unopened lipstick, because he felt that she had bought it to wear for him. And he took her gun, because he would find whoever had done this to his beautiful Mandy, and he would make that person pay.

"He admitted that he was the one stalking her?" Hank asked.

"Oh, yeah. Although he doesn't see it like that. They were in love, they were going to be together, et cetera, et cetera," Sam said.

So Tony just sulked around, Sam continued, until Mandy's funeral. Then Roy said something there that bugged him for a whole day until he figured it out.

"The lipstick," Hank said.

"Yep," Sam said. "Roy had said at the service that Mandy had been so pretty, with her dress and that red lipstick on. But she hadn't been wearing it. It had been unopened in the bottom of her purse, and then Tony had it under his pillow at home, so how could Roy have known about it?"

"So that was when Tony, our wannabe Sherlock, went after Roy, wasn't it?" said Sheila.

"Yep," Sam said again.

The three of them left the room without a backward

glance at Roy Stanton. Hank wanted to leave him there a while longer with only those pictures for company.

Sam went to type up his Tony notes. Sheila went to her desk to work on the job advertisement they would need to find a replacement for Duane. Hank stopped by the break room to top off his coffee—using his left arm, because his right one hurt like a sonofabitch—and took a minute to gaze out the window. It was starting to cloud over again. They'd probably have snow by morning. There'd be no boat plying the lake on its Sunday luncheon cruise, though. And there'd be no Mandy Bryson to come home for the weekend.

Hank turned away from the window and walked out of the room to see Gerald Tucker striding down the hallway. He looked as if he'd just finished his shift in the jail. He slowed when he saw Hank and started to smirk. Hank said nothing and moved to pass him.

"You're in for it now, boy," Tucker said as they passed. "You think you run things. But you don't."

Hank didn't stop. He didn't want to give GOB the satisfaction. As he continued on his way, he could hear Tucker's receding footsteps, and something else. The unmistakable sound, over and over, of a metal cigarette lighter flipping open and shut, open and shut.

He needed to call the Brysons. He needed to start the paperwork. He needed to—

He pushed forward. The door to his office swung open and bumped softly into the wall. The chair behind his desk swiveled around and creaked loudly as the man sitting in it settled himself.

"Hello, Hank." He was long and lean and wore a bolo tie.

"Hello. Can I help you with something?"

"You really should oil this chair. Once a month, and it stays smooth as silk."

"I'll keep that in mind. 'Course, you could have left that in your hand-off memo. If you'd cared to leave one."

The man chuckled.

"Can I help you with something, Darrell?" Hank asked again.

"Well, son, it's me who's needing to be helping you. See, I realize now that I should have been offering you a . . . tutorial, say, before I left for the state senate. I am regretting that. But now I am here, and I think we should be having a bit of a talk. 'Bout the way things work. 'Round here."

Hank planted his feet firmly on the thin, gray carpet and took a better grip on his coffee cup. He really would have preferred his chair, but it appeared that Darrell Gibbons had no intention of giving it up. He waited.

"I hear that you've been looking at my friend Edrick Fizzel's finances. His bank account, his campaign donations, things of that sort. Now, Edrick is a good friend to this office. He's taken care of us many a time. There's no reason to be starting to stir things up there. Do you get what I'm saying?"

Hank hadn't moved. And he wasn't moved, either.

"I get what you're saying. And I don't agree. Fizzel has been bought and paid for by Henry Gallagher, who hired his son at way more than market rates. That's not sticking to the spirit of campaign finance law. And he interfered with a homicide investigation on Gallagher's orders. That's illegal, too."

Gibbons laughed. "Ain't no way you can prove that. Gallagher never orders anybody to do anything. So you might as well put away your suspicions 'bout the other stuff, too. It's only going to be causing yourself one great big headache."

"I have no intention of stopping my investigation of Commissioner Fizzel."

Gibbons sighed and leaned forward, resting his elbows on the desk.

"Son, you aren't getting it. You got a chip in the game now. You got leverage. That's worth a hell of a lot more than some piss-ant public corruption conviction. That ain't going to get you anywhere. I'm not telling you to ignore this. I'm telling you to use it."

Hank stood there, hoping his face was impassive. His mind was churning, however.

"Why do you care if I have a chip in the game?"

Gibbons leaned back in the chair again. "I have a soft spot for this office. Was sheriff here for twenty years. You wouldn't have this new jail if it weren't for me. I'd like to see it continuing to prosper, not getting bulldozed by people richer and smarter than you. I'd like to see you care for it properly."

"To me, caring for it properly means upholding the law."

Gibbons rolled his eyes. "You are an uptight one, ain't you? The law can be shades of gray. Very little is black and white down here." He paused. "You like this job, don't you? You're good at it. Being in command suits you. You could be taking this department places. Make it what you think it should be. *If* you get elected when your appointment runs out."

Hank decided he'd had enough of this conversation. He took a step toward his desk. Gibbons ignored him.

"My, ah, endorsement would be very valuable. Of course, I haven't decided yet who I might be backing in the next election. Could be a tough call."

"Could be," said Hank, taking another step forward.

"Well, I should be getting on my way." Gibbons stood up and carefully smoothed down his bolo tie. He extended his hand.

Great. Hank knew he had to take it. He forced himself into what he hoped was the same state of relaxed nonchalance as Gibbons and did so. His arm was killing him. Gibbons came around the desk and slapped him on the back as he headed for the door.

"Oh, and good luck, son, on that murder. Those things can be tricky. Devil's own handiwork. They take time to solve, so don't go getting discouraged."

"Oh, that." Hank's nonchalance was flowing easily now. He put down his coffee cup. "I closed that."

Gibbons turned around and faced Hank again. "What?"

"Yeah. Taped confession. Walked me through how he did it. The whole deal."

Gibbons just stared at him. Hank reached around and grabbed the door, then gave the distinguished state senator a slap on the shoulder. "You take care now."

He pulled up to the house just in time for dinner. Thank God he wouldn't miss another one. He opened the door in from the mudroom and was met with clapping and shrieks of laughter from down toward the bedrooms. Dunc was at the stove, cutting into what appeared to be another kind of casserole.

"What's going on?" Hank asked.

"Oh. They're playing with—well, you'll see." Dunc pointed toward the living room with his spatula.

Hank grabbed a soda from the refrigerator and walked out into the living room. The TV was turned on to the local

news, but he couldn't hear it over the commotion Maribel
and Benny were making. They came bounding into the room
and skidded to a stop when they saw him. Benny threw himself at Hank, shouting, "Og!"

"What are you two talking about?" He bent down to
pick up Benny and stopped short. Racing down the hallway
toward him was a dog. A squat sausage of a thing, with a very
small head, a misaligned jaw, and mismatched ears. Its tongue
lolled out to the side as it stopped next to Maribel and sat
down. Hank recognized it immediately.

"What the hell is that thing doing in my house?"

Maribel just started clapping and jumping up and down.
Benny wrenched away and toddled over to stick his face next
to its muzzle.

"No—stop. Benny, get away. It's going to bite—" He
grabbed his son and spun toward the kitchen. "Duncan!"

Dunc appeared in the doorway, still holding the spatula.
He folded his arms.

"Yeah, that's right. We got a dog from the animal shelter.
This afternoon, after lunch. After you ran out on us, and
Maggie stood us up altogether. I decided they deserved a little
love and companionship. So there."

Hank sputtered. He could think of nothing to say, or at
least nothing that would be suitable in front of his children.
"You . . . you had no right to do that without talking to us
first. How dare . . ."

"I live here, too," Dunc said, waving the spatula at
him. "And I'm the one who's around all day, so what do you
care?"

Hank pointed helplessly at the thing, which had flipped
over onto its back and was wiggling in delight as Maribel

scratched its belly. "But that? That thing? Why on earth did you pick that one?"

"Well, now, that's a funny story. They couldn't decide, see. Maribel wanted one with cropped ears and Benny wanted one with floppy ears—"

Benny put his hands up to his own ears and flapped them enthusiastically. Then Maribel chimed in. "So we con-prized, Daddy."

"You what?" Hank asked.

"They compromised," Dunc said. "One ear's up, one ear's down."

"You always say me and Benny need to con-prize," Maribel said. "You proud of us?"

Hank looked at his kids, who now sat on either side of the devil-dog he'd returned to that fed-up owner earlier in the week. They beamed up at him. He could feel them vibrating with joy from three feet away. They looked up at him and waited. And he knew he couldn't create another crack. Their childhood was going to be filled with enough of them as they all went along. He couldn't add more just because they'd chosen possibly the worst pet in the history of the world. He knelt down.

"We can keep him."

He was tackled by all three of them. His kids laughed with glee, and the dog managed to lick both Hank's hands and his face while digging his claws into his stomach. He bit back a yell of pain as Benny sat on his bad arm. He struggled to sit up and asked, "So, what are we going to name him?"

"Oh, we know already," Maribel said. "I said he's pretty, but Benny said he's a boy—"

Benny shouted, "Boy! Not girl!"

"—so we call him handsome. *Guapo.* That's what Grand-pop said is Spanish for handsome. Is he right, Daddy? He's not so good on the Spanish."

Hank laughed. That was sure true. But Dunc had gotten it right this time. He looked at the dog, who was now sitting in his lap. Everything else about the mutt was contradictory, so why not?

"Guapo it is," he said.

He started to shove Guapo the Dog off his lap when, out of the corner of his eye, he saw Edrick Fizzel pop up on the TV screen. He froze. "Quiet," he said, in the even, low tone he seldom used that everyone in the house knew meant instant obedience. No one moved.

"*. . . extremely pleased to announce that the county of Branson has caught Mandy Bryson's killer. Our entire community worked tirelessly to bring this murderer to justice. The county commission wants everyone watching to know that we hold the safety of our citizens and guests as our highest priority. I, Commissioner Edrick Fizzel, will continue to make sure that this killer's court case is handled properly. We will lock him up and throw away the key. Thank you.*"

Hank stared at the screen as it went to commercial. He patted Guapo on the head. He didn't know what else to do. Throwing a chair out the window didn't seem wise.

"I didn't know you'd arrested somebody."

Maggie came into view and stared down at him. Her look changed from congratulatory to concerned as she saw his expression. "Babe . . . ?"

"No one knew. That I'd arrested someone. No one who would leak it . . . except . . ." He patted Guapo again.

"You haven't announced it?" she asked.

"No. I. Have. Not." Pat.

"Who leaked it?"

"Darrell Gibbons."

"Why would he do that?" she asked. "Oh . . ."

"Yeah. Gave the glory to his man Fizzel." He looked up at his wife. "I got to admit, it was a good play. Totally one-upped me."

"So he's playing politics?"

"He's trying to put me in my place. Show me that he still runs things. That I need to take his suggestions."

Maggie cocked an eyebrow. "Well, then, he doesn't know much about you."

Hank gave her a weary smile. "No, he doesn't. But I guess I don't know much about Branson politics. I'm going to learn, though. You can bet on that."

She reached down and ran her hand through his hair, stopping halfway.

"Wait a minute. What the hell is in your lap?"

Guapo, who had been amazingly still, looked up and saw an exciting stranger. He struggled to get his stubby legs underneath him while his tail started whirling like a boat propeller. He desperately wanted to sniff this new person. Hank started to lift him off his legs.

"Meet the newest member of the family. He might actually not be that bad."

And then Guapo piddled in his lap.

Fantastic.